THE
ANCILLARY'S
MARK

DANIEL A. COHEN

Black Rose Writing
www.blackrosewriting.com

The final approval for this literary material is granted by the author.

First printing

ISBN: 978-1-935605-76-8

PUBLISHED BY BLACK ROSE WRITING

www.blackrosewriting.com

Printed in the United States of America

The Ancillary's Mark is printed in Book Antiqua

To my brother. My talent can never parallel his, but maybe one day it will be perpendicular.

Acknowledgments

This would never have happened without the support of my family and friends. Thank you Stephanie for your love, inspiration, and indulging all of the craziness that came with writing this book. Thank you Mom for truly believing this book was good enough to get published. Thank you Dad for helping me become the man I am today. Thank you Katie for the best editing job a guy could ask for. Thank you Billy Brinkerhoff for all of your encouragement. Thanks to the management at Poughkeepsie Nissan. Thanks to all my Grandparents. Thank you Jenn, Justin, and Alex, who weren't afraid to tell me the truth, and in so doing, made my book even better. Thank you Rachel for getting the matching tattoo of the mark. Thank you everyone who believed in me and everyone who didn't, both sides were equally important in helping bring out my potential.

PROLOGUE

East Anglia, England. Circa 1000 CE

There was no conclusion, just a feeling of finality. No passing forward into the next wondrous adventure, only vacuous terror. True and utter fear. His armor had long been tossed aside for it meant nothing anymore; protection was unnecessary. Numbness had set in—his legs were being pricked by thousands of tiny imaginary needles. He brushed his finger against the smooth patch of skin just between his almond shaped eyes and the bridge of his nose. Creamy red had jumped onto the digit, but the crimson only affirmed what he already knew.

He had no flashes of previous deeds. He didn't want any; couldn't want any. The dread and panic flooding him seemed almost karmic in nature. Taking the lives of many had done nothing to heighten his fear of death; in fact, he wondered if the faces that never haunted him would at last have something to say.

Reaching down towards his bootstraps began the furious pain. His sides throbbed like they had been sliced deep, ripping at fleshy seems. Internal explosions like a barrel of gunpowder after the spark. This was the way to end a despicable life; he accepted his fate.

England was a playground, offering up women, money, all he could have wanted and more. Anyone else viewing the windswept green and collaged sky would have been awe-struck; however, the pain made it impossible for him to take in the subtle details that made the world beautiful.

A wretched man suffering a wretched death seemed oddly fitting. *That miserable last meal; the vile plant.* The poison was unstoppable. Funny, it did not feel like a foreign substance, more like a part of him that after his whole life of waiting had come home.

He brought out his blade from the tanned steer hide wrapped to his feet. Squeezing the handle tight he fell to his knees, fracturing his kneecaps. A red veil crept into his vision and he knew the few remaining grains in his mortal hourglass were soon to be shaken downward. Piercing the soft ground with his steel he wrote the beginning to his final message.

"I was wrong…"

CHAPTER 1

"The sun was setting and the world was about to end. The hero of the Elven army had only minutes to find the hidden scroll with the incantation to stop the apocalypse. The armies of darkness had amassed numbers that could crush mountains to powder and drink the sea dry. The Elven hero had reached the Tomb of the nine Forefathers and had found Tryvak's crypt. The brave hero knew that inside the crypt was his one chance to save his people from everlasting slavery and his world from eternal despair. The hero lowered his shoulder to the elaborately carved cover of the tomb that had been prophesized to contain the scroll and pushed. At any other time his eyes would have welled up in tears—for the tomb's insurmountable beauty had far surpassed all of his expectations—but he had no time for that. Every muscle fiber in his body strained as he used all the strength he had, and with a mighty give, the top crashed to the dusty floor and cracked in two. Not knowing whether or not the scroll would be there, and praying to all three of his protectors, he peered inside and with a pounding heart, which he was sure was visible through his skin, his eyes landed upon…."

Jacob quickly closed the novel. He placed his hand upon his chest and felt his heartbeat in sync with his favorite fictional hero. There were only a few pages remaining in the book and he didn't want to go any further that night.

After months of anticipation he was finally able to purchase a copy at the midnight release party the night before. Ever since the publishing date was announced—along with the news that it would be the final novel in the *Arcanian* series—

the book had rarely escaped his mind.

A wave of nostalgia affirmed that he was not ready for the series to end, so he decided not to let it. He placed a blue square piece of construction paper in the novel to mark his place.

In the fifth grade, Jacob had started the habit of color-coding his bookmarks. Although he was now eighteen, and a graduate of Franklin Pierce High School, he continued his tradition.

It was a rather simple arrangement, but was quite effective. When he stopped reading he always wanted to be able to dive back in with the same emotions and fervor with which he had departed. Since he also maintained the habit of reading many books at once, he knew how easily the plot and certain feelings could be forgotten without a little reminder.

Jacob had many colors to choose from, often adding new ones after coming across more and more unique situations. Gold meant fear, red excitement, brown was boredom, purple lightheartedness and so on and so forth. One time he came across a story about a chimpanzee that broke out of the zoo and was found by a karate master. The chimp became an apprentice, learned martial arts, and ended up fighting crime on the streets. After the chapter where the chimp started turning to a life of crime—and began to feel remorse for his deeds—Jacob inserted a piece of white tissue paper, which was simply Jacob's way of saying, 'I give up on this story'.

Monkeerate was never finished.

When he picked up an unfinished book he did want to read, he would note the color, fill himself with that emotion and ready himself to return to the story.

He very rarely used the blue slips because blue meant suspense. Jacob loved suspense. It filled him with the tantalizing feelings of adventure and anticipation, which brought him out of his mundane life into battles, murder mysteries, safaris on vast tundras and countless other destinations where time meant nothing and he was blind to the outcome. The problem was that Jacob always had to keep reading until the suspense bubble burst and the conclusion revealed itself.

He felt attached to the characters in the *Arcanian* series. They were invited into his life and wove their way into his imagination. They faced tribulations and matured together. Saying goodbye to the series would be like saying goodbye to a close friend who promised to keep in touch, but who he knew would only appear in his memories.

Not that he really ever had any close friends to compare this to.

He knew it would be almost impossible to keep his hands from grabbing hold of the final adventure and consuming every single word, but he was determined to try. The suspense would brew in his mind and ripen until he could bite into the story and savor every last flavor it had to offer.

It was good timing to finish for the night, as he needed his sleep. The plan was to get up early and walk the three miles to the Harrison Town Library. Summertime was always his favorite time of year, as it gave him plenty of downtime to pursue whatever he liked. This was the first summer he had chosen not to get a part time job in the hopes of relaxing before college.

A nest egg of past wages meant there were no constraints for a few months and he could enjoy his buffet of possibilities. The dish he enjoyed most of all was the library, which let him read to his heart's content, all for the price of a free card.

He delighted in getting up early because walking smack dab in the middle of the road was his favorite way of getting around—the reason being that he didn't want to give either side of the road special attention and could see the most that way. Although the roads he traveled were far from popular, he liked to beat the cars and reduce his chances of getting in anyone's way.

He stood up and walked over to the open window. The stars were glowing in the sky like sparks in ash. Treetops waved at him in-synch, moving to some orchestration he couldn't hear. Crosscurrent flowed freely, and with it came the warm smell of summer.

"Maybe tomorrow," he whispered, as his gaze turned outward at things that couldn't be seen.

A particularly soothing gust glided past his face and cooled the sweat beads that had sprouted. The wind continued softly, and gently lifted his college acceptance letter off the table, depositing it on the floor.

Gently placing his unfinished book next to his pillow, and with his adrenaline slowly fading, he hopped in bed and fell asleep.

CHAPTER 2

The James Bond theme song came out of the crude speakers of his alarm clock with a crackle and woke Jacob up as it did every morning. Next to the faded picture of a young Sean Connery, the face of the clock read '5:30'. He let the song finish, as even after hearing it thousands of times, he still enjoyed the tune. He got dressed and went out the door with the plan of taking a cold shower later after the heat had taken its toll.

His mother used to wake him up with a kiss on the forehead followed by a strong pull of the curtains.

"See what you already missed?" she would say.

"Won't it happen again tomorrow? Can't I go back to sleep?" he would retort. Jacob would actually want to get out of bed, but it was a ritual.

"Honey, what do you think?" his mother would call into the hallway.

"I think tomorrow will be even grander, but if you don't get up now, how will you have anything to compare it to?" his father would call in.

"Well now I'm just too excited to sleep," he would say as his mother ruffled his hair.

They would then all congregate in the kitchen for a sit-down-lets-actually-talk kind of breakfast. Eggs, hashbrowns, orange juice… the works.

This was all before the accident.

It was seven years ago they buried his father. The knot in Jacob's stomach didn't go away for months. He was eleven.

Mr. Deer was an excellent driver — or at least that's what all the family friends and relatives assured him—but the same couldn't be said for the guy behind the wheel of the truck. The doctor told his mother that it was a painless death, but the doctor was a liar.

The pain never went away.

They had moved to the town of Harrison when Jacob was born. It was quiet and his parents believed it was going be a great place for him to grow up. Plenty of swimming holes, sports clubs, ranches and isolated places where you could get away and think—the last perk came in handy.

His mother was not in Harrison at the moment. She was somewhere in Ireland. Jacob thought the name of the town was something like Dingle. After being elected, the government— for whatever reasons the government needs, or doesn't need— decided *that* was where her talents would be the greatest use. Jacob didn't like it, but he understood, and for the last few weeks he was his house's only occupant.

His mother called him every night to check in with the latest news. She told him it wouldn't take much longer to tidy up the paperwork, and she would be back home very soon.

His mother's voice always raised a pitch or two when she lied.

It was lonely in his house… another reason to spend the least amount of time necessary in it, and more time in the words of great writers past and present.

Once outside, he saw that the sun had yet to come up. He placed an upturned hand out in front of his face—just under the tree line—and closed one eye. Slowly, he lifted his hand, but the sun didn't ascend with it. It had never worked before, but it never stopped the smile from spreading across his face. Taking his place in the center of the road, he started walking.

Jacob knew that people saw him as odd—especially if they saw him walking mid-road—but it didn't affect him as much as it should have. Other people didn't quite see eye to eye with him, but in a strange way he enjoyed that. *If everyone was meant to be the same*, he thought, *we would all still be plankton.*

Throughout grade school he saw kids changing themselves to fit in. All around him kids were always trying not to say or do anything that would set them apart from the groups they so desperately attached to, like tiny remora on one giant ideal. This meant that a little slip up could lead to constant humiliation and possibly exile by their so-called friends. He held a silent grudge against his high school because he saw that, to an extent, it restricted the students' originality.

Jacob loved innovation and saw life as an opportunity to create wonders. He could thank his father for that. Although Jacob never excelled at any one field, his father encouraged him to jump right into any opportunity that crossed his path, even if it meant a greater exodus from his peers. Music, artwork, biology, mime—yes, mime—fencing, he wanted Jacob to experience it all.

Every new pursuit was a small remedy to an itch that Jacob could never best. There was always a nagging feeling that he should be doing something or going somewhere that was just never satisfied. Whether or not it was just his father's enthusiastic—and sometimes pushy—nature was undetermined.

Never truly belonging anywhere was not a pleasant feeling, so he was always trying to think of new ideas and ways to behave that were still to be thought of—or just not expressed yet. It was like coasting a bike down a steep hill after his father had provided him with a strong push.

Jacob always sat down in elevators. Not out of some sort of phobia or anything like that; it was that he loved to see people's reactions. Whenever a woman in a short skirt came in, he would of course stand up—for he was no barbarian—but other than that, it was always butt-on-the-floor. Most people would pretend to ignore him. This was one of the many ways he found out that most people don't take to unexpected or out-of-routine experiences in their carefully planned out lives. Some fellow passengers chuckled, while others scoffed, but many, seeing him on the floor cross-legged, would just wait for the next lift. Sometimes they asked why he was sitting. "Because I can, and so can you," he would reply. Once in a while, after hearing his response, other riders would plop down next to him and sport a great big ear-to-ear grin, the kind that comes with doing something you haven't tried before, and find yourself to be enjoying. It was Jacob's all-time favorite facial expression.

It was with these other sitters that Jacob would most often strike up great conversations and swap laughs. Once he convinced an elderly man named Herman to sit with him for forty-five minutes as they rode the elevator up and down trading ghost stories at lunchtime. Needless to say, it was a sight to see.

Already a good distance into his walk, Jacob sat down on a log close to the woods. This log had been part of a very old and thick tree, and as he sat down his feet did not reach the ground — which was saying something because Jacob was rather tall. While on the skinny side, Jacob had a handsome face and on the whole looked very average. His only semi-standout feature was a distinctive grouping of birthmarks on his left palm.

On the fleshy pouch underneath the thumb he had four small moles in the shape of a diamond. Within the diamond was a perfect circle of eight more brown marks. It wouldn't have looked out of the ordinary except for the thin auburn lines connecting the diamond and circle shapes, like a constellation. His mother used to joke that he was such an extraordinary boy he must have fallen out of the sky, and his hand was the proof.

The sun started peeking out of the treetops, illuminating the top half of his head. Mist often inhabited the town of Harrison, and had surrounded him as he inhaled a breath that brought with it the sweet smell of irises. Appearing in early summer, they were Jacob's favorite flower. He always liked them — especially the ones that looked like they had beards — and researched them one of his many days in the library.

Mr. Maddock, the head librarian — or 'Word Warden' as he

referred to himself — at the Harrison Town Library was a botany buff and could talk much too much about basically anything that fell in the plant category. Jacob's two favorite irises were the bulbous and rhizome variety. The rhizomes could produce leaves that look like tiny swords while the bulbous yielded beautiful delicate flowers that Jacob was sure could win a few happy tears from any woman. *How interesting*, he thought, *that the same flower could sprout both war and peace.*

Jacob got off the log, dusted the small pieces of bark off of the back of his jeans and started once more on his trip. Unfortunately, he saw little wildlife along the rest of his journey, though he did manage to catch a glimpse of a bird in the sky, perhaps a hawk or a falcon, out to catch breakfast.

The library was an old Victorian house turned into a public knowledge center. Its windows were all three-pronged, which gave them the uncanny appearance of jester's hats without the bells. It was the type of building where the floors creaked even before you took a step. The entrance was adorned with blue arched pillars, and the deck was lined with rocking chairs where the clientele were invited to sit and read. If the days got hot enough, the library's customers could look forward to Mr. Maddock producing a large cold pitcher of southern style sweet tea that never seemed to end. It was no coincidence that the library was most crowded during heat waves.

The building had a small dirt parking lot on the side, but most visitors usually walked, so it didn't get much traffic. The majority of guests didn't have the multi-mile trek like Jacob, but he didn't consider himself unlucky. Putting in all the effort made the library as much of a reward as a privilege.

In the parking lot was Mr. Maddock's '92 Ford Taurus — which its owner had grown quite fond of — and a Nissan with New York license plates which he had never seen before. He jogged the path up to the library's entrance and opened the old door.

"Why Cob, first guest as always. I swear it must be a

matter of thirty seconds after I unlock the front doors when you come bounding in."

It was true. Mr. Maddock was just pocketing the old fashioned key, the kind that looks like a tiny brass flag on a pole. 'Cob' had been Mr. Maddock's nickname for Jacob ever since he had been coming to the library, which was quite a while.

"Hey Mr. Maddock, how do you feel about today?"

A beam of happiness ran across the old man's face. "Very fine my dear boy, very fine. I was quite hoping you would be in this morning. I have more than one first-rate surprise for you."

"Well I'm all eyes and ears, which means you have to carry me," Jacob joked.

Mr. Maddock gave a deep chuckle.

"Well, I could try but with our combined weight I'm not sure this old floor would hold up, nor would my back. Now, follow me, I have something new to show you."

Mr. Maddock had become very fatherly to Jacob over the last few years and was always there with a quick bit of advice when need be. The old man's wit was inspiring, which came in handy, as he doubled as Jacob's intellectual role model.

Mr. Maddock and Jacob's father had been very friendly. Jacob remembered bedtime stories of ancient myths that his father learned about in Mr. Maddock's freshman level class. Many years before taking the position of librarian in Harrison, Mr. Maddock was a professor at a mid-sized university in Illinois. He wasn't respected by the sophisticates working there, but was greatly respected by Jacob's father. Most nights before Jacob would fall asleep, his father would relive the younger days, imparting the tales he stayed after class to learn about — the ones that kept the old cultures alive. Stories about titans, about heroes and courage; about damsels, dragons, monsters, and mayhem. Jacob never forgot a single one.

Jacob loved reading partly because he wanted to be as intelligent and clever as the old librarian some day. He once watched the old man best him in a chess game in three moves

—and that was after he gave Jacob a five-move head start. Jacob was not a prodigy in anything, nor had he ever heard the word 'genius' used to describe him, but he was nevertheless sharp and a quick learner. What he knew, however, was not nearly enough for his brain to be sated.

The old proverb 'with age comes wisdom' was very true in Mr. Maddock's case. The librarian was nipping on the heels of seventy-five years and had learned an astonishing amount about the world. If ever Jacob was to come across a topic he didn't know much about—whether it was the Spanish Civil War or radio waves—Mr. Maddock could always shed a little light.

The bookkeeper made every topic as interesting as if Jacob had been waiting for years to hear it. It helped that the old man lived and spent most of his time in the library—with learning being his main form of entertainment, as the old man did not own a television or much go out. Knowledge became his entertainment, which he enthusiastically shared with Jacob.

"Today young Cob, we have a doozy!" Mr. Maddock said. He had started walking toward his office and Jacob followed suit. Although Mr. Maddock was in generally good health, he required the use of a cane to walk after a knee injury.

"I was in Starville yesterday at a giant used book sale and I came across this." The old man's hands plunged into a pile of books—mostly about plants—and picked up an old tattered novel. It was entitled, 'The Alchemist.'

"This is a beautiful edition," the librarian boasted. "In my opinion, one of Coelho's greatest achievements, and the story is riveting. I had to have it for my collection."

The best part about his trips to the library was that every time Jacob came in, the old man would have a great book ready for him. Mr. Maddock would carefully scour his favorite collections and with great scrutiny pick out a story that Jacob always seemed to love. The librarian would hide them behind his desk in the small corner office next to the stairs. Sometimes Jacob peeked at the selection, giving him a sneak preview of what expeditions awaited.

The stories Mr. Maddock picked out originated from all corners of the literary world. There were no boundaries on the types of books he would recommend to Jacob. Some days it would be a detective story where the protagonist attempted to crack a case that seemed near impossible, others, it would be a collection of journal entries. One time it was a cookbook entirely devoted to different ways of using jellybeans. Jacob tried out the Tutti-Fruity Carp, which—although it ended disastrously and colorfully—was extremely fun to make.

The system worked wonderfully, and Jacob had grown attached to many of those books. Somewhat embarrassingly, Mr. Maddock kept Jacob's favorites in a section of a bookshelf which was labeled 'Books from the Cob'.

An oversized leather sofa that sat near the infamous section was his immediate landing pad after receiving these new treasures. A benefit of being early was being able to choose the prime spots.

Mr. Maddock handed him the newly acquisitioned old copy, and Jacob took it into his hands with great care.

"Thanks Mr. Maddock, I can't wait!"

"Read boy, read. That ancient couch is lonely and needs some attention. I think it has grown as fond of you as you of it," Mr. Maddock said with a smile. "Enjoy, as it will be some time before the other surprise is awake."

"Awake?" Jacob questioned. "Do you have guests? Is that why there's another car in the driveway?"

"If I told you, then the surprise would just be an event instead of a mystery, and I know you don't want that."

"You got me," Jacob retorted.

"Now go on and take your rightful throne."

He didn't need to be told twice.

Dipping down into a bow he said, "May your rule over the library be vast and healthy!"

Walking in between the two bookcases that held romance, Jacob turned the corner to the biography section and found the couch. After the long trudge from his house, he deservedly started his new adventure.

CHAPTER 3

It was close to three hours later when Mr. Maddock found him, and Jacob was already a good chunk of the way through the book. The old man was right—as always—it was quite good. He heard the brisk tapping of a cane on the wood floor around the corner, so he frantically pulled out a wad of construction paper from his pocket. He quickly found a red square and placed it inside his novel—being fitting as the warring tribesmen had just arrived. Along with the cane, it sounded as if there were two sets of feet walking toward him.

Mr. Maddock rounded the corner, and behind him trailed the most beautiful girl Jacob had ever seen. Shimmering dirty-blonde hair was pulled into a French braid on the back of her head. She had a small frame, and a smile that he was sure Da Vinci would have a hard time capturing. Her eyes were the shade of blue-grey that could best be described as resembling the reflection of the moon on water.

"Cob, this is my Granddaughter Sophia."

"Um, hi," she said with a tiny wave of acknowledgement.

For a moment Jacob forgot how to speak.

Mr. Maddock had mentioned in passing that he had a granddaughter, but Jacob had not expected her to be so gorgeous.

"It's nice to meet you," she said unenthusiastically. "I've heard a lot about you."

All that Jacob managed to get out was a very quiet and elongated "wow." It sounded like the air escaping from a tire.

Sophia looked over at Mr. Maddock with a raised eyebrow.

"I believe you and Sophia are the same age. She just graduated high school in New York. Sophia surprised me with a visit. I haven't seen her in so many years. Last night I was making lasagna when I heard a knocking on the door. To my surprise, there she was, right on the doorstep... Of course it meant that I had to share my cooking." As Mr. Maddock said this, his smile seemed to grow, which Jacob would have thought to be impossible. "Oh, the sacrifices we make for family."

Mr. Maddock gave Sophia a light pat on the shoulder.

"Well now, I have much to do. These books can be very needy. Cob, would you mind keeping Sophia entertained while I work? Maybe you could show her around town—just promise me that you'll walk on the sidewalk."

Sophia interjected, "But-"

"It would be good for you to spend time with a nice young man," Mr. Maddock said, his voice taking on a firmer tone.

Jacob blushed. He was still battling to push the words out of his throat. It was like crazy-glue held them inside. Mr. Maddock walked away with a light tapping and Jacob felt as if his stomach was trying to convene with the ceiling.

"Grand-Pappy, can't I just—"

"Have fun kids!" he said with a wave as he walked away.

Sophia sighed.

"So Cob," she stressed his name like it tasted funny in her mouth, "what does one do here to pass the time?" Sophia's voice was melodic and enticing. The sound of it didn't help Jacob speak any easier.

After a somewhat awkward pause, and without any control, Jacob blurted out, "You are really beautiful."

Sophia closed her eyes and shook her head. "So, Grand Pappy wasn't lying when he said you were...unique."

At hearing this, Jacob forgot how to speak again. Come to think of it, he couldn't even remember if he was ever able to in the first place.

Another involuntary "wow" escaped his lips.

"So," she said, looking anywhere but at him. "Do you have, like, a mall?"

"… Not really."

"A Starbucks?"

"There's a little coffee shop around the corner. It's really neat. They make a latte that they put in a special mug that changes colors as it cools. They call it a Mochameleon. I actually gave them the idea for it. They said that if it caught on then they would—" He realized his rambling wasn't helping, as she was looking at him skeptically. "It's really good."

She shrugged. "Fine."

Jacob put his book down on the couch to save his spot.

They walked out of the library silently. A few times Jacob inhaled as if to say something, but each time he stopped himself.

Outside, the sun was sufficiently baking the ground. Sophia popped sunglasses out of her purse and fit them snugly on her face.

"So," he said, finally breaking the silence. "What kind of books do you like to read?"

"I don't, really."

"Read?"

"No… not really. I have enough reading to do for school."

"Oh but you have to read! It's even more important to read good books if you have school reading to do. You can't let textbooks ruin reading for you. Like, this one time for class I was assigned reading about the civil war in the textbook. It was really boring so I went to the library and asked Mr. Maddock… I mean your grandfather… if he had any good novels about it, so he gave me this one where—"

Maybe Sophia thought he wouldn't be able to notice through the sunglasses, but she let her eyes drift towards her wristwatch.

"The coffeeshop is right around here," he said timidly.

"Ok," she said. "Lead the way."

They walked along the sidewalk, Sophia trailing a few

steps behind. When they reached the shop called 'Where Have You Bean?' Jacob was already beginning to sweat from the heat. As he opened the glass door—riddled with flyers for an upcoming local band—the air-conditioning hit him full blast. He held the door for her, and as she passed by, she gave a closed-lipped smile.

The interior held a high degree in trendiness. The waitress who said hello to them had a lip ring and poorly dyed red hair — *unless that was the look she was going for,* Jacob thought.

The tables were each equipped with small aloe plants, the music playing softly through the speakers was from all independent artists, and wheat-grass shots were available for just two dollars a pop.

Sophia sat down at a table that could accommodate six. Jacob sat across from her as she picked up a menu.

"Mochameleon, huh?"

"Yeah, that's what I'm gonna get."

"What's the Al CaPacino?"

"It's an Italian soda."

"Cold?"

"Yup," he said.

"Phew," she said as she took off her sunglasses. "I think I'll try that."

The waitress came over with a pen and a little notebook with skulls on it.

They ordered their drinks.

"Oh, and just so you know," the waitress said. "All the artwork is for sale."

After she walked away from the table, both of them looked at the framed paintings that hung on the wall.

It was a themed set, under the name 'War Blooms'. The first piece Jacob saw—a black and white picture of a fighter plane dropping yellow flowers—had a tiny plaque under it that said 'D-Daisy'.

"I like Cuban Thistle Crisis," Sophia said.

Jacob immediately saw what she was referring to. It was a

missile silo covered in tiny pink flowers.

"They should do one called Berlin Wallflowers," Jacob said with a smile.

Sophia picked up her menu and buried her face in it.

Jacob waited a few moments and then resigned himself to the fact that she was not really interested in having a conversation with him.

He twiddled his thumbs under the table and wished the drinks would get there quickly.

"Bay of Pinks," she said from behind her menu.

Jacob laughed.

She put the menu down, and this time had a real smile on her face.

"Hey, we should paint that together!" he said. "There's this art store not too far away, and we could make that and maybe they would put it up on the wall with the others."

"Um… maybe some other time."

"Ok."

Another minute of silence.

"Do you like painting?" Jacob asked.

"Not really," she said.

"What do you like?"

"I don't know. I guess I like animals."

"Awesome!" Jacob said just little too loudly, which drew the attention of the other customers in the far corner table.

"Yeah," she said with her head tilted downward.

"I like animals too, just this morning I saw a bird of prey. I think it was a hawk but it really could have been a falcon."

Sophia nodded.

The next few minutes were filled with awkward conversation.

"Your drinks," the waitress said as she placed them on the table.

They drank in silence until they were both finished and then left.

CHAPTER 4

Harlem

Tyson "Marrow" Gaul sat on a metal folding chair pulled up to a felt-top poker table. Cards in one hand—king high—while the other stayed hidden beneath. He was in the back room of Yun's Chinese Bistro—the room reserved for underhanded exchanges, where law was about as relevant as manners. No one flinched when he pulled out his chromium-tipped Taurus Raging Bull Revolver. On the custom handle was a silver plate engraved with the words 'Daddy's Little Devil'. The Raging Bull 45mm cartridges were usually used to hunt Cape buffalo and African elephants; however, Marrow had found new and exciting uses for them. High-powered ammunition came in handy in his line of work.

Tyson's nickname 'Marrow' had to do with his extremely rare genetic disorder known as Blaschko's lines. Normally, these lines are undetectable to the naked eye, however when combined with certain other skin mutations, they can manifest themselves visibly. Covering Tyson's full body, the lines were a tad darker than a manila folder. Along his back they created consecutive 'V' shapes down his spine, and swirls on his thighs. The feature that stood out the most, though, was a rather stark line that traveled from his right deltoid and ended just under his nostrils. It looked uncannily like a human femur, hence the nickname. When he was younger the lines served as a curse to set him apart. Other children didn't want to associate with a freak. They spat at him and threw stones. They shouted things like, "Sticks and stones CAN break your bones."

As he grew, so did his affection for the peanut-colored

disfigurations. So much so, in fact, that later in life he no longer viewed them as built on, but rather built in.

In the present day world, they served a new purpose—fear. The world fears what it doesn't understand, and he enjoyed being an enigma.

He placed the rifle on the table and said, "Call."

The four other players at the table folded. They had only been in Marrow's employ for a few months; nonetheless, they all knew how much that gun meant to him—and what he'd done with it. A fine bluff.

"Thanks, boys," Marrow said, as his outstretched hands raked the center pot his way. "Drinks on me."

A cheer of grunts grew around the table. Marrow might have been a cold-hearted bastard but he knew how to take care of his rancorous troops. Something as simple as rounds of booze could inspire loyalty. It was almost unnecessary, as most of the men were scared enough of him to blindly follow him anywhere… and to never question his *unconventional* methods.

Stocked with Jack and Devil's Springs, the private bar in the corner started shelling out shots, and Marrow knew that it was almost time to get down to business. The monk tied up in the corner had yet to say anything.

That was a problem.

CHAPTER 5

Walking outside was like entering a pre-heating oven that Jacob hoped had finally reached its desired temperature.

"Ugh," Sophia said. "How do you guys do it?"

"Do what?"

"Live in this heat."

"Oh, I don't know. You kind of get used to it. One time when I was younger I took some hotdogs out of the freezer and tried cooking them on a rock next to the lake and—"

"There's a lake!"

"Yup."

"Close by?"

"Do you see that tiny path between the oak and birch?" He pointed off to the woods. "About a mile in there's one that most people don't know about. The water's even drinkable."

"Can you take me there?" she asked, and then softly bit her bottom lip.

Jacob didn't remember ever learning words.

He managed to move his head into a nodding motion, or close enough to it anyway.

"Ok, lets go then," she said with a smirk.

When they reached the path, the sweat was already pouring out of their foreheads like a leaky pipe.

Jacob tucked the bottom of his jeans into his socks, which he thought made him look like a scarecrow.

"You should probably do the same," he said.

She shrugged again, and then copied him.

Next, Jacob tucked his shirt in.

"You never know," he said. "You should—"

"I'll be fine."

"Sure," he said, and they set out on the dirt path.

"So you're from New York?" Jacob asked.

"Yep,"

"Your whole life?"

"Uh huh."

"Ever travel?"

"Actually," she said, her voice perking up. "I went to Paris once."

"Wow, France. Did you know that in France it is illegal to call a pig Napoleon?"

She giggled. Her cute laugh made his knees weak and he almost tripped over a small brown root.

"Really?"

"I think so."

"That's pretty funny."

"So how come you have never visited here before?"

"My parents had kind of a falling out with my grand pappy—something about obsessing over his job or something like that—to be honest I never really got the details."

"So why all of a sudden did you come?"

Sophia reached into the back of her jeans and palmed something small.

"This," she said, as she revealed a brand new drivers license.

"Freedom," Jacob said, nodding his head in appreciation.

"With a couple years of minimum wage I was able to buy my first car. As soon as I got t*his* little beauty I stuffed my trunk full of supplies, and hit the road. Most of my storage space is filled with Twinkies and flip flops."

"Well as far as provisions go, I think they're perfect—"

The tail end of his word was lost as Sophia tackled him to the ground.

Jacob looked puzzled. "Normally I'm not one to ask why but... why?"

Sophia motioned her head upwards.

Above him, just inches shy of where his head had just been, was a rather large spider dangling from its web.

"Do you see the violin shape on its back?" She asked. "That's a brown recluse spider. Their bites can be, well, not very pleasant."

"Thanks," Jacob exclaimed.

Sophia was lying next to him and he could now see her eyes up close.

She got off of him rather quickly, and started brushing non-existent dirt off her yellow blouse. He stood up—making sure to stay clear of the spider, which had just started climbing back up its web—and swept away some real dirt.

"Well, I owe you my thanks." With one hand over his stomach he gave a great bow.

"Yeah… don't mention it."

"But I already have," Jacob said. "I could have spent the rest of the day trying to itch the red skin off my face, so I must show my appreciation. Would you be so kind as to follow me? We're gonna make a small detour."

"Can't we just go to the lake? It's scorching out here."

"C'mon. It'll only take a minute."

Jacob led her down the path. He walked in between two white birches that bent almost magnetically toward each other, creating an arch. He looked down and saw the makings of a small path that would be utterly impossible to discern if he didn't already know it was there. The footpath was overrun with crabgrass and waist high stalks that were determined to stop them from reaching what Jacob wanted to show her.

"It's just up ahead," he said, excitement building in his voice.

"Great," she said sarcastically.

"So how did you know about that spider?"

"I worked at an upstate local zoo for a while. That's where I got the minimum wage I was talking about. It was pretty run down and I mostly cleaned up the cages."

"Cool."

They drifted off the path and walked through the brush until Jacob came to an abrupt halt. At first glance there was nothing setting this section of the woods apart from the rest, which is exactly why he picked it.

"Look over there, do you see it?" Jacob asked as his index finger directed her eyes behind her.

Sophia stared and squinted for several seconds.

"See what?" she asked.

There was no response.

Sophia turned back around but he was already gone.

"Cob?"

She tried a little louder. "Jacob?"

"Hello down there!" he shouted.

He was resting on a large makeshift platform of cedar planks; his head peeked down to see her.

"What are you doing?"

"Come on up!"

"Really?"

"Yeah just for a second!"

"How did you get up there?"

"Magic."

CHAPTER 6

The monk's name was Kaichub.

Back in Tibet — his home country — Kaichub's father Mozu had a small barley farm, and raised dzo — a hybrid between yak and cattle. Kaichub and his family were from a small town called Tanki Lowbei, located on one of the tributaries of the Yangtze. Most of Kaichub's early life was spent helping his father with daily chores on the farm. On certain occasions when their work was over for the day — which was very rare — his father would show him old acupuncture techniques that had been passed down through their family. He never had any sort of formal schooling, which didn't really matter, as his aspiration was to become a fully ordained monk. When Kaichub turned twenty-one, he took the thirty-six vows of conduct and entered the Sagha, a Buddhist community. He began to lead a very simple life spent mostly in meditation and practicing the ancient traditions.

Oddly enough, Kaichub had come to New York to deliver a speech on new developments in condensed matter physics in the quantum mechanics field.

After a night of drinks and stimulating conversation with some of the field's finest, he went out to the parking lot to find his rented Altima. Just as he heard the beep — after pressing the locking mechanism on the key — a black bag was forced over his head and he was knocked unconscious by a sharp blow.

When he awoke, he was face-to-face with the Bone-man.

Kaichub overheard the other men calling him Marrow, *but a kidnapper does not deserve a real name*, he thought, *so Bone-*

man it would be. It was fitting because of the strange birthmark; he had never seen anything like it.

They tied him up in the corner, and for a while they played some sort of card game he could not follow. His kidnappers attempted to drink their body weights in booze, making them rowdy and eliminating all care for a motionless monk in the corner. He did not utter a sound. *It would only be a sign of weakness*, he thought. Although he had never before come across truly bad men, he knew not to show weakness.

He thought that Krinama was going to make his life better and—although the ideas were a blessing from the Gods—he wondered why they had led him to this fate.

After some time, the music began to die down and faces began shooting quick glances his way, as if all the men in the room were anxious for something to happen.

Kaichub had learned—through hundreds of hours of meditation—how to shut off anger and hide fear behind a strong layer of courage. He began to take long slow breaths and fill his lungs with precious air, hoping that they wouldn't be among his last lungfulls in *this* life.

The Bone-man made a quick motion to one of the workers, and the music shut off. Kaichub concentrated on his breathing, trying not to think about what was to come. He wished that he were one of the older monks; they were able to erase all fear and worry and not let the evils of the world get the best of them. Nothing could faze them, even the loudest noise in the darkest of rooms.

"Is it there?" The Bone-man asked him. The tone of his voice was eerily soothing, which made the man seem all the more uncouth.

Kaichub said nothing and just looked back with an expression of feigned nonchalance.

"Playing dumb?—Let me tell you what I know." The Bone man gesticulated in rhythm to the words. "I know that it is real and I know that you have had a taste."

The Bone-man's face got within a finger's distance of his

own.

So this man was after the secrets of Krinama, he thought.

"My fellow cretins," the Bone-man shouted. "This man has stolen from me!"

The other men grunted and booed.

Kaichub did not know what the Bone-man was talking about. The only thing he was guilty of was living a peaceful life and getting rewarded for it.

"Not ONLY," the Bone-man started again, "has he had a taste, he refuses to tell me where it is. This is not to be tolerated."

The Bone-man pulled something metal out of his pocket. It was a pair of needle-nose pliers.

"So," the man whispered, "a monk just happens to be an expert on condensed matter physics, huh? I know what it can do and it is meant for me...I have known since I first heard the stories. It is my destiny"

Kaichub still didn't know what the man was getting at.

All of a sudden—with uncanny precision—the pliers gripped one of Kaichub's eyelids.

The Bone-man pulled out a laminated piece of parchment with strange writing on it. It wasn't English—Kaichub could read and write English. It was a strange language, which he had never seen before.

"I will translate for you all," the Bone-man said.

A hush came over the room. The other men hung on his every word.

"The root of power in destiny holds to create or destroy. The four cycled paths will be followed as it lives. What is known to be will happen. It will reveal the language of God as if written for countless eyes to see eternal. No sea storm or devils earthly spew can hinder what will be caused. It is the final way. Salvation in righteous hands but if not—" The Bone-man paused and his chest flared outward.

"Tremble world, for thy maker weeps."

CHAPTER 7

"Magic? Well do you have a rope for us non-magic guests?" Sophia asked.

"I did happen to make a ladder for such occasions. Believe it or not—you should probably just believe it, though—no one else has ever seen this place."

Jacob turned around and grasped his provisional ladder. He returned to the edge and threw it over. Gazing over the rim, he saw that Sophia was no longer standing underneath.

"Hey where'd you go?"

He stretched his head farther off the platform to make sure she wasn't just standing directly beneath his hideaway.

All of a sudden, he felt a sharp jerk on the back of his collar. He turned onto his back and was staring up into Sophia's face.

"I guess I'm magic too," Sophia said with a grin.

"So you figured it out, huh?" Jacob said, followed by an exaggerated fake sigh.

"Well the wooden rungs you nailed onto the back of this tree were not so well hidden," Sophia looked around the platform. "So what's special about this place?"

"It's my go-to-it-all spot," Jacob said.

"Go-to-it-all?"

"Well, the way I see it, out here is how the world truly is. Everyone wants that spot where they go to get away from it all —away from the stress and commitments of their lives—but they have it backwards. That's not *the* world, it's *our* world. The one we created and changed to fit us. We don't want to work for the world anymore, we want it to work for us. It's our little box that we locked ourselves inside, that's going to be harder and harder to open if we ever want to get out." He let his eyes wander the landscape. "Everything out here just seems to work. It's not all peace and love, either. There's pain and hunger and agony and defeat but it's the way it was before we came along and it's the way it will be long after we're gone. It's all out here. It seems people don't do what we are meant for anymore and it's entirely our fault. People need to just get out of the illusion, if only for a little while, and see what it's all about."

"I like that," Sophia said. "I need to get one of my own."

"How 'bout for as long as you're in town you share mine? The world is more beautiful when you can share it anyway."

They sat and stared off into the distance, enjoying each other's silence.

There was something, however, that Jacob chose not to share with her. Something he had never told anyone. When he was in this spot, looking out into the forest, into the landscape of gold and greens, he could feel that nagging feeling more than ever. The feeling that something out there was waiting for him. It was not a pleasant feeling, sort of a low-grade anxiety, but he was grateful for it. If it took his whole life, he would do whatever possible to find that unknown. Something was trying to reel him in, but the hook kept slipping out.

CHAPTER 8

Mr. Maddock had some free time as it was a slow day and all of the visitors seemed to have placed the books back where they belonged—a rare marvel. He sat down at his desk to a stack of newspapers and readied himself for a nice leisurely edification on what was new in the world. Getting off his feet for a little while was a relief, as it was becoming more difficult to ignore the pain in his leg. Each passing day was a little more physically challenging, but he wasn't about to let a little bit of pain stop him. He was getting old, but he was determined not to let his reliance on a cane ruin what was left of his life. *People need their librarian even if they didn't know it,* he thought.

He picked up the first paper in the pile. Gracing the front page was a story about an office building catching fire after a disgruntled employee decided to microwave his fork. He cruised through the paper—he could now be considered a speed-reader after over half a century of practice—but when it came to *novels* his pace was hardly quicker then a fifth-grader. He drank in every word and savored the subtle changes in characters.

That day's issue had nothing really out of the ordinary. A couple of stories about politics, an editorial on why English should be the standard global language, a kidnapping in New York, and one particularly interesting piece on possible medicinal properties of *nymphaea mexicana*—the Mexican water lily.

The next paper was an issue of *Human Affairs*, based in Los Angeles, which consistently did a fine job of covering worldwide events. Mr. Maddock had been a subscriber since their forty-second issue when he happened upon a copy. He always enjoyed reading this chronicle, as their field research was impeccable and their fact-finding top notch.

The paper crinkled as he straightened it in front of him to reveal the picture below the fold. The headline read:

Phenomenon in Tibet: Small Town Elation
By: Calvin Thompkins

One of many celebrations broke out last Sunday by the villagers of Tanki Lowbei, a small community in northern Tibet. Though the press was kept at arm's length for the entire day of the celebration, the townspeople were happy to pass on the reasoning behind it. The songs, dance and food were in honor of the amazing advancements in certain fields by five of its citizens and the prosperity this has brought them.

Tanki Lowbei has a population of just over three hundred, and most of its citizens' lives are spent farming and herding livestock. A handful of these simple people have now captivated the world.

In an unprecedented event, these five locals have developed novel ideas in various fields, all in an unbelievably short amount of time. The have advanced the technology in the fields of telecommunications (cell towers), automobile engine emissions, physics, and architecture using plate glass. One man even created a new musical instrument he dubbed Nipadala—a lute with a thin copper body that resonates quite well. With the newfound wealth generated by these advancements, the townspeople are starting to improve infrastructure and their way of life. These five creators can attest to no reason for the spontaneous creativity other than hard work and dedication. Story continued on page 6…

Mr. Maddock's hands began to shake and his mouth went dry. *Could it be?* he thought, *could it finally be?* His breath grew short and he grabbed a paper bag. He began to steadily breathe into the bag to try and calm himself; in and out, in and out, very slowly. He hadn't felt this way since '72 when he had gotten his hopes up only to be let down by a false news story. He opened the paper as though he were holding a priceless document, and turned to page 6.

> Cover story continued… Inexplicably, most locals in this village have never even heard of the things being improved. The townsfolk claim there was no academic thievery and that every idea was original. It may be a mystery, but it is a positive turn in the fortune of this deserving town.

As Mr. Maddock gently placed the paper on the zebrawood desk, his lips started to tremble. His suspicions had the potential to be confirmed and it could very well be the culmination of countless years of research. He had never, at any moment in his life, wished for something more than for this to be true. A lifetime of dedication was going to pay off. Every molecule of his body was ready to switch from faith to fact and without any doubt, truly believe. His eyes started to tear up. It was as if a thirsty wanderer making his way through the Sahara, at the brink of dehydration, had uncovered the grandest oasis the desert had ever held. An oasis with date palms, wells bursting with clear blue water, abundant wildlife, laughing smiling faces and the promise of a wonderful new life.

There wasn't a single moment to lose. If he made the connection it was a given that others would too—he might even be too late. Bolting out of his chair a little too fast caused his bad knee to hit the sharp edge of his desk. The amount of adrenaline his heart was pumping through his body let him ignore the pain. He raced out of his office, forgetting his cane.

Rushing past the travel and global studies shelves, he hugged the corner and headed toward the basement. He opened the door marked private.

An array of thoughts scampered through his head. The preparations needed to be set in motion and he knew exactly what to do. The plans for this day had been mentally culled, and the only variable left was if Cob would actually accept his fate. *I should have told Cob about it when he was younger,* he thought. *It doesn't matter now, whatever mistakes made in the past can't be undone, and this is our only shot.*

Mr. Maddock knew he could only push Jacob in the right direction and the young man would then have to continue on his own accord. He could not begin to imagine he challenges and obstacles that Jacob would face. What he wouldn't give to be young again and guide him until the very end. It was the most exciting day of his life and it couldn't have come sooner; it was almost time to set the dream aside. The adventure that would forever change the course of history had begun.

The Ancillary had been found.

CHAPTER 9

The summer heat had finally reached the point where the flat rocks could be used to host a barbeque. The magnolia leaves radiated vibrant shades of red and yellow, and cast shadows on Jacob's face. Sophia and Jacob had been lounging on the platform for close to an hour. They didn't speak, just enjoyed the surrounding forest.

"I think it's just about time to go cool off," Sophia finally said.

"To the lake!" Jacob exclaimed.

Sophia was the first to climb down the rickety ladder and Jacob followed.

Jacob began trailblazing through the woods to get back to the original path. They reached the dirt channel and began to walk the slow decline towards the lake.

"So what's your last name, Cob?" Sophia asked after a small amount of time.

"Deer."

"Like the start of a letter?"

"Like the creature."

"So what do you like to do in your spare time?"

"New things."

"Like?"

"Everything. I like to try stuff."

"Huh."

The lake had come into view. The path ended on a low cliff overhanging the water. The rocks glinted as the imbedded quartz glowed with a kiss from the sun.

"Well, Cob Deer, I got something new for you. How quick do you suppose you are?"

"I would say on the quicker side. Why do you ask?"

Sophia was already in full sprint toward the lake. *Spontaneous AND beautiful, what a combination,* he thought.

Jacob remembered his two past girlfriends. The first was Cindy Cleveland in third grade. She stopped speaking to Jacob after William Brinkerhoff gave Cindy his sugar cookies at recess and stole her away. The second was Becky Stuart during freshman year of high school. They had lasted for three weeks, until Becky decided she couldn't handle his eccentricities anymore—to be fair, Jacob had just tried the garlic-on-everything diet. It wasn't that Jacob wasn't able to connect with women—*well maybe it was*—he just hadn't met someone compatible yet.

Jacob started running and almost caught up to Sophia, trailing by just a few strides. He almost overtook her before she reached the overhang. In the same swift motion, she pitched her handbag off to safety and hurdled off the crag. She plunged into the deep water in a cannonball that delivered a surprising splash for such a slim girl.

Jacob was bobbing in the water next to her in only a moment. It was quite a relief to get out of the heat.

"This feels amazing!" she said.

"I know! And check it out, you can see the bottom."

Sophia looked down and gasped.

"Fish! Colorful ones!"

"This lake is filled with them. Bluegill sunfish."

"Wow, the bottom looks so close."

"I know, it's incredible! Follow me and check this out."

Jacob took long strokes, swimming along the shoreline. Sophia kept right behind him. He stopped at a patch where the bottom got lighter.

"Take a deep breath," he advised.

He plunged under and—using his hands to push upwards—sank towards the bottom. Sophia did the same.

On the bottom of the lake were the remnants of a small boat. It was whitewashed by time and ended up the color of an eggshell. The mast was no longer there, and all that remained was the deck and some of the rudder. Jacob pointed to a large group of yellow and green fish in one of the holes that used to be a window. Sophia smiled, letting air bubbles pass through her lips, which she followed to the surface.

"How old is that?" she asked when his head popped out of the water.

"Fifty years or so. I figured you would like it because those fish always seem to be in the same spot."

"I did like it... thanks."

"Don't mention it. Actually, there's this cave-type thing not too far away where this—"

A loud singing voice came from the bushes.

"Some folks like to get away, take a holiday from the neighborhood," crooned the strangely metallic tone.

"Cell-phone," Sophia explained. "Can't help but love Billy Joel." She started doing the front crawl back to the shore. Her hair trailed behind her as she took long easy strokes.

Jacob continued to tread water, as it felt amazing just to be surrounded by a chilly liquid blanket on a day like this. He wasn't ready to get back to roasting anytime soon.

Jacob heard Sophia answer the call back on land. He wondered how she was able to scramble to the top of the cliff face so fast.

"Hey grand pappy! What's going... Wait slow down... Ok...We'll be right back."

Jacob's curiosity was aroused.

"Hey Cob! We gotta go right now!" she called.

"What's the news from your grandfather?"

"I'm not sure. He sounded so frantic I couldn't understand what he was saying."

"Strange... I've never seen him worked up before," he said.

"Me neither."

Jacob took a deep breath and sank beneath the surface. He

swam underwater toward shore, trying to enjoy every last moment. The ground came up quick, and with a great gasp of air he surfaced. As he pulled himself out he looked over at Sophia. The beads of water on her face caused her skin to glisten. Hair that had been in a tight French braid had now come loose, and with a twist of her neck was thrown behind her shoulders. *She belongs in a shampoo commercial,* he thought. Jacob was sure that girls did not come more beautiful than her.

"Let's get moving," he said.

"Lead the way."

They began their journey back to see what was so urgent.

CHAPTER 10

Mr. Maddock was pacing the deck floor when Jacob and Sophia returned. A handwritten sign hung from the door that read 'Closed Early Our Apologies'. Jacob and Sophia jogged up to him. The librarian's fists were red from repeatedly squeezing his hands in anticipation.

"What's so important, Grand Pappy? And where's your cane?"

"No cane necessary today! Come with me, I will explain everything," Mr. Maddock said, ushering them into the library.

The old man led them towards the basement door. Jacob knew that something big was going on. The librarian had only one rule that Jacob had always followed and never questioned: don't go into the basement. Jacob had created fun theories on why no one was allowed in this sanctuary. His favorite was that the basement was a labyrinth guarded by a giant mouse, which would blend into the stone and catch intruders to play hopscotch with forever.

Jacob didn't enjoy hopscotch.

Mr. Maddock opened the door and they all proceeded down the stairway. To Jacob's dismay the sub-level was not a magical realm at all, just a large stuffy room with piles upon piles of literature. At the bottom of the stairs, Mr. Maddock stopped and stared both the youths in the eyes with an intensity Jacob had never seen on the old man's face.

"When I was twelve years old," Mr. Maddock began, "my grandfather gave me a book called 'Myths and Legends of the Old World'. I read that book cover to cover more times than I can recall. Every time those words hit my eyes I was transported into worlds full of adventure and excitement; however, one story always stood out. It was called "Sun and the Blue Flower", and was traced back to early Akal tribes in Ghana. The story was fascinating."

Mr. Maddock closed his eyes and recited the tale from memory.

"Before time, everything was ruled by darkness. Darkness was cold and unforgiving. The stars in the heavens stood up to Darkness, however they never had enough spirit to pierce his hold, and were kept in the far reaches of the universe, cold and alone. Darkness never ate, never cried, never sang the songs of the Unawa. Darkness had no smile and no heart. During night —for you see, it was always night—a tiny star was born named Sun. Sun was no bigger than Lion but he gave off a small amount of light, and with it… hope. Darkness did not like Sun for he did not like the light. It made Darkness's thousand eyes sting.

'Sun,' Darkness said. 'You must stop giving off your light.'

'I cannot,' Sun replied.

'If you disobey me, I will send you off to the furthest reaches of my domain,' Darkness said angrily.

'Then send me away, for light is who I am.'

Darkness sucked in his cheeks, and with all his might, blew Sun into the beyond. Sun drifted and drifted, but since Darkness ruled everything, Sun floated through the black for eons. Sun began to feel cold. Sun almost gave up hope and almost gave up his light. Then suddenly, coming close to him was another small ray of light, only it was blue.

'Who is there?' Sun asked brightly.

The blue light did not answer. When Sun reached the blue light, he saw that it was not another tiny star, but a beautiful flower. Sun and the flower were headed directly towards each other. Sun could not stop, so he prepared himself to hit. As their light connected, something miraculous happened. Sun began to grow. Sun felt power, far more power then he ever thought possible. He flared and pulsed and grew. All the stars in the far reaches of the black turned their eyes towards Sun. Sun kept growing and growing until he became bigger than the stars, bigger than earth, bigger than Darkness. Sun grew so large that Darkness could not diminish Sun's light no matter how hard he tried. Sun gave birth to life. Sun gave birth to Zebra and Hippo and Giraffe and Man. Now, every time Sun sleeps, Darkness creeps in and tries to regain his hold. But every morning, Sun pushes Darkness back and keeps us all warm and allows life to bloom, including a small blue flower which Sun named Kami."

Jacob watched the bliss on Mr. Maddock's face as he finished the story.

"That's a great story," Jacob said. "But why tell it to us now?"

"Because..." said Mr. Maddock, "I believe the flower is real, and I know where to find it."

"Real?" Sophia said. "But that's just a story."

"Well aren't the best things in life most worthy of stories?" Mr. Maddock asked. "I believe that the Akal knew of this flower and created this folklore to keep its legend alive. Modern scholars of Kami — as rare as they are — call the flower 'The Ancillary'."

"But Grand Pappy, you've never told me that one before... and you told me hundreds of stories when I was little."

"There was a reason," Mr. Maddock said. "I was in enough trouble with your parents anyway."

"Wait," she said. "This can't be why you don't get along anymore with mom and dad."

"Unfortunately it is," he said. "We are not on the same page of this wonderful book. However," Mr. Maddock said, turning his attention to Jacob. "Your father and I *were* on the same page. The same sentence in fact."

"My dad?" Jacob asked, a knot immediately forming in his stomach.

Mr. Maddock must have sensed the pain behind Jacob's

eyes.

"I'm sorry to bring him up. He was my favorite student out of all I ever had. He was more of a son to me than… anyway… he too believed that the Ancillary was real… and for good reason."

"But what does the Ancillary do in the real world?" Jacob asked.

"Let me get back to the beginning," Mr. Maddock said with a stroke of his peppered goatee. "I will explain as much as I can in the short amount of time we have. Why don't you two have a seat?" Mr. Maddock gestured to a pair of dusty wooden rocking chairs. "Then I'll enlighten you both."

Jacob and Sophia nestled into the chairs and Mr. Maddock began.

"I am a devout lover of botany, as you both know, and with good reason. Plants are the main source of medicinal products, from anti-inflammatories to sedatives, and have been used as such since humanity began. The basis for most medicines comes from natural sources. Plants can give you energy and they can relax you. Some can alter your mental state… others can take it away entirely. After I read the tale of Sun and the Blue Flower, I began to wonder, if plants could be used to heal and change the body, why not the soul?"

"Soul?" Jacob questioned.

Mr. Maddock paused as if thinking how to best explain what he meant. His eyebrows rose as he seemed to reach an answer. He opened up a closet and started rustling through old clothes, tools, books and what seemed to be sports equipment. After a short investigation, he pulled out a solid blue towel and a soccer ball.

"It is my firm belief that everyone can change the world. Potential is the most powerful idea in existence and everyone has an abundance of it. This is where the idea of destiny comes into play. The soul exists as a guide to one's destiny. Destiny is nothing more than reaching the zenith of one's potential. I admit that this is in fact a flawed theory — because potential is virtually limitless—however I believe that destiny is the search for the very top. People are happiest when they are unleashing their capability and making their mark upon the world. This holds true in every walk of life," Mr. Maddock then covered the soccer ball with the towel. "Lets say the soccer ball represents a crude depiction of destiny. Every time we do something that is a positive step towards our zenith a small section of our potential is revealed." Mr. Maddock raised a tiny portion of the towel to uncover one of the black hexagons on the ball.

"The problem is that most people don't follow what they're meant to do and end up stuck in jobs that make them unhappy, and lives that don't fit right." He then let the towel slide back to cover the whole ball. "Now imagine the ball many times bigger with infinitely more sections, which is what it would be if it was actually representing our potential."

"So what does the Ancillary do then?" Sophia asked.

"The story of "Sun and the Blue Flower" is quite ambiguous as to what the flower actually does, but my years of research have led to a possible solution. The Ancillary Flower tries to lift the entire towel at once."

"Guaranteed Destiny," Jacob said, completing the thought.

"Almost," Mr. Maddock's voice lowered. "It is a guarantee that the person who finds it will have every tool they will ever need to fulfill their destiny. It is likely that limitless knowledge and an unclouded view of why humanity exists will find the user. Some even speculate that the person who possesses the Ancillary will instantly develop capabilities of a supernatural order. Imagine the power. No one really can understand the true power we all hold inside of us. My dear children, it is a guarantee that whoever finds it will drastically change the world. The one who finds the Ancillary flower will be legend."

"Why haven't you told me about this?" Jacob asked, feeling a bit left out.

"Because I didn't want to drag you into an old man's dream. Cob, you remind me so much of myself when I was younger. Always looking for the answers even when you probably shouldn't. I have spent far too much of my time on this obsession. I kept seeing references to the Ancillary in so many texts—many times when there was actually nothing there to see. I didn't want you to waste your life away on a fairy tale."

"So what changed?" Sophia asked.

"This," Mr. Maddock said as he pulled the clipping from *Human Affairs* from his back pocket, "changed everything."

Jacob took the small piece of newspaper and brought it chest high between him and Sophia so they could read it simultaneously. He quickly scanned the story and his eyes widened.

"So you believe that these people have found it?" Jacob asked.

"Yes and no. What you need to understand is that the world is alive and tries to communicate with us all the time. People don't really listen anymore, but there are certain things that cannot be ignored. This is one of them. The earth *wants* us to find the Ancillary flower. This is our first clue as to how," Mr. Maddock said with conviction.

"But the clipping says that the people of Tanki Lowbei don't know why all this is happening," Sophia argued.

"They might not, but I do. It was quite a cunning realization if I do say so myself," Mr. Maddock said with a smirk.

"Pollen," Jacob stated.

Mr. Maddock looked astounded.

"YES! YES! How astute," Mr. Maddock said while he began to dance awkwardly, with mostly arms and legs flailing. It looked like he was trying to stay atop a log rolling down the river.

"What do you mean by that?" Sophia asked Jacob while her grandfather continued to do what could only loosely be considered dancing.

"Flowers have pollen. If the Ancillary exists then like all other flowers, the male variety would have pollen for reproduction. Right?"

"Haha, you are quite perceptive," Mr. Maddock told Jacob as he finally stopped his boogying. "I have read almost everything that has been written on the Ancillary and even I didn't make the connection that swiftly. Let's face it… everyone can change the world even if they don't know how. The pollen must be having the same effect as the Ancillary only on a smaller scale. Some of these people have advanced fields which they know nothing about, simply because they had the potential to do so. The pollen has pushed them in the right direction and filled their minds with brilliant ideas, seemingly from thin air."

"Why is this plant so rare if it reproduces?" Sophia asked.

"Good question," Mr. Maddock said. "Although no one in recent history has ever seen the Ancillary, many long-lasting cultural groups—like the Akal—have legends and folklore about the subject, which have endured throughout the ages. It is believed that the pollen is not actually for reproduction but rather to draw attention to its whereabouts. Myth dictates that there can only be one Ancillary flower at a time. If no one finds it within a year of its blossom, it will perish and a single weightless seed is sent into the wind. The air stream will carry the seed a myriad of miles until it finally settles to the ground. Once the seed reaches the earth, it will stay dormant for five hundred years until the cycle repeats itself."

"Five hundred YEARS?" Sophia was shocked.

"Years," Mr. Maddock said solemnly. "This is why you must move quickly, Cob."

"Me? Why me?" Jacob asked.

"There is one very important detail I have not told you. The Ancillary is said to have a unique characteristic. A mark to be frank."

"This Mark character sounds confused," Jacob joked.

Mr. Maddock laughed and turned around. He went to one of the cherrywood shelves in the back of the basement. He stretched his arms upward and started shuffling through the top shelf until he found what he was looking for. In Mr. Maddock's hands was a leather-bound book that looked as if it could be as old as the librarian himself. He furiously rifled through the text.

"This marking is significant because it is the Ancillary's way of telling the world who will benefit most from its properties. Life is exceedingly mysterious, children. Even with all of today's advancements and accumulated information we still know so very little. We have a fact-based theory on how old the universe is. We understand how creatures evolved through mutations to become us. We have captured the power of wind and fire. We can talk to anyone we choose across the globe by simply picking up a phone. Flying across oceans and breathing underwater are now possible. Everyday, society makes advancements that are far beyond my comprehension, yet if you locked the world's best minds in a room they would not be able to explain... this."

Mr. Maddock slowly turned the book towards Jacob's face, holding the top portion in-between his palm and fingertips. The paper was yellowed and the corners dog-eared. The words *The Ancillary* in bold print tattooed the brim of a large picture of a cave painting. The flower in focus looked normal enough, dark green sepals with tall yellow anthers, however, something strange immediately caught Jacob's eye. On every deep blue petal there indeed lay a marking. Four black dots in a perfect diamond connected by thin lines. Inside the diamond was a perfect circle of eight dots, also connected. Jacob raised his open hand next to the photo. The flower and his palm held the exact same image.

Jacob's head felt light. His purpose had just dropped in his lap after so many years of searching. The corners of his lips curled toward his ears and a single word escaped them.

"Awesome."

CHAPTER 11

Diego Ramirez tossed his inhaler into the camouflaged duffle bag. It was the type of bag that could handle anything—not that it ever had to.

As he stared at the small silver-tipped device lying on top of his clothes, a strong feeling of hate surged in him. It was that tiny thing that represented the death of his dreams. His upper arm would never have the 'Semper Fidelis' tattoo that belonged there.

The dream of entering the Marine Corp. was as fresh as if he had just woken from it yesterday.

The actual time frame was close to five years.

Now in his mid-twenties, Diego lived alone in a one-bedroom apartment working security at the stadium. Sure, he was promoted in only three years—the shortest time of any past head guard—yet it felt like he was moving forward down a wrong road, and soon he would be too far to turn back.

He knew the pressure points on the body that would take a linebacker down in seconds; he knew how to find water in the desert; he could shoot a tin can off his fence from three hundred yards; yet security was where he ended up.

The pay was fine, and the benefits were more than sufficient, but weak lungs blew his one shot at glory.

At least he would get to go on this wild-goose chase, which would at least be a much-needed change of pace.

He had accepted the job from Mr. Maddock without hesitation. Sure, the old man was kind of a crackpot, but the pay was phenomenal... too high for what he was being asked to do. It was the off-season, so taking a personal week or so was no big deal. He was making half a year's pay taking this job anyway.

Mr. Maddock was an old friend of his fathers'. The librarian was the first person to offer his help when Diego was denied the right to serve. The old man gave him some books on holistic and eastern medicines that might help, but they never panned out; mostly they just sat on his shelf half-read—he never believed in any of that supernatural hooey.

All he had to do now was escort some kids to this tiny town in Tibet, look for some flower or something, and then take them home. Mr. Maddock had even sprung for the flight; all Diego had to do was show up.

Mr. Maddock tried to explain what exactly they were looking for over the phone, but it sounded kind of crazy. *No plant exists that can make you reach your potential*, he thought, *and the Ancillary was a stupid name for a flower. And what it does? C'mon, it's like looking for the fountain of youth.*

Next in his bag went his trusted bowie knife, followed by some provisions that would come in handy in the wilderness. Some energy bars, a radio, and thermals nestled on top of the pile and thankfully hid the inhaler. Out of site and out of mind, or at least until the next attack.

How a librarian had that much dispensable income Diego didn't understand, yet he wasn't one to ask.

One thing he did understand was Mr. Maddock's sense of urgency. He threw the final belongings he wanted to take in the bag, zipped it tight, and headed out.

CHAPTER 12

The sun was finally dipping behind the tree line as Jacob bolted out the front door of the library. Of all the ways this day could have gone, this was the most unexpected. His feet were in fast pursuit of his house and the rest of his body seemed to be along for the ride. The usual chatty monologue that occupied his mind was uncharacteristically quiet. The news was so overwhelming that his thoughts were in overdrive. After receiving Mr. Maddock's urgent command to pack a bag for a rousing journey, he ran home so he could return within three hours—as Mr. Maddock had already arranged a flight. How the librarian was able to do that so quickly he could not fathom, but he had a mission to fulfill. The center of the street was his runway and he took off. His attention was brought to the high-pitched chatter from the woods. The chirping from the birds was loud—much louder than usual. It was probably his imagination, but it sounded almost as if they were cheering him on.

The sunset was a beautiful array of oranges and purples eddied together, but Jacob chose not to stop and stare. The calves of his legs were sore and his quads on fire, but he couldn't care less. Until now, his life had been an endless search for meaning. He finally had a purpose.

It didn't take long for him to get to his house. In fact, it was the fastest he had ever traveled on foot between his two homes. He took a key ring out of his pocket, which he fumbled as he attempted to find the one with the crocodile's profile. His hands were shaking quite a bit.

He threw the door open and didn't bother to close it behind him. As he began racing up the stairs he stopped midway and almost fell flat on his face before composing himself and catching his balance.

His father had known.

Mr. Maddock didn't mention it, but Jacob understood it had to be true. His father must have known all along. Mr. Maddock and his dad must have gone over that story a hundred times. If the Ancillary was the ex-professor's favorite and most cherished myth, then the ex-student must have learned all about it. When Jacob was born, his father must have seen the mark and —

He pushed the thoughts to the back of his mind. A mix of nostalgia and depression was the first wave of emotion to hit when thinking back on it. It was not the feeling he craved at the moment.

He finished his stair-climb and crashed into his room. Turning his attention back to packing, he tried keeping his wandering mind focused. Tibet. *What in the world do I need for Tibet? Is it rainy? Cold?* Jacob grabbed handfuls of socks. One very important tidbit he had learned through traveling is that regardless of where you go, there is no such thing as too many socks. A fresh pair slapped on your feet can positively alter your outlook on even the hardest mornings. Four pairs of jeans went into his Adidas duffel along with long sleeved T-shirts, a flashlight, Tylenol, Spider-Man baseball cap, grey hoodie, flannel boxers, and other small accessories. His bag was bursting with supplies and Jacob prepared himself for departure. The small metal safe in the corner held a moderate amount of his cash savings. Being frugal helped to keep it well stocked. Besides food and clothing, Jacob's money would have gone to books — but they were free at the library. Another plus.

Jacob had worked for a few years as an auto mechanic's assistant, learning the trade and making decent money. Cars never really interested him, but there were not many job openings in Harrison. Gaining the knowledge of automobile basics, he was able to join a small staff and get paid a modest wage.

The last step was to make a withdrawal.

The bottom landing was a double jump away for Jacob's long legs. The Deer house held two small levels and was located in a secluded neighborhood, as were most neighborhoods in the town of Harrison. Jacob had no siblings to worry about, which made things simpler. This would have been a prime opportunity for a younger sibling to blackmail him into getting something they wanted — like a pony. The last obstacle he faced was a big one, and it had been bothering him for a while now. How would he explain this to his mom?

Had she known?

Again, he pushed the memories of his father out. His mother was open to Jacob experiencing new events, so freedom to travel was often an option given to him, but this was way too much to ask. Even if Mr. Maddock called her up to explain the situation, she would probably just forbid him from ever going to the library again, because the man who ran it was a nut job.

He always had the urge to travel; every time he did, it felt like he was closer and closer to finding what he was meant for. Even with all of the voyaging he had done, there was no way she would knowingly allow him to travel halfway around the globe — especially if he was to be going alone.

He again stopped what he was doing.

Alone.

The initial excitement overwhelmed him, the wonderment and awe he felt at his fortune had prevented him from thinking about this word.

Alone.

It would be very difficult. Jacob tried to grasp some semblance of what this would mean. Mr. Maddock hadn't elaborated on any details of the plan yet; all he knew were his instructions to get ready rapidly. Would he have to go alone? Mr. Maddock wouldn't let him go alone, right? He would have to worry about that later. He knew that bravery was a trait greatly rewarded in life, so he recited a mantra he invented that always helped him with his insecurities.

The slow repeat of "strength of a rhinoceros beetle. Heart of a honey badger" soothed his trepidation.

Now comes the hard part, he thought.

Walking zombie-esque, with slow steps toward the house phone, Jacob tried his best to think up an excuse. He hated the idea of lying to his mother, but couldn't think of a way around it. There was an emergency number left taped to the refrigerator, so calling was an option, but actually *talking* to her meant he wouldn't be able to pull off a fib; she could always tell. As he reached the phone he had an idea.

He hit the "record message" button and heard the piercing beep.

"Thank you for calling the Deer residence we appreciate being acknowledged," he started. "Jacob Deer speaking in case you were wondering. The house is empty for the moment unless ghosts are real; then it's probably not. If you leave a message then someone will get back to you. If this is my mother, then I love you dearly and thanks for checking up on me. I am currently in Tibet looking for a supernatural flower. I'll be home soon."

-CLICK- The message was over and Jacob exhaled deeply. He was probably better off telling her the truth, rather than lying.

If his mother HAD known about the story, then maybe she would understand. If she hadn't, then the next time she tried to call, she would assume he was just being his strange self and was probably adventuring only as far as the library. It wasn't an FBI- worthy plan, but it would buy him some time.

He was ready. The door swung shut as he left his home. Sweet air poured into his lungs as the night enclosed him. Things seemed different; the stars a little brighter, the wind more melodic through the leaves, and the path back to his bedroom looked like a marathon course.

Jacob was ahead of schedule, so he took a big breath and slowed down. The sky was beautiful. The connect-the-dot legends of the past stared him down. There was little to no light pollution in Harrison and the heavens appeared as they were meant to. The Big Dipper looked as if it could scoop up all the other stars. Jacob picked a nice mossy spot and sank to his knees. His hands gripped clovers and his legs squished a couple of dandelions.

"Thank you," Jacob said in a low voice. It was very simple and sincere. In Jacob's mind there were no more words necessary to show his heartfelt appreciation. Nature enticed him to stay for a moment more, so he did.

CHAPTER 13

If Mr. Maddock were a character in a video game, it would appear as if he had consumed a special item that allowed super speed. As he flowed through the basement, books soared into piles as if they were strung together on a cable. There was no time to worry about making a mess, as unfortunately time was of the essence. The telephone's chord had stretched taut, as it had spent too much time in the crevice between cheek and shoulder as he rummaged throughout the area. He refused to let Cob down. If companionship were not possible, he would give Cob all the required supplies.

From the subterranean level the doorbell barely broke the silence, but Mr. Maddock was keeping an ear fixed for it. A cane was unnecessary as his adrenaline had been in constant flow for hours. He was aware that the feeling would not last forever and he enjoyed every second of it. As if on roller-skates, Mr. Maddock glided toward the entrance.

———————————

"There's an airplane in your backyard," Jacob said as he opened the door.

"That's not just any airplane. That's your airplane."

"Before expressing my gratitude for not having to pass through airport security, I have to ask, why?"

"Commercial flights aren't able to take you where you're going."

"Where am I going?"

"To certain success," Mr. Maddock said with a dignified

smile.

"Thanks, I was a little uncertain for a while."

"Young man, this is what you were meant for. You know, not everyone can say they have a birthmark that connects them to one of the greatest mysteries the world has ever known. There is no need for doubt; it is a thing of the past. Now come with me, I have gifts to impart and wisdom to share."

"Wisdom is the best gift so impart away, I'm going to need all that I can get."

Once inside, Mr. Maddock led Jacob into the living quarters of the house. The threshold to the dining room framed an amazing feast on a long table. The delicious smell landed heavily on Jacob's nose. There were roasted turkey legs, rosemary garlic mashed potatoes, green bean casserole with bacon and crispies, jugs of the famous sweet tea and jalapeño corn bread. Waiting on the smaller table directly behind it was a banana cream pie, multi-layered chocolate cake and an array of fresh tropical fruit. As Jacob drifted hypnotically toward the cornucopia, he saw two people lingering by the table eyeing the food.

Waiting to dig into the corn bread was Sophia—looking even more beautiful than she had earlier in the day. Next to her was someone Jacob did not recognize. He was tall, muscular and standing extremely rigidly, like a metal pole had been fastened to his back. His skin had an olive completion and his hair was cropped short, almost nonexistent.

"Diego… Jacob. Jacob… Diego," Mr. Maddock said.

"Nice to meet you," Jacob said.

Diego nodded and let out a small grunt.

"Diego is wise in the ways of the outdoors and other… necessary skills," Mr. Maddock said. "He will be accompanying you two on your trip. He'll keep you safe."

"Wait… you two?" Jacob asked.

"Correct," Mr. Maddock said with one of his patented smiles. "Two."

"You're coming?" Jacob asked Sophia.

She shrugged. "I left my house to see the world. If I'm going swimming I might as well dive in head first." She smiled. "Of all the stories my grand pappy told me when I was younger," she raised an eyebrow at her grandfather, "or didn't tell me, I would never have thought one of them had the possibility of being real. And hey, look at your hand, that's a pretty big coincidence if the story is made up."

"You didn't think I would let you go alone, did you?" Mr. Maddock asked.

Jacob could not put into words how he felt. Any anxiety that had been present quickly dwindled at the thought of having this giant bodyguard and Sophia along with him. He hoped Diego would be an excellent travel companion. If Mr. Maddock had faith in him then so would he.

"What's all this for?" Jacob asked, motioning towards the banquet.

"I feel that a celebration is precisely what we need to be doing," Mr. Maddock said. "Nourishment of the body seems prudent — plus I couldn't resist the temptation of showing off my culinary artistry. I was already preparing a feast for my granddaughter, but after the wonderful news I decided to make things a little bigger. Please… before it gets cold."

Diego dived into his chair and started gobbling down a turkey leg with all the grace of a Neanderthal. Jacob grabbed the seat next to him and snatched a leg himself. Sophia sat opposite Jacob with Mr. Maddock at her side. As they tucked into their meals, Mr. Maddock raised a glass. A small 'tink' reverberated as he tapped it with a butter knife. Diego reluctantly stopped devouring the fowl to pay attention.

"Good luck," Mr. Maddock said.

In silence they all waited to hear what else the old man had to say.

"That's it?" Sophia asked.

"Well, if you insist," Mr. Maddock said. "I guess a good story always goes with good food — Eat up Diego, you look like you are withering away."

Diego's eyes gleamed with a silent thank you.

"I will tell you all one of the most popular stories among Ancillary lore that is not supposed to be taken seriously. No one knows who was the first to tell this story. Although it is absurdly silly, it is still a favorite fable of mine," Mr. Maddock said. "The world was not always how we know it today. Humanity is the dominant life force on the planet now, but long before we were around the world was run by hedgehogs."

"Hedgehogs," Diego murmured with a mouth full of green beans. "Come on."

"I warned you it would be silly," Mr. Maddock said. "Where was I—Yes—hedgehogs. Now back then, these creatures could speak and were sentient beings well aware of their surroundings. Unfortunately, with intelligence comes arrogance. The hedgehogs did not take kindly to any changes to societal norm. They were a scared race and tried their best not to upset the harmony of their environment. Anything out of the ordinary would be cast away by the regime. During this time there was a young hedgehog named Artemis who was quite sweet and kindhearted. Her mother and father were very proud and loved her deeply. Now as you know, hedgehogs have small spines covering most of their bodies. These spines would grow in gradually over their youth and be fully developed by age four—and not a day later. Artemis was five days away from her fourth birthday and had yet to show any signs of her spines fully growing in. The smooth skin on Artemis's back was covered only by a few small spines in a very distinct pattern," Mr. Maddock paused. "The exact pattern that happens to be found on your palm, Cob."

All eyes turned towards Jacob's hand, though the mark was not discernable as it was covered in gravy at the moment.

"Artemis was mortified. If her spines did not grow in by the fourth year, the higher-ups would cast her out of their community. The other hedgehogs teased and called her names like 'Glass-Back' and 'Polished Patricia'. The young hedgehogs singled her out, but they did not quite grasp what being different meant. It meant exile, which in turn meant death. Artemis decided that she would not suffer humiliation on their terms. With a short goodbye to her parents, she set off into the woods to live on her own. After a few hours alone in the forest, the hunger and fear set in. Artemis went searching for food to try and distract her from the increasing loneliness. It was getting dark, and Artemis was becoming less and less bold. She had left her family and all that she loved. She was almost ready to lie down and give up, when she saw a soft blue glow in the distance. Collecting herself, Artemis walked towards the glow. It was then she discovered something miraculous. Light was emanating from a strange flower with markings on it. The markings were the same as the pattern on her undeveloped spines. Artemis understood that the flower was meant for her and without knowing what would come next, took a small nibble from one of the petals. Everything went dark as she immediately fell asleep."

At this point in the story, Jacob's chewing slowed. Sophia set down her fork and listened closely, while Diego kept on devouring the meal in full force.

"When Artemis awoke, she felt strange. Somewhat… heavier and more powerful. She saw the gleaming of the stars in a small puddle very close by. She went over to quench her thirst and caught her reflection staring back—only it didn't look like her. Her face appeared the same, but her back was different. Quite different. Now, instead of spines, were long sharp quills that grew in overnight. She had become a porcupine; the first porcupine. Artemis went back to hedgehog society and was welcomed with open arms—mostly because no one dared pick on her again. She soon became leader of the hedgehogs, made great changes, and her parents couldn't have been more proud."

"So is Jake here going to be able to puff up like a blowfish?" She was grinning.

"I guess spikes would be pretty cool," Jacob said, puffing out his cheeks. "So these quills are a metaphor. Evolution right?"

"Ah, you caught that, huh? It's true. Theories of evolution tie in quite nicely with Ancillary legends. It is evolution in an unconventional sense. The normal notion of evolution is a mistake made by nature that works better. The Ancillary is evolution on purpose. Unlike this story, however, the myths usually dictate that the essence of a person will be affected—not the body—which I firmly believe is the truth. I think whoever invented this story meant to express the idea of inherent potential for change."

"I think whoever invented this story was bored," said Diego.

Mr. Maddock smiled. "You would be surprised what miracles are out there."

Diego shrugged and helped himself to another heaping portion of potatoes.

Jacob's eyes drifted onto Sophia. She was staring back at him with confusion. His face got warmer.

"Out of all the people in the world..." she said.

His cheeks were on fire.

"For all we know, the plant might not even exist," Mr. Maddock said. "If not, then just have some fun, but be careful overseas, your parents would never forgive me if anything happened to you... I would never forgive me. Though I trust in Diego's capabilities completely, you must promise to be ever vigilant. This is why I have taken all the precautions I could possibly think of."

"As in...?" Sophia asked.

"Due time," Mr. Maddock stated. "For now just enjoy your meals." He took a quick look at Diego. "I see you're a step ahead of me," he said pointedly.

Diego smiled and the mashed spuds came very close to falling out of his mouth. The rest of the meal was spent in laughter and good spirits.

CHAPTER 14

Beer mugs clanged. The frothy head sloshed onto the table, coating the buffet of fried chicken. Marrow's crew was celebrating. They were to leave for Tibet at sun-up — which was only hours away — and were enjoying the finer things the New York underground had to offer. Scantily clad women and drinks were the main attraction. They sat at a long table with all the cholesterol-loaded food they could dream of. Marrow sat at the head, watching his men cheer. He stayed uncharacteristically quiet as the people around him danced and sang drinking songs.

A chorus of, "Drown it down, take the brew another round, make my beer the darkest brown, send my head to hit the ground," was joined in by most of the room.

Marrow sat in silent contemplation of what was to come. These primitive followers he attracted were concerned with only pleasing their Ids. *How stereotypical*, Marrow thought. Little Paulo, one of his men, was on all fours on the table — like a dog — with a twenty-dollar bill clutched in his teeth. Not that Marrow had anything against unleashing the inner beast, it just seemed that his men had little more than that to offer. *Why is it that money, drugs and women are the only focus of criminals?* He thought. *Those are only pleasures of the flesh*. There was so much more that he wanted… like immortality.

The idiots would be forgotten of course, as time doesn't have room in its memory for nobodies. All of the people in the bar — all the people in New York…and the rest of the U.S. for that matter — could never even dream of aspiring to what he was to become.

The details and purpose of their trip to Asia had been shared with his men, but none fully understood. They couldn't care less about why they were going as long as they were getting paid. The sights of crisp, hundred dollar stacks were overpowering. This actually worked in his favor. If no one cared for what he sought, then he could forget to worry about things like disloyalty.

Through the howling and jeering, Marrow could only concentrate on one thing. He had managed to extract a single word out of the monk... Krinama. He let the word roll over in his head slowly, excited to find out the meaning. It was the only thing the monk had screamed throughout the entire... examination. He did not let go of that information easily. Marrow was still tingling from all the fun he had trying to extract it. *Car batteries and razor blades can be very compelling*, he thought. At this point, disposing of the body was no harder than children's algebra; a very simple formula that when followed was always successful.

The monk's death did not weigh on his conscious even a bit. Sacrifices had to be made in order to get what he wanted. *Besides*, he thought, *what good was a thieving monk anyway?*

Little Paulo had just taken his shirt off and was twirling it around one of the girls' heads. Marrow let his men have their fun, but if any of them chose fun over duty in the coming days he would have no qualms about disposing of them as well. He was getting quite good at his algebra.

As tequila shots were being chased by bigger shots of tequila, Marrow chose to abstain, and let the word slide off his tongue once more.

Krinama.

CHAPTER 15

"I never thought I'd see the day when an airplane would drive down Sleepy Hollow road," said Mr. Maddock.

"I've been wondering how it got back there." Jacob scratched the budding stubble on his chin.

They were standing on the Library's back deck looking out at the small green aircraft currently parked in the brush. It looked as if it were trying to camouflage into the bushes and weeds, but utterly failing. The flamboyant craft was a bright forest green with chrome patchwork that—to the untrained eye—did not inspire much confidence. On the side of the plane was the Ancillary's mark painted obsidian black.

"So a few people believe this crazy story, huh?" asked Diego.

"More than you know, and more than I'd like at this particular moment," Mr. Maddock answered.

Diego rotated his shoulder and worked out a kink. "Why do you say that?"

"We may not be the only ones looking," Mr. Maddock said. "Stay sharp."

Diego grunted.

"It may not look like much," Mr. Maddock commented, "however, me and the pilot are old friends. Old enough to know that this particular plane can handle anything. Many years back we thought we might have found it, but it didn't pan out. She has had some major modifications done to the plane as well, including being able to hold extra fuel. She's quite clever."

The side hatch of the airplane was thrown open and a woman appeared. She was short and beautiful with dark hair.

"Oi!" The woman exclaimed with a heavy Australian accent. "You three my crew?"

Mr. Maddock gave Jacob a sly grin and a wink. "Speak of the devil... and she shall appear."

"She looks young," Jacob said.

"Rosie, it's a shame you couldn't feast with us!" Mr. Maddock called over.

"Thanks, but I needed my sleep, it's gonna be a long flight!" she yelled back.

"Did you get enough rest?"

"Do Walaroos wish for stilts?" Rosie shouted.

"They do," Mr. Maddock explained to the confused group. "Grab your things children, The Ancillary awaits."

Jacob couldn't believe this was really happening, and judging by the looks on their faces, neither could his companions — possibly for different reasons than his own. They picked up their belongings and Mr. Maddock escorted them into the yard.

Rosie had a snake with angel wings tattooed on her upper arm. Jacob thought she looked far too young for Mr. Maddock to consider an *old* friend.

"And which one of these young gents has the mark?" Rosie asked.

Jacob held up his hand.

"Rosie Gruffentree." The pilot introduced herself shaking left hands with Jacob. She held on a little longer than one normally would.

"Ain't no ordinary birthmark you got yourself here. You should consider yourself the luckiest young man this side of the world... all sides of the world. And I've been there lookin' so I should know."

"Rosie here is a long devoted fan of the Ancillary legends," Mr. Maddock said.

"Got me pilot license just in case this ever actually

happened."

"That's some devotion," Sophia said.

"And who are you, young lady?" Rosie asked, pronouncing 'who' like 'ooh'.

"This is my granddaughter Sophia, and this other young man is Diego," said Mr. Maddock.

"Strapping," Rosie said, looking directly at Diego's biceps.

"Thanks again, Rosie," Mr. Maddock said.

"Why you thanking me for? You know as well as anyone that helping to find it is all I could ask for."

Mr. Maddock turned his attention towards his wards. "Good luck you three, make me proud. I have taken the liberty of packing you some extra items — including mud-resistant sleeping bags. You'll find them already inside. I have also packed all the important information I have learned regarding the Ancillary, to help you track it down and recognize it."

Sophia and her grandfather embraced, and the old man firmly shook hands with Diego. Rosie began ushering them inside the craft.

"Hold back a second, Cob," Mr. Maddock said. "I have a few more words of wisdom for you."

The others went in, leaving him and Mr. Maddock alone. The old man put his hands on Jacob's shoulders. "First off, if you are feeling under-prepared...don't. One can never be certain of anything. Some of the greatest plans can go awry, while some of the greatest stunts can become the most treasured memories you hold. If you are feeling homesick... don't. I know you of all people are a believer that the whole world is your home, not just where you grew up. Don't forget this. Last, if you are feeling unsure...look at the situation you are in. Not many people still believe the stories, and of all the people who could have been your librarian, it was me. I know you have probably been wondering this but have been too afraid to know the answer... Yes... your father knew about the Ancillary... and knew you were meant for it. You should have seen his face when we searched through countless books looking for clues. Whenever he talked about you, it was as if he won the lottery every day of his life—if the lottery was giving out something much more important than money. By the way, although you posses the mark, that is not the reason why I believe in you. I believe in you because of who you are, not because of what is on your skin. If the world got anything right, it's trusting that you can handle this."

"Thanks," Jacob said as he too gave Mr. Maddock a hug.

"Here, you'll need this." He handed Jacob an old tattered map.

Jacob unfolded the paper and glanced inside. It was mostly lines and green blobs, with a small compass rose in the corner.

"Where did you get a map?"

Mr. Maddock winked. "Good luck."

Jacob said goodbye and entered the plane. The interior looked much like Jacob's closet—if somehow a tornado could strike it. Clothes were strewn everywhere, books and granola bars were on the ground with trinkets scattered all over the place. The inside walls were graffitied with maps and pictures. Towards the rear were three red duffel bags clearly marked with each of their names. Jacob placed his own bag next to them. Sophia and Diego were already sitting in two of the four available seats. An abundance of duct tape was holding the seat's plush innards from spilling onto the floor. Up front, Rosie was in the cockpit fiddling with dials.

Her voice boomed over the old P.A. system—which was unnecessary as the cockpit was only a few feet away.

"G'day. This is your captain speaking," squawked the speakers. "Since we are flying… well, illegally… we're cleared for takeoff. Buckle up mates, we'll be there faster than a king brown can catch a yobbo."

Jacob sat down and all three nervously strapped themselves in. The engines woke up violently, which caused the plane to vibrate. The seats all faced towards the center of the craft like military planes, which allowed the three passengers to face each other.

"So what do you think would happen if someone bad found the Ancillary?" Sophia asked.

"What do you mean?" Jacob said.

"I only know as much as you two about this flower, but I think I got the gist of what grand-pappy was saying. The flower makes you reach your potential, right?"

"Right," Jacob said.

"What if someone has the potential to do terrible things? I mean, not everyone's good."

"I... guess I hadn't thought about that."

"If this flower really does what the legends say," Sophia said, "then wouldn't it be devastating in the hands of someone evil? And like grand-pappy said, everyone has limitless potential, so doesn't that mean someone could be capable of limitless evil?"

"I wouldn't be too worried about it," Diego interjected.

"Why not?"

"Because there is no such thing as a magic flower."

"How would you know?"

"Because it can't possibly exist. Our world has rules and no matter how hard we try or how bad we want... there will always be rules."

"Well there's always the exception that proves it anyway," she said.

"Like the platypus," said Jacob.

"And my grand-pappy may be... eccentric, but he's no fool."

The ground began to move. Jacob looked out of the window and saw the library rush past. They were now cruising along the road. Luckily, there were no cars in their path when Rosie decided to punch it.

The acceleration was brutal. If not for the old leather seatbelts, all three would have slid off their seats into the back of the plane from the g-force. The wheels left the ground and with a roar, they were flying. Jacob had never been in such a small plane before, and the stomach-in-throat feeling was more potent and nauseating then in the larger counterparts.

He looked out of the small oval window and down at the ground. They were rapidly ascending, reaching cotton-candy clouds in a matter of minutes. As the plane leveled out, Jacob's ears popped and the skull-crushing pressure was equalized.

"So is it just me… or does this feel completely unreal?" Jacob asked.

"It's like I'm living someone else's life," Sophia said. "I can't imagine what it must feel like for you. Waking up one morning and finding out that you are destined for something great. I still don't even know what I'm going to major in."

"You make him sound like some sort of savior," Diego joked.

"It sounds a bit ridiculous, but it's not that far off. You heard what my grand-pappy said. The mark shows who stands to gain the most from the Ancillary. Cob, of all the people in the world…it's you. The world is pretty messed up right now and could use some change. Unemployment rates skyrocketing, attacks from the religious right—you must be meant for something huge."

"Maybe I'll turn into Godzilla."

Sophia chuckled. "Maybe not that huge."

"You seem to be believing this fairy tale pretty easily," Diego said to Sophia.

"What's not to believe? All the proof I need is on his hand."

"Its just a funny looking birthmark—no offense Jacob."

Jacob gave a closed-lipped smile.

"I don't think regular birthmarks look like that. And if my grand-pappy was so obsessed with this that he let it get between him and my parents, the least we can do is help him indulge his mystery-tooth."

"What are your parents going to think when they find out you took his side?" Diego asked smugly.

"Well if we find it, then there doesn't have to be sides."

Outside of the aircraft the light finally seemed to fade. In the distance they could see neon jagged lightning bolts coming from dark storm clouds.

"Hey Rosie," Diego called. "We're not flying through that mess, are we?"

"Yessir. Don't worry though, a couple little sparks couldn't take down old Artemis."

"You named the plane Artemis?"

"After one of my favorite stories."

All three passengers looked at each other and smiled. Then reality hit.

"Is she crazy?" Sophia asked. "Going through a storm like that in this rust-bucket?"

Jacob tightened his seat belt. He normally loved flying, but was beginning to feel less and less comfortable as they approached the black clouds. Apparently the trip wasn't going to start as smoothly as he would have liked.

At first it was just small vibrations resonating through the cabin. It was like going over the tiny bumps on the side of highways that keep you awake if you start to drift. Then, the small tremors grew big.

The first jolt caused the interior to look even more like a warzone. The lights flickered and all the items on the floor were momentarily suspended in mid-air. Jacob was hit in the head by a running shoe. Sophia's tight grip on the armrests made her knuckles white. They could feel the energy buzzing around the hull, the pent up power ready to unleash itself in a fury of lightning.

-BANG- The second jolt caused a little more devastation than they were ready for. Everything went completely dark and Diego's strap snapped open. He was thrown onto the floor, stumbling as he tried to stand. Jacob's head was hurled violently into the headrest of his seat and a blinding light entered his vision.

Sophia didn't scream, even during a barrage of heavy mystery items flying through the air. Something sharp caught her on the side of her face and caused a small stream of blood to run down her chin. There was no time for recovery, as the storm was not calming down. The wind tried to tear out the rivets, causing the metal to scream. The plane shook with a ferocity that seemed far too capable of taking them down.

As Diego was flailing on the ground trying to get his hands on something, the atmosphere suddenly seemed to relax. He was able to stand up and make his way back to his seat. Jacob was fine, but the blood still flowed freely on Sophia's face.

Thankful for the current peace—and for continuing to live—they all silently prayed that it would remain that way. Diego tied the broken sections of the straps together across his lap.

Jacob noticed the blood trickling down Sophia's face and landing on her legs in small dots. He reached into his pocket and pulled out a handkerchief—he was the only person he knew of that still carried the old-fashioned cloth.

"For me?" Sophia asked.

Jacob nodded and went over to her. He placed the handkerchief gently against her skin and put pressure on the cut. She placed her hand upon his and squeezed it tightly towards her face. They locked eyes and an unfamiliar feeling welled up inside of Jacob.

"That was fun," Diego said.

"Sorry 'bout that," Rosie called back. "A little hiccup."

"By hiccup, do you mean explosion?" Diego asked.

"Are we through it?" Jacob asked.

"The worst of it, as far as I can tell," Rosie said.

"Why didn't we just go around it?" Diego asked.

"I'm sure a sturdy young man like yourself doesn't back down from every obstacle thrown in your way, do you? Besides, the more time we lose, the more likely it is someone might find the Ancillary before you."

"Touché," Diego said.

"Also, we've got Jacob with us. I wasn't too worried," Rosie said.

"What do you mean? It's not like I did anything except almost become a human bouncy-ball."

Rosie burst out laughing, full-on Santa Claus belly laughs.

"That old codger never told you?"

"What's so funny?" Sophia asked.

"When was the last time you broke a bone?"

Jacob thought about it for a few moments. "Never, I guess."

"Last time you got ill… I mean really ill? The kind that keeps you in bed for weeks and creates a bedside mountain of tissues."

"… I haven't."

"Last time you were in a near death situation?" Rosie said solemnly.

"About five minutes ago."

Rosie burst out laughing again. "Yes, yes. Sorry 'bout that. But you're a croc in a pond, aren't you?"

"I don't get what you're playing at," Sophia said with a hint of contempt in her voice.

"The world is not going to let the one go so easily," Rosie stated proudly.

"Especially now that the Ancillary has blossomed. I'm not saying that you're invincible… no, no, not by any means. But what I will say is that you must be very lucky when it comes to getting hurt. Am I correct?"

"Um…I guess so."

Diego reached over and gave Jacob a sharp punch in the arm.

"Ow!"

Sophia shook her head. "Testosterone at its finest."

CHAPTER 16

Candles lined the lip of the well, casting long shadows upon brick. The flickering light projected the cloaked native's images into puppet-like shadows across the walls. For as long as anyone could remember, an underground river had constantly replenished the well by means of cool water with a deep blue hue. Things had changed. A place that was long renowned as the town's reserve water supply recently had taken on a whole new purpose; a greater purpose.

Crowded did not begin to describe the state the small building was in. This was a very important ritual, not to be missed. A small figure—quite eclipsed by lofty shoulders and festively decorated gourds—shivered in the corner.

It was his time.

The only form not facing the well was dressed in a uniform unlike the rest of the hooded masses. A fur cap sporting antlers and golden trinkets rested on top of the chief's skull. Though it looked like an ancient heirloom passed from generation to generation, it had only been created sixty days prior when the first miracles had begun.

"GODAKH!" boomed the chief. "Step forward!"

The ongoing chatter and excitement quickly halted. The small figure slowly shuffled forward; the thin light revealed it to be a young boy.

"Come child, the vision water will not drink itself!"

This was meant to be an exciting day, but the recipient was always nervous. The well had been restricted since the first miracles had started. The townsfolk decided that this was a gift to be earned and not given lightly. On certain days, someone from the village was presented with the reward, and today the worthy recipient was Godakh.

The boy finally squeezed his way through the crowd and stopped before the chief. His eyes gazed up towards the hulk of a man addressing the crowd. The chief looked quite silly in his hat and Godakh let out a small giggle.

"Good boy, laugh, do not be afraid, for this is a time of celebration."

The chief then started chanting a ritual in their native tongue.

"Mnyam du kha phye 'dzam bu kling!"

A small porcelain bowl attached to a long rope was lowered into the well. It was dipped into the water below and raised very cautiously and with great precision. The chief took the bowl in his hands and slowly passed it to Godakh.

"Your new life awaits," he said quietly to the boy.

Godakh gingerly took the bowl and raised it to his mouth. He felt the cool liquid pass his lips and soothe his scratchy throat. As he gulped the water, the crowd of people began a chant of their own.

"Krinama…" they spoke in unison.

A little louder. "Krinama."

They chanted louder and louder until the noise was deafening.

Godakh finished the water and wiped his palm across his mouth.

"KRINAMA!"

The young boy dropped to his knees.

Nothing happened.

CHAPTER 17

The crinkling of a Twinkie wrapper raised Jacob from his slumber. Across the aisle, Sophia was trying her best to quietly remove the plastic sheath from her confectionary treat, to no avail. He felt like he must have been out for some time. The flight hadn't been unpleasant, as the three passengers talked all through the night. Mostly it was Jacob and Sophia talking, with Diego putting in his two cents here and there, consisting mostly of negativity and survival tips. Jacob was fascinated with Diego's knowledge: that you shouldn't lie down during the middle of a storm if you can't find shelter; rather crouch on the balls of your feet. After imparting that particular tidbit of wisdom however, the topic of storms was quickly dropped.

The conversation ranged from New York politics to southern fads, including mudding—which Jacob explained is where you take your four-wheeler or truck into a mud field in the rain and try and flip it. Sophia and Jacob talked about past pets and favorite guilty-pleasure foods. There was even a friendly debate on how often aliens must visit the earth.

"Good morning, sunshine," Sophia whispered.

"Is it morning? Where are the roosters?" Jacob asked.

"I don't think roosters can fly at thirty thousand feet. We've been sleeping for a good five hours, so it should be morning... unless I've gotten this whole time difference thing wrong." Sophia pulled out another Twinkie from her bag. "Breakfast of champions?"

"Absolutely!"

She tossed the sugary treat, which Jacob caught and began

devouring with the savagery of a junkyard dog. Diego started moving slowly and began to awaken. Sophia pulled out another Twinkie and threw it at Diego's head. This promptly knocked Diego out of his fading dream.

"Morning," Diego said sluggishly.

"Eat up. Today's a big day and we're going to need all the sugar induced energy we can get," Sophia said.

"Are we there yet?" Diego called out.

The pilot turned around, looking all too awake for someone who'd been flying for almost a full day.

"You all have a nice nap, then?" Rosie inquired with a coy smile.

"More like hibernation. I feel like a million bucks," Jacob said.

"Good, because we're getting close."

Jacob liberated himself from his chair and walked toward the tiny bathroom at the rear of the plane. A good splash of water in the face always supercharged him. He pulled the small door back and entered the cubicle-sized lavatory. The sink was dirty but the water that poured from the faucet was surprisingly clear. Splashing repeatedly rendered a nice chill throughout his body.

He thought of his father and what he would say about all this.

Jacob used a towel to dry his face and returned to his seat.

"What's wrong?" Sophia asked.

"Nothing... I guess that Twinkie wasn't the best idea for a first meal."

"Oh well, I have more snacks in my bag. I think I have some pretzels—"

"No thanks. I'm not really hungry."

"I'll take them," Diego exclaimed.

Sophia gave them up, and Diego wolfed them down very quickly.

Rosie's voice resonated through the cabin. "Ok folks, it's approximately one o'clock in Oshimiru and we will be landing shortly. I hope you all enjoyed your flight, and thank you for choosing the Ancillary Express."

"What's Oshimiru?" Jacob called. "I thought we were going to Tanki Lowbei?"

Rosie turned around in the cockpit. "Artemis can only take so much without fuel... we're pretty lucky we made it all the way here. A jumbuck can't run on hot chips, and we can't run on fumes."

"So we're getting fuel?

"Quick and easy," Rosie said. "Oshimiru is a small island off the coast of Japan. I know a spot."

Sophia looked impressed.

"We'll touchdown, cadge some fuel, and be back in the air in twenty."

Jacob looked outside the window and saw the endless blue reach a small green slab. His ears began to pop as they descended towards the island.

He took out a stick of gum and popped it in his mouth. "Gum?"

"Please," Sophia said, and he handed her a piece.

Diego held up a palm in respectful refusal.

Jacob had to admit, Rosie wasn't half bad as a pilot. The drop was smoother than most of the commercial flights he had been on.

They came upon the island and Jacob saw many small huts and shacks. The roofs were more rust than metal, and he noted plenty of people working rice patties and what he assumed to be tea fields, as the plants were only knee high. The workers were wearing wide brim hats and mud covered clothes.

There were grey roads that looked like they had only ever been paved once. Most of the vehicles on the side of the road were missing wheels or didn't have any at all. They just lay there, desolate and abandoned. One old looking car was flipped over and the underside had a white marking that Jacob couldn't make out.

The runway was no more than a field of dirt. Rosie made

do with what they had to work with and she gracefully landed Artemis, coming to a stop perfectly in the center. There were no other planes on the runway, which made Jacob feel a tad uneasy.

Rosie turned around to address them once more, thankfully not using the squawky overhead speakers.

"A few ground rules," she said, this time with no smile, "that building over there is where you will go to get food." She pointed to a red pagoda on the out-skirts of the dirt field.

Unbuckling herself from the small cockpit, she finally joined them in the back. She started handing out colored bills that looked similar to dollars. "Here are some Yen I got from the bank before we left. Go only to that red building and nowhere else. Order some food, bog in and then immediately return. No barney. Got it?"

"I'll take care of this one," Diego said forcefully.

"Good," Rosie said. "I am going to drive to the building on the opposite side of the landing strip and refuel."

She grabbed the handle and opened the door.

As Jacob exited the craft, he felt a slight chill in the air. Sophia followed and wrapped her arms around her chest.

"Oh," Rosie said. "It gets colder on the island than on the mainland; all the more reason to go quick. Off with ya!"

Their footsteps dragged dry earth into the ground behind them. Over Jacob's shoulder, he heard the door slam and the plane engine grumble. Diego led them quickly toward the pagoda.

Jacob looked in his hand. They each received a thousand-yen banknote. He had no idea how much that was worth, but he hoped it would by him a decent meal.

"Who do you think the man on the bill is?" Jacob asked.

"I don't know," Diego answered. "But I bet he probably had a lot of these."

"He was a writer. Soseki Natsume," Sophia said.

Jacob's eyes widened. "How did you know that?" he asked, astonished.

She opened her arms, palm up, "Anime. It's been mentioned."

"You like anime?" Jacob asked.

"Yeah, when I was —"

"Enough chit-chat," Diego interrupted as they approached the building. "Let's stay quiet, I don't want to draw unwanted attention to ourselves. I'm good at my job, but I'd rather not have to do it."

Jacob licked his lips and nodded.

The entranceway was adorned with carvings of small dragons and golden lions. The door itself was bright red, with two silver handles shaped like phoenixes. The building looked less decrepit then the other buildings he had seen from above.

"So remember," Diego said coolly, "in and out." He slowly opened the door to the sound of song and loud chatter. As they walked through the portal, the chatter stopped and all eyes drifted towards them. After a few awkward moments, even the music shut off.

The interior was small and smelled strongly of salty fish. There were only a handful of tables, and most were occupied by small crowds of older men. Yen were scattered on the tables — bills much larger than the ones they were given — and it looked as if they had interrupted a gambling game of sorts.

A fat man with a brown stained apron stood behind the old wooden counter. Behind him was a small stove, roasting white fillets of fish and green stringy material. There were no signs with any indication of food choice or price.

Diego held his head high and it appeared that a little silence was the last thing in the world he had to worry about. Jacob tried to emulate him and give off a strong presence. He was aware that his hands were slightly shaking, so he slid them into his jean pockets.

Diego walked right up to the counter and slapped the bill onto the table.

The obese man looked at the bill and then back at Diego's face. The yen was slowly removed from the table by the rotund figure and placed in a small box with no lid.

He turned around, proceeding to pull some translucent noodles out of a pot and into a bowl. Then, some opaque brown liquid was ladled on top, with a piece of fish finishing it off. The man handed Diego the concoction and a pair of pearly-white chopsticks.

Jacob nervously turned his head back and forth and realized all eyes were focused exclusively on him.

Diego took his bowl, plopped down at an empty table and voraciously tucked into his meal, expertly using the two polished sticks.

Jacob realized it was his turn.

He went up to the counter and removed his hand and the yen from his pocket. Mirroring Diego, he placed it upon the counter. The man took his money and began dishing out a generous portion of noodles and fish. He turned around and held out the bowl for Jacob to take.

All of a sudden, the bowl crashed onto the floor. Before Jacob could register what was going on, the thick hand grabbed his left wrist. He tried to struggle free, but it was like the hand was tightly screwed on. The plump man's face was turned down to look at his catch, whispering to himself.

At the sound of what he said, all the older men in the restaurant stood up.

The fleshy man behind the counter repeated what he said a little louder.

A gathering began.

They circled Jacob and slowly moved inward. He continued to attempt to wrestle himself free, but his opponent was far stronger.

Diego leapt over and grabbed the chubby man's arm with both hands. With a strong twist and pull, the man screamed and finally let go of Jacob.

The man bellowed his message again.

The patrons all held their arms out, ready to scoop him up. The locals might have looked a tad frail, but Jacob's group was outnumbered five-to-one.

A door swung open from behind the counter. The door was uniform in color and style to the wall, and Jacob had not noticed it before.

Two more overweight men with stained white shirts came out.

"I think that's our cue to leave," Jacob said.

Diego let go of the man and scooped Sophia over his shoulder with one arm.

"Follow close behind… Now!"

Jacob's large guard started barreling through the tables, people, chairs, and noodle bowls while keeping his free shoulder forward as a weapon. Jacob ran right behind him, as close as possible without a collision.

Tables toppled over and chairs flew apart like wooden shrapnel. They made it through the door and back outside. Just as they escaped the room, they saw Rosie pulling back onto the dirt tarmac. Diego didn't slow down his stride as Sophia bobbed up and down over his massive frame. Jacob took long strides and kept up as they made their way towards the plane.

They still had a few hundred yards to go and Jacob could hear the noises trailing behind them getting louder.

"Open the door!" Diego bellowed.

Nothing happened. *Rosie couldn't possibly hear us from that far away,* Jacob thought.

"Open the damn door!" Diego repeated.

Jacob turned around and saw the mob of locals chasing after them. A few were wielding kitchen knives and thick wooden planks.

"Let's pick up some speed," Diego belted. "Move those legs, kid!"

After a few moments they were almost at the plane. The metal hatch was still sealed.

Diego gently placed Sophia on her own two feet and began ramming the hatch with the vigor of a sledgehammer.

"Open up!" he shouted. "Rosie!"

Slowly, the hatch opened on creaky hinges, audible even over the ruckus behind them.

"Get in," Rosie shouted as she let out the small ramp.

Diego ushered Sophia in and then barreled in with Jacob. Rosie quickly retracted the metal incline and slammed the door closed.

It was just in time, as the second the metal clicked into place, there was a loud banging on the side of the plane. After that, many more pairs of hands were trying to break in.

"Get us up," Diego stated calmly.

"Can do," Rosie said as she made her way toward the front.

Another loud smack.

"What was that all about?" Sophia asked.

Jacob sat down and strapped himself in tightly.

"He saw my hand," he said quietly.

"Do you think?..."

"What other reason could there have been?"

A deafening bash caused them both to wince.

"Let's get going," Diego said irritably.

"You saying that is about as useful as an ashtray on a motorbike. I'm flat out like a lizard drinking," Rosie shouted over the thuds and clanks. "She's not as young as she used to be."

"What are you saying?" Jacob asked, not sure if he wanted to know the answer.

"It might take her a few tries," Rosie said sheepishly.

"Well keep trying!" Sophia shouted. "I think there's more of them now!"

The hand slaps and localized explosions now surrounded the entire plane. Angry shouts were coming from all directions. A large metal pole hit the glass window next to Jacob, which spider-webbed on impact

"What did you all do in there?" Rosie shouted while fiddling with some dials.

"Nothing!" Jacob said.

"Well remind me to do *something* next time I stop here."

The roar of the engine drowned out the locals.

"Let's do the Harold Holt!" Rosie shouted, and she thrust a lever and they lurched forward.

Jacob squinted to make out the figures racing behind him, and saw that the few that chased them out of the restaurant had now become dozens. They shouted and waved their sharp and heavy items in the air, but fell behind as Artemis took to the sky.

"That was close," Sophia said.

"What did they want?" Jacob asked.

"I think we're not the only ones who have heard about the Ancillary."

"I don't get it," Diego said. "They couldn't possibly believe that nonsense."

"They grabbed him right after they saw the mark," Sophia argued. "What other explanation could there be?"

Jacob unbuckled himself and pressed his face against the window. An uneasy feeling crept into his limbs. He needed to get another look at something.

As they passed the dilapidated buildings, Jacob caught another glance at the overturned car. This time he could see exactly what the white graffiti was.

There—standing out against the dark underside of the automobile like a lone snowball on asphalt—was the Ancillary's mark.

CHAPTER 18

It was surprising to Jacob how short the rest of the flight was. After only a few hours they were nearing their destination. It was late afternoon — or at least that's what Rosie had told them — and his internal clock was off.

As they got closer, Jacob felt a stronger and stronger urge to be on the ground. It was like the magnetic pull was getting heavier as they approached the other side of the world.

"You look happy," Sophia said.

"It's really happening," he replied. "I just can't seem to believe it."

"As well you shouldn't," Diego said.

"You know," Sophia huffed. "You really should get on board if we want to have any chance of finding it."

"Me believing that a mystical flower exists isn't going to help it magically sprout. You and those crazy islanders are all wasting your time."

"Regardless," Jacob said. "I'm having an adventure across the globe... I think it's time well spent."

Sophia smiled at him.

"Oi! We're about there!" Rosie asserted. "Go ahead and grab your parachutes!"

"... huh?" Sophia said.

"Parachutes."

"You've got to be kidding me," Sophia said.

"Tanki Lowbei doesn't have an airport, it's a woop woop. What did you think was going to happen?" Rosie asked. "You want me to beam you down, Scotty?"

Sophia looked perplexed. "I don't know, maybe we drive from somewhere *with* an airport. I don't know how to skydive."

"Easiest thing in the world. Just jump and pull," Rosie stated matter-of-factly.

"Sounds simple enough," Jacob said.

"It is," Diego said. "But you sure it's the safest thing to do? They've never even gone tandem before. I'm being paid to keep them... intact. Maybe she's right, maybe we should find an airport."

"A... we would never get clearance for landing because no one knows we're up here; all we would get is a rack off. B... as you have already seen, it is not just us who know about the Ancillary and there's no time for smoko. And C... what's an adventure without a little risk?"

"Fine," Diego said. "But no word of this to the old man."

Rosie saluted.

"Right then, those duffel bags have your parachutes in 'em. I didn't know how big you were—especially you Diego—but they should fit right."

Jacob hurried over and began humming the James Bond theme song. Sophia opened her red duffel and took out her chute. It was a small green backpack with a giant yellow label that simply said 'Warning'. Along with the chutes, the red duffels held very dense coats which all three quickly put on. Rosie put the plane in autopilot and proceeded to help get the right straps in the right places.

"Warning about what?" Sophia asked.

"Warning you that if you don't remember to pull the red tab, you're looking to be pavement pancake for the crows."

"Fair enough," Diego said, as he pulled his arms through the shoulder straps.

"Now listen closely. Make sure to jump away from the plane so you don't hit anything. You might be a tad frightened at first but don't let it get to you. It's all in good fun, mates!" She slapped Diego on the back, which created a surprisingly loud thud. "Now, after you jump I'll send your stuff down attached to a chute of its own."

All three had their packs on and Diego was the only one who didn't look sorely out of place. Jacob could barely move his arms because of how thick the coat was.

"My advice to you all is, go into town and yabber with townsfolk to find out any clues you can about its whereabouts. Mr. Maddock said they claim not to know anything, but I have a sneaky suspicion that they're not letting on what they know. Here's a compass, a map, and a two-way radio. Call me when you find the flower and I'll pick you up in a rent-a-car. Don't do anything with it until I get there, if you don't mind, I would like to watch."

"Of course," Jacob said. "It's the least I can do."

"But there's no airport, how will you get us?" Diego asked.

"You let me worry about that, sweet thing," Rosie said.

Jacob looked at his companions. "I don't suppose either of you speak Tibetan?"

Rosie tossed him a brand new English-Tibetan dictionary with the stickers still attached. "Call it a good luck present."

Their bags were then bundled up with a tent and supplies, and threaded with a large rope, which was attached to another parachute. Rosie grasped the side hatch handle tightly.

"We descended to about five thousand feet, so release your chute quickly…remember… pavement waffles."

Jacob smirked. "Pancakes."

"Right, pancakes."

"Be seeing you soon," Jacob said. "And thanks for everything."

Rosie readied herself to open the door. "My honor and privilege."

The world was revealed in a frame of wind and noise. The hatch was pulled back and the wind roared past them. The icy air bit at Jacob's face.

"You ready?" Jacob asked Sophia.

"This is nuts!" Sophia said.

Jacob inched his way toward the opening. "Call me a squirrel!"

He jumped.

CHAPTER 19

Marrow loved flying first class. Enough legroom to fully extend, a great steak and potatoes dinner, and no small children staring and gawking at his deformity all added to its superiority. The trip was long, but the small comforts made all the difference.

Marrow beckoned the stewardess. "Another whisky."

She was very attractive and was rather interested in him.

"Sure…is there anything else I can do for you?"

"No…not now."

She turned and sauntered away, making a point to gracefully swing her hips. Marrow felt that old primal urge, but didn't let it take hold… yet.

She had been staring at him since he first stepped foot on the airplane. Even with his condition, it was not rare for women to throw themselves at his feet. It seemed that good girls always wanted that little taste of danger, and lust was easily brought out by his mysterious aura. Not only did Marrow give off the bad-man image, he lived the part.

An untitled book lay flat upon his lap. He opened past the cover to where the Ancillary's mark was sprawled across the first page. The intricacies of the book were the only thing Marrow knew better than his revolver. The air slowly leaked from his lungs. Regardless of how many sessions Marrow underwent with the book, the craving was never lessened. It was like heroin to a methadone addict. The book held all his favorite stories about the Ancillary. Bound together and set in a single volume were all sorts of tales from all different times and places, all about the Ancillary. Distinctive titles had been used to describe the plant, including the Flower of Destiny, The Perennial Apocalypse, Hwana Gotiva, Divine Bloom, and many others. The fact of the matter was that so many ancient civilizations independently knew of it's existence that it was either real, or antiquated communication was a hell of a lot better than anyone could imagine. He began to read it for what must have been the hundredth time.

"Your Jack Daniels, sir."

"Thanks." He flashed her a smile. This always had the same effect.

She blushed a scarlet red. "Is there anything else I can do for you?"

Marrow thought for a minute. The reading could wait. Why not give the girl what she deserved? If they wanted to experience the dark side of things, why not indulge them. It was the least he could do.

"As a matter of fact there is. What's your name?"

The stewardess perked up as if it was Christmas morning.

"Veronica. What's yours?"

"Veronica…beautiful name. My name is Tyson." Again a smile. "I seem to have developed an intense kink… here in my neck."

Marrow took her hand and placed it on the spot. Her delicate fingers were trembling.

"I see what you mean, Tyson."

"You have a wonderful aircraft and it would be a shame if I couldn't enjoy the flight because of this… kink."

"You're right sir. That would be just dreadful."

"Is there something you can do for me?"

Veronica turned around and craned her neck, apparently looking for something. "There *is* an extra room that is used by us flight attendants for sleeping on these long flights. Why don't I take you back there and see if I can't work that kink out for you?"

"Very kind of you."

Marrow unbuckled himself and followed the beautiful stewardess into the private room.

The door locked behind them.

CHAPTER 20

It was unlike anything Jacob had ever experienced. The world was rising toward him, as opposed to him falling toward it. It was incredible. Floating in midair with the sun shining down was an experience he always wanted to try, and it turned out the actual act was better then he had dreamt it to be.

"WAHOO!" he screamed.

Jacob let his body rotate through the air, giving him a three hundred and sixty degree view of the scene around him. Snow-covered mountain peaks ascended while the rush of wind kept his cheeks pinned back. Tilting his head, he saw two other bodies diving from the plane. The smaller body was flailing around, while the other seemed completely composed, tucked in an aerodynamic pose, like a bowling pin.

In the distance he could see a mountain so large it had to be Everest. The peak was a giant white crown perched atop the huge pile of green earth. The mist encircling the precipice created a mystical quality that was utterly breathtaking.

The ground was coming faster than expected, so he yanked hard on the red tab. The chute failed.

Panic came upon him like a fast-acting poison. Another yank, harder this time, resulted in the same outcome. Behind his shoulders the flap was waving wildly, yet the chute would not come out.

Frenzied, he kept pulling but nothing happened. He couldn't have been more than a thousand feet up, as he could now make out individual trees. Reaching back with his hands, he stretched to the point where his shoulders burned and rummaged in the open flap. The bulk of the coat held him back from full extension. The gale-worthy wind wasn't helping either. He rummaged around, getting a fingernail inside the chute. He felt the nylon cloth in his grasp and pulled it out as hard as he could. The red chute raced past the back of his head and he felt a strong yank as the wind took its grip on the fabric.

It was over. It worked.

Jacob had never been more relieved. The panic that took over his mind was unlike anything he was familiar with. Two near death experiences in one day made him wonder how lucky he actually was.

Drifting downward towards a bed of green, his ticker had yet to settle down. Above him, four red ovals hogged the sky. Diego and Sophia must have had no problem, and their stuff seemed not too far behind.

The target they were aimed toward was an open grassy field. His landing was surprisingly graceful, and with only a small thud he hit the ground. As he landed, he bent down and immediately kissed the ground—he finally understood why people did that.

Diego was next to touch down on the meadow. His chute fell neatly behind him, and for a minute he looked like a superhero—until Jacob heard the wheezing.

"You... my friend... are quite the daredevil!" Diego exclaimed between the gasps. "I don't think you could have waited any longer to open your chute."

"Believe me, it was not by choice," Jacob said. "Are you Ok?"

Stronger attempts for air. Diego dug into his pocket and pulled out a small white object. After a quick puff, Diego swiftly stashed the inhaler. "Fine. What do you mean not by choice?"

"It wouldn't open."

Diego's face went pale, "WHAT?"

"Let's say my parachute was sky shy."

This brought a snort, and a little color back. "Ok, that

wasn't bad. But you shouldn't joke about that."

"If you take life too seriously, then the joke's on you," Jacob said.

On that note, Sophia landed with her knees buckling. The red material covered her like a space blanket while she lay on the ground. She was uncontrollably giggling.

"That…was… INCREDIBLE!" she screamed in between chuckles.

"I'm glad someone enjoyed it," Jacob said.

She stopped laughing. "By the way, why did you wait so long to pull the tab?"

Jacob and Diego both looked at each other.

"My pack had a little stage fright," Jacob said.

Sophia looked like she was about to explode.

"I am gonna STRANGLE Rosie."

"Hey, it's not her fault, there's no way she could have known."

Sophia didn't let that deter her anger. "She should know how to pack a parachute. She has a plane! If anything would have happened to you then—" She stopped herself and cooled down a bit. "Let's just get our stuff."

Their belongings hit the ground only a few yards away, and unfastening themselves from their parachutes, they walked toward them.

Diego began working on the ropes that bound the equipment.

Sophia and Jacob hung off to the side.

"Are you… OK?" she asked with concern in her voice.

"I'm fine, it was no big deal."

Diego finished his work and divvied up the supplies. He took the tent and the items Mr. Maddock gave them and swung them around his back. The other bags he bestowed upon their respective owners.

"You fine with all of that?" Sophia asked.

"Absolutely."

Jacob took out his map and compass.

"So it looks like... That's north, toward that river over there." Jacob unfolded the map and stared at it for a minute. "It looks like we have to go west."

"Very impressive," Sophia said enthusiastically.

"Boy scouts. At least until I got kicked out."

"What for?" Sophia asked.

"Apparently, if you find a baby bear cub you aren't supposed to bring it home as a pet."

"Who knew?" Sophia said.

"Yeah well, after all I pulled I guess that was the clincher."

Diego leaned in towards the map and Jacob pointed out their route.

"He's right." Diego looked surprised. "Let's get moving. We have a lot of ground to cover."

Jacob neglected to tell the others, but it wasn't just his short-lived career as a Webelo that let him know the direction. It was strange, but he could feel the right direction, like when you are turned about under water and the bubbles rolling against your skin tell you which way is up.

He followed the bubbles.

CHAPTER 21

"OH MY GOD!" the stewardess screamed, bringing the pilot out of the cockpit to see what the commotion was about.

He was a short, squat man, with flight wings attached to his lapel. His neck swiveled as he tried to locate where the sound was coming from. Rushing towards the back of the plane, he found what the commotion was about. Standing inside the flight attendants' on-call room was Becky—one of the newer flight attendants. Piercing shrieks were fleeing from her vocal chords. The door was wide open, and his eyes quickly found the cause.

"What's going on?" he asked.

"She's not breathing! Veronica! Wake up!"

The pilot removed his aviators and scurried over to the mattress Veronica was lying on.

She was covered with a thin blanket, and not moving. Her neck was exposed and the pilot gasped. Around her throat was a thick ring of raw skin. Placing an index and middle finger against her trachea, he failed to find a pulse.

Nothing.

Her arm lay limp over the side of the bed and he quickly moved his fingers onto her wrist to see if maybe she had a radial pulse.

Nothing.

"Becky," he said calmly but firmly, "please call the paramedics. You have to stay composed. Tell them we are pulled up to gate forty five and then tell them to bring the heavy defibrillator."

Becky stood motionless with her jaw slack.

"Becky," he said a little louder. "Now!"

She pulled herself from the scene and rushed towards the on-board emergency phone-line.

The pilot lowered the blanket down to Veronica's navel and saw that she was unclothed.

He placed his left hand upon his right and fit them in the center of her rib cage. Fifteen quick thrusts later, he tilted her head back and blew steady puffs of air into her chest. Lowering his ear to her lips, he listened for breath and again tried to find a pulse.

He repeated the process over and over, hoping for resuscitation. Becky raced back into the room.

"They're on the way," she said. "Is Ronnie going to be alright?"

"To be honest, I'm not sure. If you would like to help, make sure the path is cleared for the E.M.T's. They're her best shot."

The pilot continued C.P.R, pushing through sore shoulders and empty lungs. While physically exhausting himself, his mind drifted towards how awful the situation was. Who would do this to Veronica? She was dedicated, friendly, and had a wonderful personality. He took a short break to try and get some answers. Becky was huddled in the corner, still watching in horror.

"What happened?" the pilot asked her.

"I- I'm not sure. The door was locked, I came in to rest and I saw her lying there. She didn't look right... just sitting there limp and pale. I went over to see if she was hurt. When I tried to wake her—"

"Did you see anyone with her?"

"No, she disappeared halfway through the flight. After her double shift I figured she just needed to sleep."

At that moment the paramedics rushed in. The pilot quickly filled them in on the situation and they began their work. Two pads were placed on either side of her sternum and they sent stream after stream of electricity in order to jump-start her heart.

The pilot got out of their way and hustled over to the phone. He dialed franticly, dreading the news he had to give.

"Hello, security? This is Pilot Greg Bromson, code GBREG42. We have a situation…"

CHAPTER 22

Jacob, Sophia and Diego sat under a large conifer to take refuge from the surprisingly strong sun. Getting their bearings wasn't exactly difficult, but the heat was much more than expected, causing a delay in their search. The grass was dry and very comfortable under Jacob's feet, so he suggested they relax and check their inventory while they were storing their jackets.

"Do these trees look shorter to you?" Jacob asked no one in particular.

"Actually, yeah," Sophia said, "I wonder why?"

"Higher altitude," Diego replied confidently.

"I wonder if that will affect the height of the flower, too." Jacob said.

Diego rolled his eyes.

Jacob ruffled through the bag Mr. Maddock had given them and found some useful items. There were freeze-dried meals — the kind used by astronauts — water-filtering straws, a well-used hatchet, books labeled with their different uses, LED flashlights, and other small items.

"I think we should check these out while we're sitting here," Jacob said, and tossed a couple of books into Diego and Sophia's hands.

"I'll take care of keeping you safe, but I'm not going to help with that end," Diego said.

"Think of it this way," Jacob said. "If you help, the faster we'll be able to search, and the faster we'll be able to go home — whether or not it is real."

Diego ran his tongue against his top teeth. He stretched out a hand.

Jacob winked at Sophia.

The old text Jacob chose to rummage through had a large post-it note on the front that simply read 'check page fifty one'. Flipping through the brittle yellow pages, he eventually reached the suggestion:

… text shows that the seed will most likely settle in a cool secluded area. The rhyme of the Cronapians goes as follows.

Look in the place where the blue light will glow
Under moon will find shadows never to show
In the place where it starts will be never the same
By worlds surface will flow untitled to name

A taste and will find a new life in store
The blossom will spur and creating of more
Golden floating will spark the fire ignite
Of mind eye and knowledge of mightiest might

Though one for it's meant to deny is a trait
Anyone for it will define the innate
Ground is the lock for man's quest for the key
The root of it all will be man's destiny

On the bottom of the page was another note from Mr. Maddock. It had bullet points on what evidence he had gathered from this poem. They included: *glows blue, brightest during night, anyone can use it,* and *look by water.*

Jacob shared this knowledge with the others.

"You guys find anything?" Jacob asked.

"My book is really only full of prophetic mumbo-jumbo," Sophia said.

"Mine is about frogs and how they may or may not croak louder near the Ancillary," Diego said. "I think I'll file it under the mumbo-jumbo section as well."

"How far from Tanki Lowbei are we?" Sophia asked Jacob.

"Rosie's aim is good, but not great. I think we have another day's walk ahead of us."

"This is really exciting," she said, dancing with her shoulders.

"I know. What do you think is going to happen?" Jacob asked her.

"If I guessed, I'm sure I couldn't be further from the truth. It's a big mystery."

"I just hope we can conclude that it's not *real* relatively quickly," Diego said while picking dirt from his shoes with a stick. "That way we won't be searching around aimlessly for longer than we have to."

"Don't worry," Jacob said. "If we can't find it in a few days, I'll be perfectly fine with going home."

In truth, he wouldn't be. He wanted... needed to find the flower. Even though he had only just learned about the Ancillary, it felt like he knew about it his whole life. Like when a words are on the tip of his tongue and then someone says it, saving him restless hours lying in bed that night—but in this case, it saved Jacob restless years.

"Speaking of home," Jacob said to Sophia. "What did you tell your parents?"

"I... I kind of didn't."

"Really? I guess that was the smarter thing to do."

"I figure they'll be furious when they find out the truth, but if they can tell their friends that their daughter helped the famous Jacob Deer reach the Ancillary... I think everything will smooth over."

"Famous?" Jacob asked.

"Of course. If this flower is all it's cracked up to be, then I think fame is only the first step," she stated.

"Cracked up being the operative word," Diego mumbled.

"I hadn't really thought about that."

"Well, start thinking," she said. "You're going to need some good hiding-from-the-paparazzi techniques."

"I don't think they'll be that interested. It's not like I'm some rock star or actor."

Sophia grinned. "You do realize that this is the greatest and most important treasure ever, right?"

"I knew it was probably really pretty."

"Think about it. People see treasure as silver and gold and material items, but in the grand scheme of things all that really doesn't matter. Those things are all just *things* when you die. But imagine a treasure that guarantees you're remembered through time. People will be saying your name for years to come. I just wonder what they're going to be saying."

Jacob mimed giant objects pressing him down and Sophia giggled.

They decided to brave the heat, and began a slow trek across the unknown land. After a half hour or so of silent pacing, they reached a thin river that rambled and wove down a valley. Fast flowing current had carved the rock walls smooth over the years. Jacob wandered down a few boulders and reached the waters' edge. He removed his sneakers and sat down on the closest rock to the water that he could. Dipping his feet into the current, he let out a long sigh of relief. Though his quest had just begun, everything happening so fast was exhausting. Sophia came down and sat next to him on the flat rock. She took her shoes off as well, and dropped her feet in the water just inches away from his. *Even her toes were cute*, he thought. They were painted all different shades, making them look like little tropical fish. She pulled them up and down, breaking the surface and causing individual small splashes.

"So how are you holding up, Cob?"

"Like the leaning tower of Pisa at the moment... which I guess is fitting if I'm to be a tourist attraction. Where's Diego?"

"He wanted to take a look around and see if he can find any landmarks. I figured I would come and talk to you. By the way, you're in store for much more than a tourist attraction. And unless you *do* end up getting spikes, I don't think people would pay the entrance fee... let's just hope you grow some giant quills, like Artemis."

"You are very sweet."

"It's all the candy."

She smirked and looked straight into his eyes. He felt electricity surge through his body. He could feel every piece of skin tingling.

"I think you're going to be great," she said.

"I don't feel like a bad person, but what if I have the potential inside of me?"

She turned toward him, grabbed both of his hands, and her face lit up.

"Listen, I consider myself a very good judge of character. I have been my whole life. It's a gift. When I look at you I don't see an ounce of evil — anyone can see that after talking with you for five minutes. You are going to do great things and change the world... for the better."

"Do you really think so?"

"I know so." She gripped his fingers a little tighter. "You might not be normal, but who wants normal? Normal is boring."

"You are really something."

"I know." Flicking her hair like a supermodel, she flashed a smile. "The *best* something."

They both cracked up laughing. She splashed Jacob with a good-sized handful of water, which Jacob retaliated in spades.

Both sat soaking — with the water taking its sweet time to evaporate off their skin — as they relaxed in the warm weather. The sunshine caressed their faces, and Jacob felt as if a warm, comfortable vice embraced his head and wouldn't let him go. Out of his peripherals he saw her face in pure ecstasy. Blonde hair glistening, and sparkling blue eyes through half-shut lashes made Jacob realize he wanted nothing more than to lean over and kiss her.

"Hey! We should get moving!" Diego called from above.

Sophia broke from her reverie and put her footwear back on. The two scampered back up the boulders.

"Find anything?" Jacob asked.

"There are a few remnants of a shack beyond that ridge, but nothing that we can really use."

"So we keep following the map?"

"Let's just hope it's current… where'd you get it anyway?"

"Mr. Maddock," Jacob answered.

"How does the old man have a map of this region of Tibet?"

Jacob opened his palms. "How did he get us a plane?"

Diego nodded. "Good point."

"I think we should take another look at the books before we go scampering off," Sophia said.

"Yeah, good idea."

"Fine," Diego said. "But quickly."

They divvied up the next wave of literary infantry. Like the previous books, they were full of notes and bookmarked pages. After a few minutes, Diego exhaled a small puff of air from his nostrils.

"What?" Jacob asked.

"Check this out," Diego remarked. "I can't believe all these people accepted this nonsense."

"What's the news?" Jacob asked.

"Turns out that the Romans believed that the Ancillary pollen is a sparkling golden color. Bright enough to be distinguished from other pollen."

"That's what the rhyme could have been talking about!" Sophia exclaimed, "Golden floating will spark the fire ignite!"

"So we look for golden pollen in the air," Jacob said.

Diego looked smug. "And follow the trail!" he said sardonically.

"Exactly," Sophia said. "So we… oh right, there wouldn't be a trail."

"Well, it's still is good to know," Jacob said. "Now if we see golden pollen we know we are on the right track. Good work! Plus we can ask the locals if they have seen anything golden floating around…if we can figure out how to ask that in

Tibetan."

"We have clues!" Sophia stated enthusiastically. "How great is that!"

Suddenly, their attention was drawn to the valley. Something down there was moving.

CHAPTER 23

Marrow stepped into the back seat of his rental Escalade. Russell had taken it upon himself to do the driving, and Frankie was in the front passenger seat to help with the navigation. At his request—and with a large cash deposit—they had acquired a brand new Cadillac, which were quite rare in the town of Fu Huanxi.

"Only a few hundred miles, boys!" Marrow said.

"Y-Yes sir. Right away, sir," Frankie said.

His men were shaky and unfocused. These were not characteristics that Marrow prized in his employees.

"What is with you two?"

Frankie muttered, "Nothing sir, it's just…"

"Just what Frankie?"

"Just… something Shully said."

"And what did Shully say?"

"… About what happened on the plane. With the stewardess."

"Shully has to learn how to keep his bloody mouth shut."

"What if the Feds track us down?" Frankie asked.

Marrow reached into the inside of his three-piece suit jacket and pulled out a pair of gloves, a rope, and a fake passport.

Russell smirked. "Always thinking, boss."

Frankie seemed unconvinced.

"Covering your tracks doesn't mean they can't find you. What possible reason did you have to kill her?"

With the swiftness of a rattlesnake striking his prey, Marrow pulled out his raging bull revolver. He flipped the gun so he held onto the barrel and struck the handle across Frankie's cheek. A sickening crack, and Frankie's mouth was dripping crimson.

"THE SAME REASON I DID THAT FOR!" Marrow roared. "DON'T QUESTION ME."

Frankie tried to make a sound, but the pain held him back. As he spat, four teeth hit the floor mats. Marrow got out of the car and opened the driver-side door. He grabbed Frankie by the shirt and pulled him out and onto the pavement.

"Russell, get over here and drive. Put Frankie in the trunk so he can think about the definition of loyalty." After finishing this order he kicked Frankie in the ribs.

"Right away, boss."

Russell proceeded to aid a limping Frankie to the trunk and put him inside.

"Don't worry buddy," Russell whispered to Frankie when they got outside of Marrow's earshot. "He'll get what's coming to him."

"Hurry up!" Marrow called.

Russell slammed the trunk hatch and took the driver's position.

"Drive quick," Marrow said.

"But I don't know where I'm going," Russell murmured.

"Well, you better learn. I'm through being patient."

Russell pulled a map out of the glove compartment. Though rather tattered, the map showed the main highways and streets they would have to take to get to their destination. Russell quickly memorized the necessary path and started driving. The rest of his men trailed behind in several smaller, less luxurious sedans.

Fu Huanxi was the closest town to Tanki Lowbei with a decent airport. Marrow decided to drive the rest of the way, and maybe have some… fun with the locals. He could barely wait for his prize, but he knew the men needed a small amount of entertainment.

After driving outside of the airport borders, the first thing

Marrow noticed was the extreme poverty. To his right was a shack with a roof made from a children's blow up pool. A family of three flocked underneath their crude shelter, attending to a pet pig. They were feeding it a small bowl of something that could have passed as rice.

"Swine," he scoffed.

"The pig?" Russell asked.

"That too."

On the opposite side of the street were children—who wore more dirt than clothing—playing with a soccer ball. Most didn't have shirts, and the few that did looked like they were wearing large slices of Swiss cheese. The ball was semi-deflated and there were no goals, but they seemed to be making up the rules as they went along. It appeared that the object was to kick the ball through another player's legs, then tackle that person.

"A bunch of heathens."

Marrow held down the power window button until the glass was fully lowered. The revolver poked its edge out into the clean air. There was a loud crack, after a single shot was fired.

The ball exploded.

CHAPTER 24

Halfway around the globe, Jacob's mother picked up the phone. She hated being away from her son for so long, and every phone call she made caused the longing to worsen.

Mrs. Deer severely missed the fireflies.

Her little boy would sit with her on the porch on warm summer nights, and they would watch the light show. The fireflies in Harrison were special—just like her son. Thousands would congregate at the large conifer in the back yard and glow almost in unison.

It was like nature's Christmas every day.

She would look over at her son and give thanks that he was still there with her in an otherwise lonely world. She would tell him stories and he would look out at the tree in wonder. They tried to make out shapes of light coming from the thousands of tiny bugs. It was their private fireworks display. One time, Jacob swore he saw the Mona Lisa in bioluminescence.

In the many weeks there, she had yet to see a firefly.

Ireland was beautiful, however. All the hearsay was correct. The rolling green hills and giant stone boulders covered in fine mists fit all the majestic descriptions the media had portrayed. The food was wonderful and the drinks were warm. The rumor was true that the Irish could tell quite the tale, and many nights she was regaled with stories of banshees and magical sidhe.

Outside of Dublin—where she was staying—was a small town where the people were friendly, and most of them quickly learned her name. On certain days, she would make her way into the capital and conduct the bureaucratic work she was there to perform. She had a lot of downtime, so naturally she gravitated to the cultural displays. The museums were world-class, the shows were beautifully conducted, but nothing could ease the penetrating stab of loneliness.

Her accommodations were like something out of a fairy-tale. A small log cabin — complete with award-winning cuteness accessories, including hand-knit curtains and local oil paintings on the walls — was her temporary place of residence.

It was her final day in Dublin, and it was about time that it came. Jacob meant the world to her and being apart was like being in outer space without a ship. She couldn't wait to get back and hold him tight.

She dialed the fourteen numbers needed to reach him. It was astounding how many buttons she had to press. While the phone was ringing, she thought about what he was doing at that very moment — probably trying to make toast with a hair-dryer.

The ringing didn't stop, and she let out a long sigh. He couldn't *always* be home, she thought.

Strange… the message on the machine was different than when she left. She let it finished and started to giggle. To that day, her laugh was still the high-pitched squeal of a high school cheerleader.

A supernatural flower, she thought, *it was like something my husband would make up.*

"Hi my darling boy," she said into the receiver, "I'm sorry I missed you, I wish we could have talked. I love you so very much. Call me back when you get this. My number is still on the fridge… but of course you already know that. I can't wait to see you and I have a surprise for you. I love you, love you, love you…. and good luck with the flower…. I hear Tibet is beautiful this time of year."

She hung up the phone and looked around the room.

"Goodbye," she said to the room. "It's been nice."

She headed into the bedroom and packed her things. She had a flight to catch and a son to see.

CHAPTER 25

"Don't run over to it!" Diego called after Jacob. "We don't even know what it is! Get back here!"

"You worry too much," Jacob shouted back as he started hurdling over berry bushes and small trees. "C'mon, I want to find out!"

Diego and Sophia looked at each other and shrugged.

"Why not?" Sophia said.

"We have no choice either way... I have a feeling I'll be earning every dollar I'm being paid... And I'm being paid a lot."

They started chasing after Jacob down the hills toward the stirring object. The brush was dense and the grass was high. They scrambled through bamboo cane and tried to catch up to Jacob, who was surprisingly agile in this environment. As they started making headway towards their destination, they could see the object coming more and more into focus. It was large and dark, and they couldn't quite make out the details.

Jacob was still a hundred feet in front of them. He could see the back of the object; it was nestled in-between a small, circular patch of cane, and was black with a shiny tinge. Jacob slowed down and approached the mysterious entity. As Jacob began pulling open a space just large enough to peek his head through, there was a loud crunch of twigs under his foot. The thing jolted as if startled, and turned around.

"Jeez, don't sneak up on people, man."

Jacob was astounded. He was face to face with a boy in a tuxedo. Jacob had not expected it to be a person, much less a person who spoke English. Jacob slowly stepped through the bamboo.

The boy was of Asian decent, yet his accent was not heavy. Being a head shorter, the boy had to angle his face backward to meet Jacob's gaze. He looked to be around Jacob's age and appeared uncomfortably tense.

"I apologize," Jacob said.

"No worries, dude, you just startled me, is all." The boy stuck a hand in his double-breasted formalwear. "But I think I might lose my lunch."

"You speak English," Jacob said.

"So do you, bro."

"That's true. I just… I mean… the last thing I expected to see out here was a boy in a tux who speaks fluent English."

"Get with the program, man, everybody speaks English these days. It's the universal language. My names Chi Chung Hupuenang, but you can call me Clark."

"Clark?" Jacob asked.

Without missing a beat, Clark ripped open his jacket and underneath was a blue shirt with a giant 'S' on it.

"Superman!" The boy said. "Clark… Get it?"

Jacob immediately knew he was going to like Clark. Sophia and Diego came crashing through the bushes, and Clark almost jumped out of his expensive looking shoes.

"Don't you people know not to ambush someone like that?"

Both Sophia and Diego didn't know how to react. All three stepped across the border of cane.

"Uh… hi?" Diego said, extending a hand.

"Hi yourself, pal," Clark said, shaking Diego's hand vigorously. "I'm Clark."

"You speak English?" asked Sophia.

Clark's eyes widened. "Is that so surprising?"

In unison all three said, "Yes."

Clark laughed, "Well it's not every day I come out to the Sinung and meet three …Americans?"

"The home of the brave," Jacob said with a nod.

"And the Man of Steel!" Clark said.

Jacob's eyebrows pinched inward. "You said Sinung... What's that?"

"Look around, dude... you're in it!"

Everyone's eyes surveyed their surroundings and noticed that the patch of land they were standing on stood out from the rest of the immediate nature.

The cane field that Clark was originally crouched in was in a perfect circle, encompassing a red earth. Above the circle, the cane made a natural roof. In the center of the soil was a small garden made from tiny bonsai trees. The dwarfed trees were beautiful in their defects. The looked aged, and the branches were twisted and gnarled. A small pair of clippers was set down next to a bonsai with white bark that looked bleached.

"Sinung is a tradition that I intend to keep regardless of the new... developments. Even if I am missing the ceremony," Clark said poignantly.

"How long have these trees been here?" Jacob asked.

"Generations, man... like forever. My father entrusted their care to me before he passed."

"They're wonderful," Sophia said.

Clark pointed to his chest. "Superman."

Sophia and Diego introduced themselves and started asking Clark questions about the area.

"Do you know how to get to Tanki Lowbei?" Diego asked. "It's a small town somewhere around here."

"I should," Clark said. "I grew up there. It's pretty awesome, a lot's happening."

"What luck!" Sophia said. "Do you think you could take us there?"

"Sure, I just have to finish up here." Clark hesitated for a moment then blurted out, "You're not spies, right?"

"Spies? Why would we be spies?" Diego asked.

"Never mind. Just checking."

Something bothered Jacob about the boy's dialect. "Where

did you learn to speak English?"

Clark hesitated for a moment. "…We had classes in school… but mostly from comic books. The Americans used to ship them to us."

"Hence the affiliation to Big Blue."

With a thumbs up, Clark said, "You got it…Hey, if you want, you could help me. Things will go faster with four pairs of hands."

"Sure," Jacob said, "but I don't know the first thing about taking care of tiny trees."

"I can teach you… here," he handed Jacob a small spray bottle full of an opaque green liquid, "grandpa's secret formula. Spray a small amount on the leaves of each tree." Clark pointed towards a small, rather naked looking tree. "You can start with the bald cyprus, I named him Ernie."

"I'm your man!" Jacob saluted. "I hope you're thirsty, Ernie."

"What can I do?" Sophia asked, eager to learn a new skill. "I've worked with plants before."

"I have the perfect job for delicate hands. Each tree will need to be pruned. This is very tricky, so pay attention. If you cut off too little, the plant will grow and invade the territory of its neighbors. That's a no-no. If you cut too much it will die." Clark hung his head low and lolled his tongue out. He grabbed the small clippers and cut one or two leaves off of a Japanese white pine.

After showing Sophia exactly where to cut, he passed the scissors like a small torch and she took over, clipping miniscule leaves one at a time.

"I don't think we have time for this," Diego huffed.

"C'mon, dude," Clark said airily. "You help me, I help you."

"The silver rule," Jacob said.

"Fine," Diego grunted. "But then we go. What do I have to do?"

"Man, I got the perfect job for you. The soil needs to be

aerated. Dig with your fingers and make the ground nice and soft so water can easily seep in. Sinung was designed so only a certain amount of water can pass through the bamboo, and they need all of it, bro. "

"I guess I can do that," Diego said as he got to work. Looking back he asked, "What job are you going to do?"

"The most important task of all, man!" Clark said.

The boy bent over to one of the trees and burst into song. As he sang, he danced around the perimeter of the garden, enunciating so all the plants could hear.

"Little beauties in the earth, humdidy humdidy doo
So aged but you feel just like new, humdidy humdidy doo
Fragile in the grand old eye, humdidy humdidy die
But stronger than the ocean tide, humdidy humdidy die
So perfect found in every way, humdidy humdidy dee
You will live eternity, humdidy humdidy dee"

"It's catchy right? I wrote it myself," Clark said.

All three stopped what they were doing. Diego looked at Clark as if there were three polka dotted heads writhing on his shoulders.

"I love it!" Jacob said. "Why do you sing to them?"

"They're living things, man, much older than all of us combined. They need love and respect and songs just like everything else."

Jacob pondered this for a moment. "Hmm… interesting"

"This work leaves you pretty dirty. Why are you wearing a tuxedo?" Sophia asked.

"Because it's Ernie's birthday. He's one hundred and sixty three today." Clark laughed. "I guess it doesn't make any sense since they don't have eyes; I just thought it would be nice."

"Well, aren't you sweet," Sophia said.

Jacob walked over to Ernie the bonsai tree and got down on his stomach. In a tune that sounded a lot like 'Take me out to the ballgame,' Jacob tried a song of his own.

Ernie oh it's your birthday
Your turning one sixty three
I'll sing to you the whole day through
Because you're my favorite tree

"Don't let the others here you say that!" Sophia quipped.

With a quick flick of the index finger Jacob corrected himself. "*One* of my favorite trees."

Each continued on with their assigned jobs, and as they were working dutifully, struck up a conversation.

"So you said a lot is happening in your hometown… what did you mean?" Sophia asked.

"The gods have chosen us."

"For what?"

Clark thought for a second. "I'm not quite sure, but it's pretty cool. We have always been a simple town… very low key, and we have always been very happy. I'm not one to question the will of the gods, but I guess they have decided that we need to do more."

"More…" Diego said.

"More everything. I really can't explain it. When we get home… you'll see. You can crash with me for a while if you want. I'll show you my comic collection. I have one where Hurricommando blows apart an enemy tank with his breath. It's killer!"

Sophia's eyebrows rose. "You're very trusting. Not many New Yorkers would be so quick to take in strangers."

"Like I said…simple people. I guess we were raised differently. Maybe that's why we were chosen… who knows?" Clark shrugged. "Nice job with the pruning, by the way, it's actually considered a deep spiritual art. You must have a large soul."

Diego removed his fingers from the earth. "Souls come in different sizes?"

"Of course. Haven't you ever felt yours growing?"

Diego eyed him suspiciously.

"How can you tell?" Jacob asked.

"You can feel it." Clark patted the center of his chest. "I'll try to explain as best as I can. The soul is there to guide you, but it also needs you. Just like the bonsais. If I were to ignore them and never return to Sinung, then they would surely wither away. They are here to inspire and help me, but they also need me… to care for them and love them. Just like my soul, the bonsai grow how I want them to. In this case—" He pointed to a particular twisted looking tree. "—The caretakers before me wanted it to be asymmetrical and serpentine to show how beauty isn't always found in perfection. The soul works the same way… it grows how you let it. That is why there are evil people in the world, they have abandoned their souls."

Jacob was taken aback. "Asymmetrical and serpentine? You speak *really* good English."

"A lot of comic books, man," Clark said. "A lot of comic books."

CHAPTER 26

"So what are you three doing way out here, anyway?" Clark asked.

They had finished their individual jobs and had set off toward Tanki Lowbei. Clark had affectionately said his farewell to the bonsais with a bow—which the others mirrored—to show respect.

"That's a long and crazy story," Diego said.

"Good thing. We have a nice long walk ahead of us."

"We're spies," Jacob teased.

Clark laughed. "Ok, maybe I was being a little paranoid earlier, but once we get to my town you'll see why."

Sophia chimed in, "I think we already know why. The news of some of your townspeople being... chosen... well, a somewhat less metaphysical version hit the newsstands all the way in America. I'm sure all sorts of people have been asking questions."

"Right you are. It's quite annoying really; they don't appreciate the beauty and spiritual nature of it all. They are either here to try and uncover a scandal, get a story, or steal some of our ideas. Although it's most likely that some people have come to try and receive the blessing themselves."

"Blessing?" Diego asked.

"Did I say blessing?" Clark laughed nervously. "I meant... dressing. We are known for making some of the finest garments in Tibet. Sorry my English isn't as good as I would like."

"Oh," Jacob said. "Well get ready to add another reason to that list."

"You are here for something else?"

"Yup, let's just say that the people in your town were not the only ones chosen."

"You mean… you have had a taste as well?"

Diego butted in, "Taste of what?"

"Oh, nothing," Clark seemed uncertain, as if he should not have mentioned it. "So how were you chosen?"

Jacob held out his left palm for Clark to see. They all stopped walking, and the boy examined Jacob's skin, looking perplexed.

"I don't understand. It's just a birthmark," Clark said. "An interesting one, but a birthmark just the same."

"That." Jacob exclaimed. "Is where this long story begins."

As they traveled along vast fields of beautiful yellow flowers, through expanses of grey rock face, and even a tunneling fissure with blue stalactites, hanging menacingly from the ceiling, Jacob explained to Clark everything he had learned so far about the Ancillary.

Taking one of the grainy hardcover books out of his pack, he opened to a page with a picture of the Ancillary's mark upon it. Sandwiched between languages Jacob could not decipher, the picture caught hold of Clark's attention.

"The biggest chalice," Clark whispered to himself.

"Huh?" Jacob said.

"Oh nothing…so the Gods chose us to help you?"

"I guess if that's the way you want to look at it… yeah. By choosing you, I could find my way here."

"This is amazing! It's like a comic book. I have Mutant Mayhem issue forty where Senzar the flamible meets and helps an aggrandized version of himself who can create molten volcanic conflagrations that can burn through the earth's crust —"

"I think we get the picture," Diego interjected.

Clark beamed. "I have to take you to Fuki."

Brushing off a rather large beetle that had landed on her elbow, Sophia asked, "What's a Fuki?"

"In America, you would deem Fuki a chieftain, or at least the American natives would. He needs to hear your tale of wonderment. This is wicked!"

Jacob couldn't help but think that there was something strange about Clark, though he couldn't quite put his finger on it. This didn't set off any panic, however, as it wasn't a feeling of distrust, but rather curiosity. The boy seemed oddly cultured and gave Jacob the feeling that Clark still had a lot to reveal about himself.

At that moment, they had finished passing through a particularly dense passage of sticklers, when a wave of enthusiasm hit Clark. Increasing his speed, he moved swiftly towards a large wooden arch hovering in thick brush. Once he was below the arch he turned his head and with a coy smile said, "Welcome lady and gentlemen…to Tanki Lowbei!"

Passing through the arch was like stepping into a different world.

"Wow," Jacob said. "My kind of town."

CHAPTER 27

"Strange," Mr. Maddock muttered to himself. The aged librarian had uncovered a text about the Ancillary that had been long forgotten amongst his mammoth collection of books. While rummaging through shelves—and reeking mayhem on his organizing system—he found the small book hidden in a bottom corner. He ran his fingers over the small text about the Ancillary.

"I don't remember you," he said as he perused through its pages, discovering that the book couldn't have been more than a hundred unnumbered pages. It boasted a spectacularly simple cover, beige with a fine textured binding that was pleasing to the touch, and a small picture of the Ancillary's mark on its spine. He must have picked it up one day and never got around to reading it—which was very unlike him. Stopping randomly on one of its pages, Mr. Maddock came upon some ancient lyrical prose he could not remember ever reading.

"You've been hiding from me all this time."

Much like when one savors a fine meal, Mr. Maddock took his time reading this, as it had been a long time since he had the opportunity to explore new knowledge about the famed flower... or rather, esoterically famed. The footnotes at the bottom of this page noted that the text above was found written in the dirt with a small blade in East Anglia, next to a dead traveler's body circa 1000 CE, and later translated. Next to the writing was the Ancillary's mark carved deep into the firm soil:

I was wrong
In the end breathe not, for the blossom itself was Satan's plume
I had been beckoned by fortune and glory, my name abiding
Ended by prospect of light like the day sky in darkness times
The black stars on petal coax the seeker
As my pedigree weeps and reunion is hastily forthcoming
It seems the treasure is a buried one
Only found by the worthy
I pillaged and terrible things I did
I was drawn for the mark was drawn on me from birth
I chose death

Mr. Maddock sat down at his desk for a while, reading and re-reading this passage. It was unnerving. *Why had this person died?* All sorts of scenarios flashed through his mind. *Did a jealous rival also seeking the flower kill him? Did he die looking for the Ancillary instead of living his life? Starvation? Dehydration? What does it mean?*

As he scanned the lines very carefully, he stopped at a particular word.

"Oh my God," he whispered to himself.

Everything clicked into place. It was the placement of the final puzzle piece, revealing the hidden image.

Mr. Maddock sprang from his chair and leaped over obstacles, ignoring the pain in his leg.

Dashing to the phone and almost knocking over the receiver, he dialed Rosie's cellular phone number.

Several rings later, no one answered.

CHAPTER 28

Tanki Lowbei was unlike anything they could have imagined. Passing into town was like taking a portal into an alternate dimension much like our world, but where things are a tad off. The town itself couldn't have been sprawled across more than fifty acres; however, it was jam-packed with outlandish sights. The houses were small and seemed to be initially made out of brick and wood, yet there were space-age additions on every domicile. Some had giant satellite dishes on top, others, sunrooms with sunken Jacuzzis. In front of one home lay a swimming pool acting as a moat around the entire area— complete with a drawbridge and medieval turrets. Two of the houses in the distance had Ionic Greek columns outside with beautiful marble statues, and stone fountains spouting clear water in fabulous forms. Along the side of the roads were restaurants with French sounding names and faux grapevine spiraling up pillars. On the outdoor patio of the one called 'L'amore du croissant' a young couple was sitting, sipping cappuccinos and eating pastries. The foot traffic reminded Jacob of a street condensation only Mardi Gras or a hometown Super Bowl championship could attract.

Diego was dazzled. "Is that…Is that a monk driving a Lamborghini?"

"Yes," Clark said nonchalantly as the bright yellow automobile passed. "That's Huang Fei Chi, he had a major breakthrough in fiber-optic technology for phone companies, which reduces chemical pollution. He left the monastery, but still values many of the Buddhist traditions, like nonviolence and kindness to everyone."

"Are Italian sports cars a tradition as well? Diego said. "If so, you can shave my head right now."

Clark sniggered. "No, sorry dude. It seemed the Gods chose him to help humans communicate easier with each other... kind of like me."

"What do you mean by that?" Sophia asked.

Clark nodded slightly. "We'll get to that."

Across the newly paved road were two businessmen of Tibetan descent dressed in fine suits, talking on cell phones. Their shoes were Italian leather and they carried expensive looking briefcases. They gave Clark a wave and passed by, not seeming to mind at all that there were strangers in their community.

"Why does it seem like everyone here is rich now?" Diego asked. "I thought only a few of you were... chosen."

Clark smiled mischievously. "That's what we tell the reporters. In truth... a lot more of us are doing great things."

"Doesn't the media wonder why it looks like everyone has money?"

"We spread the wealth," Clark said with a shrug.

"And you guys are raking it in, huh?" Sophia said.

"Actually, yes... this is the first time these families have had disposable income, which leads to them spending it on unimportant or aesthetically pleasing items. To tell you the truth though, the people here care more about what they are actually doing with their lives than what they own... they just wanted to have a little fun."

"So most of these people have inhaled the pollen?" Sophia asked.

"Pollen?" Clark look bewildered. "I'm not sure what you mean."

"The way you were chosen, isn't that what happened?"

"No that was because of —"

Clark was suddenly interrupted by a small boy running towards them, waving his arms and shouting, "CLARK...

CLARK!" The young boy kept it up until he was just mere feet away from them.

"Oh." The boy looked abashed. "Who are you people?"

Clark was quick to respond, "Don't worry Namala, they're my cousins… from America."

"Cousins?" The boy replied. "They don't look like you."

"Distant cousins… this is Namala. What's going on, little dude?"

Namala pulled Clark a few feet away, apparently not wanting the three strangers to hear what he had to say.

The small boy whispered something into Clark's ear, with his hand creating a barrier between his words and the newcomers. Jacob could have sworn that Namala's eyes darted to his palm, but he was probably just being paranoid. Clark jolted upward, a look of panic on his face.

"You three need to hide."

"What… why?" Diego said.

Clark had lost the friendly, happy-go-lucky expression that seemed natural to him, which had been replaced with shock.

"My house. It's the one over there." He pointed. "The one with the writing on the walls. I have a spare key under the golden Buddha that welcomes guests. Wait there for me." And with that Clark sped off towards an unknown destination, with Namala nipping at his heels, trying his best to keep up.

Jacob, Diego and Sophia were left standing in the street.

"What do you think happened? Sophia asked.

"I'm not sure, but I hope we don't get caught in the middle. We need to keep these people on our side if we expect to get any help," Diego said.

"Shall we then?" Jacob held both hands, palm upward, in the direction Clark had designated, letting a very silly grin slip onto his face.

"We shall," Sophia said, doing her best to imitate a queen. She wrapped her arm through the crook of Jacob's and they swiftly walked toward the house.

As they began to stroll, they noticed the streets were now

abandoned. The chairs where the young couple had been sitting only moments ago were now occupied only by air. The businessmen that had been calmly walking were nowhere to be seen, and cars were missing from the street. The hustle and bustle had turned from a Louisiana celebration to an old spaghetti-western ghost town.

"This is weird," Sophia said. "What just happened?"

Diego's head turned from side to side like a bobble-head doll. "It must have been something big. Lets get moving… quick."

They hurried towards Clark's house and stopped at the front door.

"Oh no," Sophia exclaimed.

There were hundreds of Buddhas outside of his front door. They were in all sorts of positions. One was feeding baby Buddhas, one was carrying something over his head, one was playing some sort of instrument; there were so many different kinds.

"How are we supposed to know the welcoming one?" Sophia groaned.

"Lets start looking," Diego said as Jacob bent down to shake hands with one of the small statues.

They picked them up by the handful, but after a minute had only uncovered about a third. There were Buddhas with bowls, fruit, candles, cupcakes, coins, baskets and even one that appeared to be holding firecrackers—Jacob had no idea where you would find one like that.

All of a sudden Sophia burst into a fit of laughter.

"What's so funny?" Diego asked.

"This is the one."

Diego and Sophia bent over the small figure to take a look. They too started to chuckle. The small Buddha was in the exact pose Jacob had been in while ushering them towards Clark's house; it even had the same silly grin on its small rotund face.

"Coincidence?" Sophia asked as the hilarity subsided.

Jacob lifted up the small statue and found the key hidden

beneath. "Fate."

It was then Jacob noticed how unusual the building that stood in front of them was. The side paneling of the entire house was speckled with different languages written in thick, gooey black paint. The walls themselves were made of a brown adobe-like material, with the inscriptions making it look like something out of an eighteenth century manuscript. Of all the languages displayed, they recognized only a few of the dialects.

"Bienvenido Los Amigos," Diego translated. "Welcome friends."

"Is that French?" Sophia asked herself. "Accueillez ceux qui cherchent l'amitié"

"I think so." Jacob read aloud. "Begrüßen Sie meine Freunde... I bet it says something about comic books."

It seems that no major language was left out: Italian, Greek, and even Latin. There were even dialects written with symbols, like Mandarin and hieroglyphics.

Sophia spoke hesitantly, "I think we have made ourselves an interesting friend."

"Lets get inside," Diego said. "This is getting very eerie. I feel like I've entered the suburbs of the Twilight Zone." He fit the small key into the lock and they entered an even stranger world.

Not only did the inside also have the multi-lingual wallpaper, but all sorts of papers were tacked up to the sides of the room. From ceiling to floor, there was no space left blank. In the far corner, stacks of white rectangular boxes were placed on top of each other, labeled things like 'Spiderman' and 'Astonishing X-men'. Beside the mountain of comics lay a heap of books, the most prominent being many varieties of dictionaries.

Pages upon pages were ripped out of books and placed upon the walls for a nontraditional decor. A connection was made from the diagrams with sharpie tracks and twine trails. It looked like the standard for mock movie sets about either serial killers or lunatic detectives.

"Do you think he's a mass word murderer?" Sophia asked.

"I think he reads more than just comic books." Jacob said. "Let's have a look around."

All three placed their travel bags on the floor. The small flat had three bedrooms, a half-kitchen, and a small lavatory — none of which looked much different from one another. Clark had all the basic necessities: food, fresh water, clothes and a twin mattress. Any empty space was filled with strange writings scattered across the floor.

Jacob was thoroughly enjoying this, as he had never seen anything remotely close to it in his life. The cascading sentences swirling around him were surreal. It was like living inside the mind of a mad genius. He envisioned himself tucked into this mastermind's cerebellum, staring at the neighboring lobes and watching the knowledge flicker and pass by.

"You know," Jacob started, "this actually explains a lot."

"How could this possibly explain anything?" Diego asked.

"Did you notice the type of English words he used to talk to us? I didn't even understand some of them."

"That's true," Sophia said. "I thought it was awfully funny how he was talking, it was like his speech kept slipping back and forth. Sort of like a California surfer switching to a Harvard professor."

"Maybe it's just the fact that most people around the world speak English. He did tell us that, and that small boy spoke it very well, too," Diego pointed out.

"Maybe you're right... or maybe we have been sucked into an alternate dimension where little worldly Buddhas with interesting tastes in decorations control everything," Jacob joked, adding a 'Woooo' while shaking his hands in front of his body.

This seemed to break some of the tension, allowing the three travelers to relax a bit and settle into this bizarre house. They sat around and examined some of the documents while waiting for the arrival of their host.

They waited for over an hour.

Jacob was right in the middle of telling a story when it happened.

"So there he was. The knight held his sword high and gave a slight nod to his opponent. The princess was watching in tears, hoping Sir Bob wouldn't be hurt."

"You named the knight Bob?" Diego asked.

Jacob shrugged. "It could happen. Anyway he slid down his visor when—"

A blast echoed throughout the entire house. It sounded like someone had thrown open the door, trying to forcibly release it from its hinges.

"NO FUKI!" they heard someone yell. "It wasn't them!"

Rounding the corner was one of the largest men Jacob had ever seen. Diego might as well have been a dachshund looking up at a German shepherd. He crashed through the first room with the ferocity of an irate rhinoceros. When the man reached the area they were lounging in, Jacob's limbs went stiff.

With a face like driftwood—and the type of muscles that come with loads of outdoor work—he towered over the three of them, covering them all in shadow. He had a round face, with a nose that looked many times broken. His teeth clenched and muscles flexed. He looked almost ready to pounce, like a lion stalking a baby antelope.

Clark came running in behind the sizable foe and started yelling.

"They weren't even here. They had nothing to do with this!"

The giant man raised a finger the size of a sausage.

"You have brought this upon my village."

Clark kept shouting, "It couldn't have been them, Fuki!"

Jacob could tell that this man was holding himself back.

"You need to answer some questions!" The giant boomed.

Diego was already in front of Jacob, with a hand grabbing something metal lodged between his pants and belt. Jacob's bodyguard was tense and looked ready to jump on the intruder, though he doubted it would do much good.

Jacob stood up and, without missing a beat, shook the man's frankfurter finger. He put on his best smile and said, "Sure, no problem…Welcome to the Word Kingdom. Can I get you something to eat?"

"What?" The giant man said. His fierce demeanor had subsided and he looked confused.

Clark was in the background, covering his mouth with his hands, trying his very best not to laugh. It was like a wooden dam trying to hold back the Mississippi.

"Just trying to lighten the mood," Jacob said, making a face like a wide-eyed puppy dog.

The dam burst. Clark was hooting and hollering as if all the laughter was trying to escape his body at once. He clutched his stomach and his eyes welled up in tears.

Fuki couldn't have looked more confused. All of a sudden the gigantic man joined in on the laughter and soon found himself embracing his own belly as loud foghorn whoops pervaded the room.

Sophia leaned over and whispered to Jacob, "Apparently you're very funny in Tibet?"

"Who knew?"

Fuki calmed down and the tension diminished.

"I needed that, young ones. Something very bad indeed has occurred." He turned towards Clark. "So you say these travelers have nothing to do with our misfortune?"

Clark, too, had stopped howling. His face turned serious. "To be truthful, I don't think we would have had our miracles in the first place if it weren't for them…at least partly."

"I don't understand. What do these foreigners have to do with our town?"

"I will explain everything, but first let's relax and drink tea."

Clark lit a small stove in the corner and brought out a tiny teakettle with jade cups to serve it in. He then led his guests into a small stone-tiled courtyard behind the house with a few mahogany chairs and a stained glass table. Everyone settled in, and Clark provided the introductions. After that, Jacob tried his best to clear up the situation.

"First off... how does everyone around here know English?" Jacob asked.

Fuki's chest puffed out with pride. "Everyone is taught how to speak at least limited English when they first enter for schooling. I make sure of that," he said, jabbing his thumb into his sternum. "We honor the ability, as it is a connector."

Clark smiled. "Like I said, universal language, man."

"Ok, but how do you," he pointed at Clark, "speak such amazing English... and what appears to be every other language known to any man... ever."

Clark smirked. "You figured that out, huh?"

"It was either that, or you have a strange taste in Feng Shui."

"Well, I was chosen by the gods to—"

Fuki hushed him before Clark could finish his sentence.

"Before young Chi here-"

"CLARK!"

"Yes... Clark. Before young Clark here spills the immense secrets of our town to you, I have a few questions of my own," Fuki said.

"Shoot."

"Clark mentioned that you have some connection to what is happening here."

Jacob inhaled a large breath and started recounting his journey thus far.

CHAPTER 29

"So you had to jump?" A look of envy flashed across Clark's face.

Jacob took a sip from his dark green cup to build the suspense. The warm drink was quite pleasing. If he guessed correctly, it was oolong with honey and some other ingredient that Jacob couldn't place... maybe vanilla? "Yup... and my parachute didn't come out. I had to wrench it free."

Clark threw his head back. "No way, dude!"

"The truth is being told."

"Before you go any further," Fuki said sternly. "I feel I can trust you now. You're story is far too wild to have been falsely crafted." He paused in reflection. "So the gods chose us so we can help you find this flower?"

"If you look at it like that," Jacob said.

"STAND UP!" Fuki bellowed, "ALL OF YOU!"

Fear once again struck Jacob. All three quickly rose.

"Over here!" He shouted and pointed at one of the stones.

They jolted from their seats and crowded into the designated area.

In one swoop, Fuki bent down and embraced all three in the biggest and firmest hug Jacob had ever received in his life.

"FRIENDS!" The vibrations from Fuki's deep voice rippled through them. "It is so good that you have come."

Fuki released them, and precious air could now fill in Jacob's lungs.

"Uh... thanks?" Diego said.

"So it will be as heartbreaking for you, then, when I say

that the Gods no longer see fit to bless our people."

"What do you mean by that?" Sophia asked.

"Please… sit back down. This is very tough news. I know nothing of the flower you mentioned, but I do believe you when you say it exists. The Gods chose you through the… Ancillary was it?"

Jacob nodded.

"We have been chosen through another means…. Krinama."

"What's Krinama?" Jacob asked.

Fuki opened his arms wide. "It is when the divine bless our minds."

"C'mon," Diego said. "This can't be real."

"How else would you explain my people," Fuki said patronizingly. "If not the Gods?"

"And you think that they have stopped?" Sophia asked.

"I know so. I called a meeting just moments ago, and when Namala told me three strangers were in our land, I believed you must have created sabotage or angered the gods. You see… we are tolerant of outsiders coming in to our home—though most of them don't wish us well. Most are here to document us or try and steal from us; however we are all the Gods' children and must treat each other with respect. We have but one rule on which we remain firm… on the days of the ceremony, the outsiders remain beyond our borders. We don't explain why we ask them to leave, just that they have to temporarily go."

"Yeah." Clark slapped his forehead. "In all the excitement it slipped my mind."

"This morning another young boy was to receive the heavenly award… nothing happened. We figured the first time was a mistake, but it has been confirmed. The gold has disappeared."

"Did you say GOLD!" Sophia exclaimed.

"Yes. Do you know such things?"

Jacob's eyes widened. "I think we might have some idea. Can you take us to wherever you have your ceremonies?"

The jade cup—which looked as if it was a dollhouse accessory in Fuki's massive hand—was placed on the table. "In dark times, it is my duty to protect my people. In great times my obligation remains the same. I see that I must be trusting so we can figure this out together." Fuki exhaled through his nose. "I will show you."

"Great," Jacob said. "I promise that if there is any way I can help, you can be assured that I will do it."

"Thank you. My doubts will now be put to rest." Fuki stood from his chair a little too quickly and sent it toppling over. "Follow me."

Once back inside, Jacob picked up his bag and pulled out a few of the books Mr. Maddock had given them.

"Think we will need them?" Diego asked.

"Hey, you never know. Better to have sore arms than a sore day."

They followed Fuki back through Clark's eccentric house and started walking down the road. They walked in a line, like baby ducklings following their mother. People were now back in the streets, though their faces were riddled with mistrust and fear. Jacob understood... the greatest event to ever happen to their town had ended, and Jacob, Sophia, and Diego must look like prime scapegoats.

"It is OK!" Fuki roared. "These three outsiders are to be trusted and respected! They are here to help. Pass the word along!"

It seemed that this only alleviated some of the long faces among the crowds. Jacob saw that these people were truly worried. Still though, the townspeople were carrying out their daily activities, which got odder and odder as they trotted onward. To their right was a small, older man in bright orange robes solving incredibly complex math problems on the blacktop with yellow chalk. A few yards behind him, a young girl was completing amazing feats of gymnastic strength. She proceeded to do a triple back flip and landed in a perfect forward split. A woman was sitting cross-legged on the grass in front of her house with a portable computer. This was neither an ordinary laptop nor an ordinary house. The outside of the house was crawling with wires, all feeding into a small paint-chipped shed on the side of the house. All types of lights and sounds were coming from the inside of this house, with the woman typing away. The power notebook she was using had some additions of its own. It had sprouted antennae — the kind on old-fashioned television sets — however, they were glowing neon green. Additional motherboards were also placed along the outside of the monitor, making it look like a tiny metallic city.

"That's Quen," Fuki pointed out, noticing the baffled looks on the outsider's faces. "She created these for us." Out of the pocket of his animal-skin overcoat came a small object that looked like a beeper. "This is how I announce the time for the meeting ceremonies secretly, so no foreigner with questionable motives will know. We then have plenty of time for everyone to politely ask the intruders to leave before they can find out where the miracles are performed."

"So most of the locals here have gone to... Krinama?" Sophia asked.

"Most... but not all. This is why it is such a blow to us that it has ceased now of all times."

"This is wild!" Diego said.

"Yes," Fuki murmured. "Krinama *was* the highest of blessings."

"Have you done it?" Jacob asked.

Fuki stopped walking. Jacob could only see the silhouette of him against the sun, but he knew Fuki was taken aback.

"No," he said solemnly. "A leader must look out for his people before he thinks of himself. I was to be the very last."

"That's very noble of you."

Fuki said nothing more on the subject and resumed walking.

More and more amazing sights were theirs to behold. Someone had sculpted a beautiful, life-size statue of a dancer out of bronze. There was a middle-aged balding man who was playing with three golden retriever puppies. The canines were able to follow commands that they didn't even know were possible.

"Karate-chop," the man called out to the puppies. All three — in perfect synchronization — stood on their hind legs and made a swiping motion with their paws.

"Awww..." Sophia stopped walking and stared with her mouth in an 'O' shape.

"Come," Fuki beckoned to her. "There will be plenty of time to enjoy our town later."

Under a pine tree sat a young boy writing things down on a legal pad. His face seemed temporarily paralyzed in an expression of stoicism. Crouching on the other side of the tree was a group of schoolgirls, looking at the young boy with the same face Sophia had made while looking at the puppies.

They walked towards a less populated section of the town. The wild houses faded into the distance as Fuki led them up to an aged building. It looked very old, older than most things Jacob had seen so far. It was simply designed, with dark brown lumber that was amazingly well kept for a building so ancient. There were strange symbols also made out of wood around the front entrance: an eye with two retinas, a pair of hands, and a wonderfully intricate, multi-colored mandala.

"This was an old temple used long before any of us were born," Fuki said. "No one knows why it was abandoned as a place of meditation. In the past, we have only used it as a backup water supply. As of late it has been the sight of the transformations. Clark was actually the first to discover it. It was the one time his mischief led to something beneficial."

Clark smirked. "What can I say?"

"Can we go in?" Jacob asked.

Fuki nodded and walked over to the large double doors. Their handles were golden and had a knocker expertly crafted in the shape of a lion. Fuki opened both doors, which let out creaks of refusal, and they followed him inside.

Jacob noticed that the townsfolk had taken the liberty of decorating the inside. Balloons, ribbons and streamers were all hanging from the ceiling, making it contrastingly festive compared to the exterior. The ceiling was not high, but it looked able to accommodate a fair share of the townsfolk. Roses, lilies, small trinkets, colorful origami and all sorts of other items were lined up in the corner around a circular stone structure.

"After a transformation, the recipient will bring a small gift to express their gratitude to whomever saw fit to grace us with wonderful knowledge."

Jacob ambled over to the rounded granite and peered inside.

"It's a well!"

"Yes, that is where it happens."

"So let me see if I have this down… Clark—" Jacob counted off his fingers. "—You find this place, drink from the well and you suddenly know how to read and write all sorts of languages."

"Si, signor!" Clark said.

"Then, you show the place to someone else and they drink."

"More or less," Clark continued.

"Then Fuki realizes that this is a divine presence choosing you all to receive this blessing through water?"

"Yes."

"This continues," Jacob said, "giving the honor to someone different and you create a ceremony. This is how so many people here are making groundbreaking discoveries and developing marvelous talents."

"I can see why you are meant for this flower," Fuki said. "However, I have seen no flower that has the mark you bear."

"You mentioned gold before?" Jacob asked.

"In the well, there were golden flecks. They are now gone, the heavens have now taken them away."

Diego started frantically looking around the building for

something. He checked in the darkness created by shadows and in the hidden crevices.

"What are you doing, little one?" Fuki asked.

Jacob assumed this was the first time anyone had referred to Diego as 'little'.

"Searching for the flower! It's got to be around here somewhere!"

Jacob placed a hand on Diego's shoulder. "You can stop looking."

"What do you mean? We're so close!"

"So you're starting to believe then," Sophia said.

Diego was taken aback. "No... I... It's just that if we find it, then you can see it is just a flower and we can go home."

Sophia tried to hold back a smile.

Jacob still hadn't mentioned the perplexing feeling of directional magnetism, and this place just didn't feel right. The bubbles hadn't settled yet.

Sophia stepped over to Jacob. "You know something, don't you?"

"The pollen didn't fall into the well here."

It took a few seconds, but it seemed that he and Sophia had the same realization. "The Ancillary must be close to water... the pollen traveled and ended up here!"

"Exactly!" Jacob said. "We are getting closer!"

"Wait... that rhyme mentioned water — or at least hinted to it," Diego said.

"You're right," Jacob was stunned. "You were paying attention to that?"

Diego cracked his knuckles.

Jacob placed the books he had been carrying gently on the ground. It was a relief, as even the smallest amount of weight became cumbersome after a while. He picked up the text he was reading earlier and again flipped to page fifty-one.

Jacob scanned the lines until he found what he was looking for. "In the place where it starts will be never the same, by worlds' surface will flow untitled to name... flowing surface...

never the same… that sure sounds like water to me."

"Maybe it always settles by water?" Sophia said. "I think we should pay close attention to that poem, it might have a lot more to—"

In the far corner of the abandoned temple, a whimper cut Sophia off mid-sentence. The sound came from far in the darkness, behind a stack of old planks. It was muffled, but Jacob was sure that it had been a sob.

"Who is there?" Fuki yelled. "Come and show yourself."

The sobs became a putter, like the sound of an old lawn mower trying its best to wake up. Out of the shadows came a small boy.

"Godakh," Fuki said gently. "Why are you here? You should be with your family."

When the boy spoke, his words were broken by sobs. "W-Why me Fuki? W-Why G-Gods hate me?"

"Dear child," Fuki bent as low as possible so he could be eye level with Godakh, "It has nothing to do with you. The Gods love you… it was just bad timing."

"B-But Fuki," choked Godakh. "It h-happened at my turn. They h-hate me Fuki. They h-hate me!"

Fuki picked the young lad up and embraced him—the child's feet ended well off the ground.

"Hush now, child, I promise it wasn't you."

Jacob walked over and introduced himself to the boy.

"Hey, I'm Jacob, but you can call me Cob if you want."

"H-Hi Cob."

"I'm going to help your town. It wasn't your fault; it turns out the golden specks were from a flower… far up the river. I guess the gods—" Jacob paused. "—Well, it's hard to explain, little man. But long story short, you had nothing to do with the gold disappearing."

"P-Promise?"

"I swear by all the stars in the sky and grass on the ground. Fuki, I am going to find that flower and when I do, I'm going to bring it here and give it to you first."

"Huh?" Diego muttered.

"I want you to take it and shake every last bit of pollen out and divide it amongst your people. I don't know why all of a sudden it stopped — maybe a shift in the winds — but I sure won't let you not finish what has started. I owe you all that much at least."

Fuki looked as if he wanted to give Jacob another hug, which he was very much hoping wouldn't come to pass.

To Jacob's delight, Fuki remained where he was standing. "You really are going to change the world, young Cob. It seems the Gods chose right."

CHAPTER 30

This is taking much too long, Marrow thought. It had been hours already, and although Marrow had been enjoying every second of his inebriation, a nagging feeling had been pulling at him for some time now.

Along the drive, Russell had spotted a small dive bar on the side of the road. He had convinced Marrow to stop and let them have little bit of long-awaited fun. Their entourage pulled into the parking lot and all but one had entered into the establishment.

Frankie was still locked in the trunk.

They had tied the owner to a chair with duct tape, and stuffed a dirty sock into his mouth, so he wouldn't ruin the fun by babbling on in whatever language they spoke in Tibet. The floor was now covered with broken glass from smashed liquor bottles, and pool balls were lodged deep into the walls. Chairs had been busted over backs, and little wooden stakes littered the ground as if there had been a massive vampire slaying. They had held the women there against their wills and kicked out the local men, who would have spoiled their fun. One particularly angry patron had tried to put up a fight and stop their merrymaking…his body was limp in the corner.

"Whoo! Shake it!" Shully said.

The women were dancing on the bars. Marrow knew they were only in the spirit of things out of fear, but they were in the spirit of things nonetheless. Marrow and his men had been having a grand old time, but he had decided that enough was enough. Not because they had done enough damage to the bar

—including emptying most of the whisky bottles into their stomachs—but because he couldn't wait any longer to get what he had come for.

"Time to get moving!" he roared.

Little Paulo let out a whine. "Oh c'mon boss, just a little longer."

Marrow said nothing—little Paulo got the message.

"Cut the music," Marrow said calmly.

One of his men kicked the rusty jukebox, and his foot went through the glass. This didn't stop the music, so after removing his leg from the mess of audio disks, he unplugged the machine.

As the place got quiet, the women snuck off the bar and tried to shy away into the back room. Marrow couldn't have her calling the authorities. He snapped his fingers and little Paulo scooped her up in his arms.

"It is time you help me reach my destiny."

He caught a glimpse of Tony rolling his eyes.

"I'm sorry Tony, is something wrong?" Marrow asked politely.

"No boss… but… a flower? C'mon, I know you're not that naïve."

"Why is this naiveté?"

"Because it can't be real."

"Ah, very fine argument indeed… however." He stood up and started pacing the room. "Let's put this logic to the test."

He pulled out his revolver and let it hang on one finger. "There are tribes in the Amazon that do not keep in contact with the outside world. They hold *their* secrets as well as vice versa. They have lived simply for hundreds of years, without the need for anything fancy."

"In 1836, Samuel Colt issued the first patent for the revolver." Marrow ran his hand over the smooth barrel. "It contained six bullets that could be consecutively fired without having to reload after every single shot. Colt was a visionary. At the same time, do you know what these Amazonian philistines hunted and warred with? Hmm…. Anybody?...They fought with pointed sticks. Now if someone was to tell them that something as sophisticated and elegant as the revolver actually existed, do you know what their answer would have been…?"

Marrow smiled. "Probably something like a roll of the eyes."

All around the bar, there were hearty laughs. Even Tony chuckled.

Marrow raised his gun towards Tony's face and the laughing immediately halted.

"You know something else that's unbelievable? A cockroach can live weeks without its head. It will actually die of starvation first. I wonder if it's the same with humans?"

A blast shook the room.

CHAPTER 31

Clark had called it momos; Jacob called it delicious. It was dinnertime and Jacob was famished. The steamed dumplings on his plate had been presented in a dark tomato sauce with basil and cumin. After one bite, he felt he knew a little bit about what heaven's restaurants would serve. They had been taken to a small house-to-restaurant convert, owned and operated by a dainty old woman named Mau. People were crowded in, side-by-side along three long tables, sharing a glorious meal together in the buffet style. Anyone that *could* fit, *did* fit, as it appeared that Mau's was the first choice of restaurant for all in Tanki Lowbei. The plan was, at first light tomorrow, they would set out along the river with Clark as a guide.

"Mau," Clark said between bites of samosa, "was one of the first people here to drink from the well of visions." He took another heaping chomp. "Good thing too." The food rolled around in his mouth. "The gods chose to bless her with the talent to cook the finest meals we have ever eaten. She was always a wonderful chef—many times making me great meals after school when I was younger—but now she's cooking on a whole new level. Great thing for her and an even better thing for us!"

Sophia picked up a large helping of tenderized yak meat and placed it onto her plate. Gently stabbing a small piece with her two-pronged fork, she brought it into her mouth and slowly chewed—letting the juices roll gently into her stomach. Her entire face lit up, and she momentarily gave up her girlish manners to start shoveling mounds of the food past her lips.

She was sitting next to Jacob, and after chewing the mass of meat, grasped his thigh. "Have you ever tasted ANYTHING this good?!"

"I can't say that I have—and your grandfather makes a mean pot roast."

"This is incredible," Sophia said. "If the pollen can make this happen, imagine what the flower itself can do. Just think… if Mau already had the potential to create this, I can't fathom what all of us have inside. People always tell you that it's possible to do anything, but I've never really believed it until now. It's a glorious feeling."

"I'm happy again," Jacob sang. Together they roared with laughter. Sending wave after wave of delicious food into their bellies had further enhanced the day's joyfulness.

While Diego and Clark were in a heated discussion about which superhero would win in a fight—Superman or the Incredible Hulk—Jacob and Sophia were able to talk to one another freely.

"I really like your hair," Jacob commented. "It reminds me of a story I once heard about spinning straw into gold."

Sophia's teeth sparkled when she smiled. "You really are a straight shooter aren't you?"

"I'm so glad you came," Jacob said.

"Me too, I've never done anything remotely like this before. This has been the best couple of days of my whole life… I'm sure that it's the first thing I'm going to tell my grandchildren about… probably before they even know how to speak."

"This really has been some adventure so far…and we really just started. I bet tomorrow holds all sorts of new…"

"New what?"

"Just new," he stated.

In a voice that sounded much like an Australian naturalist, Sophia said, "That's true, bright and early we venture out into the wilderness facing wild bears, avalanches, poachers, booby traps, quicksand and worst of all… those pesky little mosquitoes."

Jacob laughed, "If that's true, count me out... I'll just wait another five hundred years until the Ancillary chooses a more *convenient* location."

"You know what... I'll go with you then, too."

Suddenly, shouting overtook their conversation. "But the Hulk wouldn't know about kryptonite, so he couldn't defeat him no matter what!" Clark said defensively.

"But the Hulk gets stronger the angrier he gets! Can you say that about Superman?"

"Superman is invincible! It doesn't matter!"

Most of the dinner guests around the table had no idea who either of those fictional characters were, so they just stared and enjoyed watching the friendly debate.

"ENOUGH!" Fuki hollered. The whole table went silent.

Fuki flashed a cunning smile. With a flex of his monstrous biceps he said, "It doesn't matter. I would beat them both!"

Everyone roared with laughter and the chatter began again. Up and down the table everyone was enjoying their meals and each other's company. Songs were spontaneously composed and everyone was pretty quick to learn the words. Soon enough the food dwindled, but their morale was high. Jacob noticed that these people were determined not to let the Krinama disaster lower their spirits.

"Is every dinner like this?" Jacob asked Clark.

"Actually, yes. Our town has an unparalleled level of joy. Ever since Krinama, all the little problems have seemed to melt away. Even now, in the middle of a crisis, everyone seems to be getting along... great town, man."

Jacob and Sophia were quick to resume their conversation and talked about past experiences, hobbies, and reminisced about the day's uncanny events. Before Jacob knew it, an hour had passed and most of the guests had already left the restaurant.

Jacob looked around; the only people left sitting were the three Americans, Clark, Fuki, and a few other locals who were pleading with Mau for one more course. She happily obliged.

"When did it get so empty in here?" Jacob asked.

"I hadn't noticed," Sophia said. "So anyway, I can't believe you have never been to a Broadway play!"

"I've always wanted to. I hear the Lion King changes lives, but I've never made it over to the east coast."

"One day, when you come and visit me, I'll take you. Afterwards we'll go to Central Park and we can eat in the Lower East side."

"That sounds great."

"I think it's time to get moving," Clark said. "My stomach feels like a balloon about to rupture." He took out a wad of colorful paper currency that Clark explained was called the yuan. "It's on me, friends."

"Thanks! Are you sure?" Diego asked.

"In Tanki Lowbei it is a dishonor not to buy the first meal for new friends… actually I made that up, but your Princeton University has paid me handsomely to attempt a translation of some ancient tablet one of their archaeology professors found. My skills are not going unnoticed."

"How do you keep the media from finding out about all of your town's achievements?" Sophia asked. "I'm sure that they are asking a lot of questions."

"More and more every day," Clark said. "But with Krinama no more, I guess we have no more reason to hide."

"Don't go giving away your secrets just yet," Jacob said. "We still have time to find the Ancillary."

They all thanked Mau and left the table with their stomachs and hearts full to the brim. It was now approaching twilight, and the town was quieting down. In the distance they could hear the hum of Quen's technologically advanced house. The dim light hitting the fountains and scattered artwork gave a special ambience to Tanki Lowbei, which Jacob couldn't help but take to heart. The world had brought him here. This beautiful mysterious place, and it felt right. Mr. Maddock was correct, in some way he felt home.

"You've got a little something." Sophia began brushing her hand through his hair. "Right… here. Got it."

Her fingers making their way across his scalp sparked a fresh ripple of yearning. "…Thanks," he said.

"My friends," Fuki said with grandeur. "I will see you in the morning to help you prepare for your quest." With that, he turned and walked into the distance.

When the colossal man was out of earshot, Sophia whispered to Clark, "He must be disappointed. As the leader of your town he must have been looking forward to everyone getting to drink the pollen water… himself included."

"Yes, though if he is devastated, he will not show it. Of all the people in our community, we look to him for strength and courage. He passes his aura off to us and we feel safe."

"Cob," she said. "I can't wait to see the look on his face when you bring back the flower and give him the pollen."

"Me neither… me neither."

"We should get going, you all need your sleep if you're going to keep up with me tomorrow."

"Oh really?" Diego said playfully. "We'll see about that!"

Ready to surrender to their food-related comas, they followed Clark back to his wordy house. As they passed the tiny Buddhas, Jacob made a small bow to the one welcoming them.

They pulled out the thin vinyl sleeping bags Mr. Maddock had provided for them, leaving Jacob grateful not to be sleeping in the mud, as was the intention. Along with their slumber gear were toothbrushes and floss.

"You all can sleep in here," Clark said. "It was my father's room."

"Thank you Clark, this means so much," Jacob said.

All three travelers went into the bathroom and started attacking their teeth with the brand-new brushes. The sink was equipped with homemade fresh mint toothpaste, which was far superior to the brands they normally used. After all three had finished, Sophia noticed what was in the corner of the bathroom.

"Oh my lord… a shower!"

The look on her face rivaled every young child's grin when they get their first puppy. She pulled a towel from a fresh stack off the ground. "You gentlemen mind?"

"Ladies first," Jacob declared.

Both boys exited the bathroom and let Sophia get acquainted with the hot water.

"You are so into that girl," Diego said with a grin.

"It's that obvious, huh?"

"Like hay in a pin stack."

"Very clever," Jacob said. "Problem is, I'm not sure how she feels."

"Nothing in life comes easy, my little friend, especially when it comes to a girl that beautiful."

Clark ambled around the corner. His night clothing consisted of a fresh superman shirt and pajama pants spangled with superman logos.

"I think you might be on the verge of obsession," Diego joked.

"No… just limited wardrobe. I got a discount on the t-shirts because I ordered more than fifty."

"You're serious?"

"Free shipping too… which is saying something because we sort of live in the middle of nowhere."

After a few minutes of planning the next day's journey, Sophia opened up the bathroom door, wrapped up in a towel. Her creamy skin was radiant, and her hair was tossed to the side. Small droplets of water were falling to the floor, but Jacob assumed that Clark couldn't care less. All three young men stared slack-jawed and googily eyed.

"Would one of you fine young men care to toss me my bag?"

It took a minute for the request to register with any of them, as their minds had been lost in a sea of hormones. Jacob almost reverted to the mental stage of when he had first met her. It was as if they were ancient Greek sailors being drawn toward an unknown destination by beautiful song. Diego was the first to break away from the siren-like trance and retrieved Sophia's bag.

"Thanks... I'll only be another minute," she said as she shut herself back inside.

Jacob took a deep breath. "Why am I in Tibet again?"

Clark swallowed, "I don't know... but I'm sure glad you brought her."

CHAPTER 32

The bonfire was the perfect way to finalize the day. Jacob, Sophia, Diego and Clark all sat around the brazen flames that penetrated the darkness and cast long flowing shadows upon the land. Clark had whipped up this localized inferno in a manner of minutes. The cracking twigs and splintering logs sent the smell of burnt wood flowing to their nostrils. This is quite relaxing, Jacob thought. Small outcrops of flames cracked like tiny orange whips, leaving only a blurry image ingrained in their sights.

"What did it feel like?" Diego asked. "When you drank from the well."

Clark looked unnaturally serious while trying to answer this question. "At first, everything around me went black. I think I may have passed out because I can't really recall the beginning stages. The dreams were uncanny... if they could even be described as dreams." He paused. "Everyone has certain moments in their lives when they are not distracted and can just feel the earth breathing around them. No music or conversation or books or television... just... life. It was like that... only a hundred times stronger. The sun's position had told me I was not under the Gods' spell long, but in the other place... it was months. I couldn't possibly vocalize what happened, I couldn't do it justice. The only possible way to describe it is through... sound." He fell silent for a moment. "I'll be right back."

Clark went into his house and left Jacob and the others contemplating by the warmth of the fire. No one said anything until Clark returned, as they were too preoccupied with their thoughts. He brought along a small drum. Clark explained that it was called a djembe and was played with the bare hands. The drum itself had patterns: diamonds, triangles, panthers, and arrows, among others, all working together to form a story.

"Listen… just hear the noises around you."

They all tried their best to clear their minds of all their needless internal chatter and just listen. To Jacob's surprise, it actually worked. The chirping of crickets, the sound of the wind kissing the trees as it passed through, owls calling to one another — these things all rose in crescendo and he could feel nature surging.

"Now think of the sounds of the earth around us as the small day-to-day learnings the gods are hoping we notice. Not always do we focus on them… but they are always there… waiting."

The sound of Clark's soft voice echoed through their minds as they felt peace and tranquility gushing freely.

"This, my friends… is the music of where we start."

Diego looked like he could sink into the chair and try a round of hibernation.

BOOM. B-BOOM. BADABOOM. Clark began striking the drum hard with an open fist. Jacob, Sophia and Diego all jolted forward and were brought out of their transfixion.

"What did you do that for? I was enjoying it," Diego said.

"You asked what it felt like," Clark smiled.

"Like a headache?"

"No, you missed the point. Do you see what happened? You all couldn't concentrate anymore. The drumming is today's hectic world. Even here in the middle of nowhere it is hard to concentrate on the things that matter. After that water touched my lips, it conditioned my mind to finally relax and I was given the gift of communication. '

"And when you woke up, you could read and write all sorts of languages?" Jacob asked.

"… Not quite, but I rose a different man. I could feel that

something had changed, but I didn't know what yet. It took a couple of days to figure that out. But all of a sudden I had the unquenchable thirst to read. Any unfamiliar word I came across, I suddenly knew the meaning. Opalescence, undulation, dalliance, I understood them all. So I tried French, Latin, Japanese, Swahili; they were all mine for the taking. When I read these strange and foreign idioms it was like they were all lying dormant in my brain just waiting to be unleashed. Nothing else has changed, just this amazing gift of lingo."

It was Sophia's turn to let out an elongated 'wow'.

Diego looked pale. "So… this is actually real?"

"If my story and abilities can't convince you, then I don't know what will."

"It's just… stuff like this can't happen."

"It already did," Clark said. "Even though I was the first to stumble upon the well, it wasn't frightening. I knew I had been part of something divine. I told Fuki what had happened, and the rest, as you would say is history."

"That's amazing, Clark. So why did you hide it from us?" Jacob asked.

"With all the people snooping around, I have to disguise my ability."

A look of revelation dawned on Sophia. "So that's why you talked the way you did when we first met."

"That… and using bombastic language isn't nearly as fun as surfer lingo." Clark stood up and pretended to catch a wave. "Hang ten, bro!"

Jacob, along with the others, laughed until waves of exhaustion came crashing down.

"I guess we should turn in for the night," Diego said mid-yawn.

Clark bent down and started piling sand onto the fire pit. "Good idea, we have a long day ahead of us."

Smoke danced above their heads as the fire was extinguished and they followed the interior lights of Clark's home back inside.

Clark said a quick goodnight, threw some papers off of his mattress, and fell asleep as soon as his Superman apparel touched the Superman sheets.

Diego set his sleeping bag up close to the door — *probably feeling the need to be closest to danger,* Jacob thought. Jacob pushed away some photographs of the Rosetta stone and made a small nest for himself on the floor. Even though it was thin bedding on hard wood, it looked more comfortable than a puffy comforter and goose down pillows. Zippering open the bag and sliding in, he stretched out and relaxed.

Sophia set up her bag as close to Jacob's as possible without them actually overlapping. She had changed into pink satin pajamas that shone in the dim light. Getting into her bag, she curled up on her left side and faced Jacob.

He could see the tolls of the day in her expression; however, it didn't make her any less stunning. In fact, Jacob thought it only enhanced her beauty. She didn't let a little thing like being tired slow her down. Loud, nasally snores were coming from behind him and he knew Diego had already fallen asleep.

Sophia ruffled her body some in an attempt to find comfort. "Some day, huh Cob?"

"Some day," Jacob said.

"You know," she said after settling in, "you have nice eyes."

"Thanks… but they're just brown."

"It's not the color," she said quietly. "It's what I can see in them."

"What can you see?"

"Hope, excitement, adventure … love."

At that last word, Jacob's stomach tightened.

"You have amazing eyes," he returned. "Blue is my favorite color."

"I got them from my grandmother."

Jacob was caught off guard. He had never met Mr. Maddock's wife, as she had passed away before Jacob ever stepped foot in the library. It wasn't like it was a sore subject, it was just that Jacob never brought it up. From time to time he would catch the librarian staring at an old black and white photograph of his wife on the mantelpiece. Now that Sophia mentioned it, he could see the resemblance. She inherited the sandy blonde hair and the same smile that filled the polished silver frame.

"Were you close?" Jacob asked, hoping to learn a little more.

"No... she died when I was little."

"Sorry."

"It's ok. If you believe it, she loved books even more that my grand pappy."

"I didn't think that was possible. What was her name?"

"Maggie." Sophia's teeth pulled in her bottom lip. "I wonder if she knew about the Ancillary too?"

"I bet she did. I bet her and Mr. Maddock would stay up late — sitting next to each other just like this — and tell tall tales of hedgehogs and African spirits."

"Do you think anyone found one in the past?" Sophia asked.

"I'm not sure, your grandfather never mentioned it... if someone did we probably know their name... right?"

"Right." Sophia let out a deep yawn as her eyelids sloped downward as if pulled by invisible hooks. "Hey Cob?"

"Hmm."

She leaned in closer, "I think —"

BANG. A deafening blast was heard off in the distance.

Diego jolted out of his sleep. "What's going —"

BANG. Another one.

"Is Clark banging his drum again?" Diego asked.

"I don't think so, that sounded way too loud," Sophia said.

Through the walls, more thunderous roars broke the night silence. They could vaguely hear crashes and what sounded like men laughing.

Clark came racing into the room.

"Did you three hear that, too?"

"Yeah," Jacob said, "It sounds like it's getting closer."

They could now hear the explosive noises clearer, and they had a definite resemblance to gunfire.

Jacob quickly got out of his cocoon. "So I'm guessing this isn't a normal nighttime occurrence?"

"Not even in this town," Clark said. "Hurry, lets go see what it is. I hope everyone is alright."

Clark raced back into his bedroom and returned holding an aluminum Louisville slugger in one hand and an LED flashlight in the other.

There was no time to change out of their pajamas, as they could now make out distinct screams. In a flash, they all donned footwear and prepared to see what the commotion was about.

They heard a muffled yell. "Wake up everyone. No more dreaming… It's nightmare time."

"Do you have any more of those bats?" Diego asked Clark.

"Sorry, non-violent town. Grab what you can but hurry."

The Spaniard pounced into the kitchen and grabbed three sharp cooking knives. He returned with one he tucked into the back of his belt and extended his hands for Jacob and Sophia to take the other two.

Sophia looked nervous. "I don't think I could."

"Yeah, I'll take my chances," Jacob said.

"I'm being paid for you not to have to take chances," Diego said as he turned the front door handle. "Now you should all wait inside —"

Clark raced out the door before Diego could finish his sentence.

"No!" Jacob called, and bolted after him.

Jacob heard the objection bellowed by Diego.

He stood next to Clark on the front stoop and noticed the neighbors were all just as scared and confused as they were. Two slim men were exiting the house with solar panels on the left.

"Clark!" one of the neighbors called. "What's going on?"

"I'm not sure. It sounds like it's coming from the courtyard. Follow us!"

Diego crashed through the door. "No, you should stay here. I'll go—"

From the front of Clark's home they couldn't see anything out of the ordinary, but they could hear a commotion coming from behind the houses across the street. It couldn't have been more than a few hundred feet away. There was loud shouting and a cacophony of noises that could only have been made by someone forcibly shattering something... or some things. The outlines of the houses across the street glowed a sick yellow as the sound of gunfire was heard.

Jacob would never have guessed Clark could move so fast. His short friend was already making his way toward the ruckus before Jacob was able to get a thought across. He chased after Clark as fast as his legs would carry him, several times almost tripping or falling from buckled knees.

"Get back here!" Diego yelled.

"Clark! Stop!" Jacob screamed.

A woman screeched from somewhere in the distance.

He followed Clark behind Quan's labyrinth of wires, and passed onto the next street behind them. Across the road was the courtyard Clark had mentioned. He was not ready for what he saw. It was a dimly lit, wide stone piazza with beautiful ceramic and clay sculptures of the Buddha and other deities, currently being blown to pieces by semi-automatics.

Six or seven men were using these artfully crafted figures for target practice; however, there was one man hidden in the shadows, standing completely still with his arms behind his back.

The sight of these vandals didn't deter Clark from keeping his pace. Jacob followed behind him and noticed that the rest of the townsfolk were emerging from the woodwork, all with the same intentions as Clark—stopping these monsters.

A cherub head exploded. The uninvited men were emitting

roars of laughter as if defacement was their premier form of entertainment. The townspeople surrounded the scene and slowly moved in towards their foe, as though they were one entity, like a school of fish or swarming bees before a cell.

"HALT!" Fuki's deep booming ricocheted across the courtyard and surprisingly the men stopped shooting. They slinked their way behind the man standing still, who was presumably the leader.

Fuki's large body was a menacing sight in the dark. The locals still circled around, and Fuki moved into the ring towards the invaders.

"I do not care who you are or what you want. You are to leave immediately! Get out and never return here!"

Slowly the leader brought his hands from behind him. One of them was holding a large revolver. Jacob saw a flash of writing on the handle, but couldn't make out what it said at that distance. The eerie man still said nothing but raised the firearm in the direction of a particularly aesthetic carving of an eagle and squeezed the trigger. The right wing blasted into a thousand pieces.

The stranger's voice was smooth and velvety. "You speak English? Great. So you'll understand me when I say we have no intention of leaving yet. We came for something and we will stay until we get it."

The man stepped forward into a patch of light from a streetlamp. The face that was revealed had thick brown lines running across the entirety of it. One line looked uncannily like a bone and ended just under his nose.

"We have nothing for you," Fuki said as he walked closer. "Turn around and go."

"You would be the leader of this pathetic excuse for a town?" The disfigured man asked in a silky voice.

"Yes."

With the speed of a viper the man lifted his arm and fired a single shot.

Fuki's head jerked back and with a horrible thud, his

massive body crumpled to the ground.
    The bone-faced man smiled.
        "Who's next?"

CHAPTER 33

His bat held high, Clark charged like lightning.

"Nooooo!" He cried. "Fuki!"

The bone-man was uncannily fast. Clark's momentum kept him going forward, which the intruder used to his advantage. Like a professional baseball player cradling a particularly fast line drive, the bone-man scooped Clark into his grasp and managed to disarm him all at once. One arm shot under Clarks elbow and a hand twisted behind his neck, locking the young boy into a hold.

"Good, we have a volunteer." The trespasser slammed the barrel of his revolver against Clark's temple and pushed it deep, causing Clark to wince in pain.

"My name is Marrow. Me and my men are completely willing to be civilized if you all cooperate... you people do know what civilized means, correct?"

As he said this, a swimming pool of blood was assembling around Fuki's lifeless head. In the shadows it was slick—like oil—and gave Jacob a nauseating feeling in the pit of his stomach.

An old monk hobbled out of the gathering and shuffled in closer to the action. His knees were as shaky as his back was hunched. He had a freshly shaven head and red tattered robes that swayed as he staggered forward. Jacob was surprised he could stand at all.

"We peaceful people," the feeble man said pleasantly in broken English. "Please let Clark go. We talk private and give what you want."

"I don't think so old man." Another thrust of his firearm into the side of Clark's head. "I will make this very simple for all of you. I want the Ancillary... now... and if you all play dumb and don't hand it over," Marrow looked down at Clark's clothing, "we are going to find out if this young boy is actually faster than a speeding bullet."

Jacob's heart stopped. The Ancillary. So that's why he was here.

There was a muttering in the crowd, their faces skewed with confusion.

The aged monk spoke again, "We never heard this. You must be mistake."

"The Ancillary... the flower... the pollen you all have been stealing. Do you really think I wouldn't notice what was happening? My whole life has been dedicated to finding it and you rice peddlers aren't going to keep me from it."

Even standing next to a dead friend, the monk kept his cool. "I know nothing of Ancillary flower. You have wrong town."

"Wrong town," Marrow scoffed sardonically. "Do you think I'm that naïve?" His face contorted in rage. "Do you think I'm a damn fool?!"

Little Paulo chimed in. "I think they do boss."

Marrow released the gun from Clark's forehead and waved it around.

"Do you think I'm just going to look around and not see it all? Satellite dishes, Ipods, expensive suits, and fancy cars, in a town of FARMERS! Obviously the Ancillary has been a lucrative take for you all. Am I supposed to believe all those brilliant ideas that removed you from the Stone Age just... fell out of the sky?"

His men all laughed at this remark.

Someone from the crowd yelled, "The Gods chose us!"

"The gods," he said mockingly, "have nothing to do with this. Now hand over the flower or this young man here will change from the 'Man of Steel' to the 'Man full of lead'." This time he gently replaced the barrel back on Clark's face.

"We don't know what talking about. You kill us all but won't get what you want," the monk said calmly.

"Does that go the same for all of you?" Marrow shouted out to the rest of the huddled masses.

There was barrage of nodding heads and affirmations.

"I guess I'll have to try something else." He paused. "What is Krinama?"

There was a unified gasp as Marrow spoke the word.

"How do you know time of the Gods?" the old monk asked.

"There is that whole 'gods' thing again. You heathens will believe anything. As I said before, they have nothing to do with this. Now I'll try again... what is Krinama?"

"It's a ceremony," Clark said. "But we don't negotiate with the enemy, you're just going to have to kill us all."

"Sounds fair to me," Marrow answered.

"WAIT!" Jacob shouted.

"No," Diego whispered from behind him.

Marrow's head turned toward where the shout originated from.

"Cob, NO!" Clark yelled back.

Marrow pulled the trigger.

Click.

Clark vomited.

"I guess I forgot to fill that chamber... Oh well, care to press your luck?"

"Stop!" Sophia yelled. "They don't know about the Ancillary... but I do."

Jacob hadn't noticed Sophia behind them and immediately his stomach plummeted.

Marrow released his prisoner and Clark fell to the ground, sobbing. The bone-man walked closer to Sophia and his men followed.

"Well I'll be... Cob was it? You three don't look like you belong here," Marrow said, his voice back to being smooth and melodic. "Two Americans and… a Spaniard?"

"Three Americans," Diego snarled.

"So what would three Americans be doing in a town of yak herders?"

Sophia started talking but was cut off by Diego.

" — We love yaks. My aunt has one, we named him Sam."

At this, Marrow's cronies all laughed.

"A funny guy, huh? Well, funny guy, you have exactly three seconds to tell me what you know about my flower, or you won't be telling jokes for a very long time."

Diego laughed. "Threaten me? I'm going to — "

"If you promise not to hurt anyone else, I'll tell you what we know," Sophia interjected.

In a patronizing tone Marrow said, "Cross my heart."

"Ok, well, first off, I was telling the truth before, these people know nothing about the Ancillary, but that's why we're here, we are searching for it, too. I read about it and thought it would be fun to take my friends and go search for it. After reading the article in human affairs we knew to start here."

"If you read about it, then you must know it doesn't belong to you."

"What do you mean?" she asked.

"I assume you know about the mark?"

"No," Sophia lied.

"There's a mark on the Ancillary, a four pointed diamond with eight connected dots in a circle. It tells the world who it is meant for, who has the most," Marrow paused, "potential… Who's name it will make immortal. "

"So?"

In one quick swoop, still holding his revolver, Marrow ripped open his button down shirt underneath his jacket.

There on his chest — in the same tan color as the lines on his face — was the mark of the Ancillary.

CHAPTER 34

Jacob's left hand involuntarily slid into his pocket. Luckily, Marrow didn't notice the odd reaction. A million thoughts exploded inside Jacob's head all at once. He had a hard time deciphering any of them as his brain went into overload. There was no uncertainty; on Marrow's body was the exact mark that Jacob currently had residing in his jeans.

Jacob managed to pin down a question in his spinning head. *How do we both have the mark?*

"You see… it is mine," Marrow said. He turned around and faced the crowd. "You see… you people have been stealing from me." His voice was booming. "The reason I was generous and only killed one of you is because the pollen itself doesn't affect the potency of the flower." Marrow bobbed his head side-to-side as if weighing his options. "Problem is… I was going to give the pollen to my men here. I assume they all must be very disappointed."

As if on cue, his lackeys all moved into the crowd and violently wrestled out hostages of their own. Not surprisingly, all were women.

"Oh no," Marrow said in faux shock. "I guess if you don't tell me where my property is, I'm just going to have to let my people have a different sort of reward."

In the middle of the circle one of the men brought out a buck knife and ran the blunt side slowly against the cheek of his hostage.

Marrow opened his shirt wider. "So I guess it's safe to say none of you have laid eyes this mark? Ever seen it at

Krinama?"

"Hold on!" came a tiny voice from the crowd. "I've seen that before."

Out walked the young boy that Jacob recognized as Namala.

Marrow ran over and grabbed the small boy by the shirt and lifted him clean off the ground.

"You better not be lying to me, boy!" He grabbed tighter.

"I'm not." Namala squirmed around trying to get free. "I've seen it."

"Where? Where is the Ancillary?" Marrow bellowed.

Namala's body wrenched in the air until he was staring straight at Jacob. With a tiny finger he pointed. "There!"

Jacob's heart sank. If Marrow was so quick to kill Fuki, he didn't stand a chance if this madman saw that his mark had a twin.

"NO!" Clark cried out, still crouched on the ground next to his fallen leader.

Marrow took a few steps toward Clark and kicked him square in the jaw. This knocked Clark into the edge of the puddle around Fuki. He scampered out, in shock, trying to wipe the blood stains from his shirt onto the ground.

"I think I've heard enough out of you," Marrow said while dragging Namala behind him like a wiggling sack of potatoes. He slowly walked toward Jacob.

Malice filled his voice. "Show me."

"Him!" Namala pointed again. "Check him!"

Sophia's eyes dilated in fear. Jacob noticed her hands trembling beside him so he locked his free fingers with hers. He squeezed reassuringly, half to calm her down, and half because if this was going to be his last moment on earth, he wanted her to know how he felt. She firmly pressed her palm back into his.

Marrow marched up to the three travelers and jerked Namala in front if him, like a tiny human rag-doll.

"You're telling me one of them has the Ancillary?"

"Yes."

"Who?"

"Him. The shorter one."

"You have been holding out on me, huh?" Marrow spat on the ground in front of them. "Just hand it over, and all will be forgiven."

Diego stepped in front of Clark. "Look." Diego turned out his pocket. "I don't blame him for making things up to save his people, but we don't have the flower."

Marrow raised his revolver up to Diego's face. He didn't flinch.

"I believe my little accomplice here said the shorter one. Now get the hell out of my way."

"It's alright, let him by," Jacob said calmly. He thought of what Rosie had said on the plane. Today he could handle anything.

Diego was unfazed. Like a sentry guarding the front gates of a tower, he stood rigid and proud.

Marrow tucked his gun into a holster hiding under his jacket. "Now look... see... no threats. Cob there is going to be just fine, now move aside and let me speak with him."

Diego remained where he stood.

"Just let him through," Jacob pleaded. "Please!"

Diego turned slightly so he could speak with Jacob. "Sorry, no can do."

A glint of silver was visible in the back of Diego's belt. This was just the opportunity Marrow needed. He snatched the knife with such speed that it looked as if it had materialized in his hand out of thin air.

When Jacob's protector turned back around, Marrow plunged the blade deep into Diego's stomach.

CHAPTER 35

It was a gruesome sound. Though it wasn't loud, it was a noise that would forever haunt Jacob. A sucking sound, like pulling something out of Jell-O. The knife was removed from Diego's abdomen, and started a leak. As if in disbelief, Diego looked down to the spot where red was streaming out, and brought his fingers to the large slit.

All rationale was lost to Jacob as he watched his bodyguard hemorrhaging profusely. His mind in a hazy white light, he was sure that he had to be dreaming. That was it! This was just a nightmare. He fell asleep at Clark's and this was all just in his head. It had to be.

Diego slowly lowered himself downward, and like a ship sinking into the cold, merciless ocean, he hit the stone.

Reality struck.

Jacob hadn't noticed, but Sophia was squeezing so hard her fingernails broke the skin on the back of his hand.

"Now look," Marrow said breaking the silence. "I am very good at what I do. When I want to leave someone alive, I know exactly how to do it. No arteries or organs were pierced. He will not die, if I finally get what I want... cooperation."

Sophia cried out, "You monster! How dare—"

"Uh-uh!" Marrow said with a wag of his finger, "Cooperation."

He stepped around Diego and came face to face with Jacob. "Give me the flower."

Through clenched teeth, Jacob said, "I... don't... have it."

"Check his hand!" Namala screeched.

"Take your hand out of your pocket," Marrow commanded.

He indulged the order and brought his hand out, and with it his pocket. Opening his fist—so his palm was facing away from the murderer—showed that he was indeed not hiding anything.

Marrow turned toward Namala. "You lied! Bad move."

"No!" squealed Namala. "The other side!"

Diego tried speaking but all that came out was a muffled wheeze.

An inquisitive smile came across Marrow's distorted face. "Turn it around."

With a reluctant twist, Jacob's palm—along with the mark in all its glory—stared Marrow in the face.

"See! There it is! The Ancillary," Namala squeaked. "Now take him and let us go."

Jacob couldn't place Marrow's reaction. Was it fear? Anger? Excitement? The swirls running across his face made it near impossible to tell.

"Is… is that a tattoo?" Marrow questioned.

Jacob figured there was no point in trying to hide it now. "No, a birthmark."

The lined face remained quiet for a few moments, as if Marrow was silently concocting a plan. Being that their boss had stopped talking for the moment, his men became flustered.

"What do you want us to do?" A muscular redhead in a calfskin jacket called out.

"Nothing yet," Marrow answered. "Give me a second to think."

In the confusion, Sophia chanced bending down to help Diego. She took off her pink wool socks and placed them upon her protector's wound, creating a firm pressure. The pink soon morphed into a darker shade. Marrow didn't stop her; he just kept staring at Jacob's palm.

Jacob finally broke the silence. "Why would you go about it this way?"

Marrow ignored his comment. "Of all the problems I thought I could run into, this was far out of my realm of possibilities... another chosen...very interesting."

Marrow absentmindedly ran a hand over his chest. "In all my research I've never heard of two before."

Jacob could tell that Marrow was inwardly debating what to do. For a man with a shoot-first, leave later attitude, Jacob felt as if he might be in luck.

"Tell me..." Marrow said. "Do you feel it too?"

"Feel what?"

"The little tug... pulling you. Sort of like a fisherman hooked you and is slowly spinning the reel."

"I'm not sure what you mean."

"Hmff," Marrow sneered. "I think you do. That instinctual feeling of where to go."

Jacob thought of the bubbles.

"I have read a theory about it," Marrow continued, "it is believed that the truly chosen would feel compelled to find it. It is almost as if something is guiding you... luring you in. The problem is that it is relatively weak, but apparently it gets stronger the closer you get. And I'll tell you, it's grabbing my attention. So tell me... do you feel it too?"

Jacob hesitated. "Yes."

"What is he talking about?" asked Sophia.

"I didn't mention it because I wasn't sure what it was."

Diego was able to mutter a few words, "You should have told us pal."

"I know... it was stupid of me to hide it," Jacob said.

So that's what it's been, Jacob thought, that sensitivity that he never seemed to satisfy. It made sense. When he was home it was always small, easily pushed into the back of his mind. His entire life had been devoted to trying new things, hoping he would find something to scratch that itch of his. Now, he could feel it growing, a drive to move forward, a train set in motion, hell-bent on finishing its route. Only one giant problem, his new friend had been gutted and revenge took over the box seats of his mind.

"I'd like to thank you," Marrow said.

"For what?" Jacob sneered.

"You have just made my life a whole lot easier... and to think I assumed the people here were going to make this harder for me."

Jacob had a funny feeling he knew where this was going.

"What do you think is going to happen?" Sophia said with no attempt to conceal the venom in her voice.

Marrow didn't take his eyes off of Jacob.

"Cob here is going to find the Ancillary for me."

CHAPTER 36

"Honey?" Mrs. Deer stepped across the threshold and flicked the lights. Same place as she remembered; it felt good to be home.

In her arms were grocery bags full to the handle with the ingredients for her famous sweet and sour meatballs, Cob's favorite lunch.

Beep-beep. The headlights flashed and acknowledged the rental Maxima being locked by her remote key. It was around eleven in the morning on a glorious summer day.

"Sweetie?" she called louder. Cob must have been upstairs. He was going to be so surprised, she hadn't told him that she would be coming home earlier than they had planned. It turned out that she had more pull than she thought.

Following the passageway into the kitchen she placed the bags down on the granite countertop.

"I'm home!" she chimed as melodic as a bird.

There was no response from anywhere in her home. Even though she had lived alone for the last few weeks — and had become accustomed to silence — it was still unnerving.

She first began the search in the lower level of the house. The den, the sunroom and the basement were all empty. Sometimes Jacob would go down there and practice pulling apart old appliances to see what made them tick.

Nothing.

She checked his bedroom, the living room, even the garage…still nothing.

Using all her strength, she grabbed the twenty-foot

extendable steel ladder and laid it against the house. She climbed to the top rung and peered across the flat part of the roof. On warm summer afternoons such as this, her son would often sprawl out on a madras beach towel, stare at the blue sky, and nap to his heart's content. Though the ladder was stowed under a pile of boxes in the garage, it was worth a shot. This too failed.

Next, she hurried over to the phone.

She looked on her list of contacts and found the Harrison town library.

Several rings were heard through the receiver, followed by a pre-recorded message from the librarian himself.

She returned the phone to its hook.

On a long shot she decided to call Mr. Maddock's cell phone. His number was listed in her book, but it was rarely used; most of the time the old man never left his book-lending duties.

"Hi Mr. Maddock! How are you?" Mrs. Deer couldn't believe she got through. "Yes the trip was great... I can't hear you that well, the reception is very fuzzy...No, I think haggis was a little too adventurous for me... Yes, I kissed the Blarney stone... I were able to settle some of the disagreements rather quickly..."

Mrs. Deer cut his next question off. "You don't know where my Jacob is by any chance do you?...Your granddaughter you say?... Sophia, that's a beautiful name... they hit it off? Camping—that's moving a little fast isn't it... yes I know they're almost grown up. Oh, well can you give me a call when you hear from them?... Ok, thanks a bunch Teddy."

Relieved, she hung up.

Theodore Maddock flipped the newfangled cellular phone closed. It was only the third call he had ever received from the device, but it was reasons like that he continued to pay the forty dollars a month. Although the kids were in fact camping, conveniently leaving out the location was close enough to lying that he felt a twinge of guilt in his gut, but it was for the better;

there was nothing Jacob's mom could do for her son now — hopefully the same couldn't be said for himself.

With resolve, he shouldered his bag and set out under the Tibetan stars.

CHAPTER 37

"And what makes you think he'll do that for you?" Sophia's glossy eyes wouldn't look down at her hands, now covered in blood.

"I think he'll have a very good reason to get it for me," Marrow insisted.

"What's that?" Jacob asked.

"First, I think you probably don't want any more people to get hurt... and I assure you, that *is* a distinct possibility. If that's not enough... I'm sure I could think of a way to persuade you." Marrow grabbed a fistful of Sophia's blonde hair and pulled her against his body.

"Now," he said calmly, "if you don't want her to look like your Spaniard friend," Marrow waved his knife toward Diego. "And your Spaniard to look like their leader," he motioned toward Fuki's motionless body, "then I think you're going to want to cooperate."

Jacob had no choice; in fact, he would gladly give up all of this destiny crap just to see Sophia safe.

"Done," Jacob responded rather quickly.

"So you have an idea where it is then."

"If you act... how did you describe it... civilized, you can often find out what you want to know."

"Careful boy." Marrow was no longer smiling. "I'm giving you a fair deal. You have the chance of a lifetime; you get to keep these lives intact. I could kill you now and then you wouldn't even have that. I'm sure my men would like that opportunity... it's been a long trip and killin' is the most potent amphetamine… and believe me when I say it's near impossible to kick the habit."

The slimy men all grunted with delight.

"Fine, I'll bring it to you," Jacob said. "On one condition."

"You are in no position to make demands."

It was Jacob's turn to ignore this comment. "I need your word that no one else will get hurt."

Marrow menacingly stroked Sophia's hair. "And if they do?"

"Then you'll never find it."

"You do realize I could just go get it myself. It's just more… convenient this way."

"I don't think so, because earlier today—after days of searching—I found the Ancillary, and it wasn't easy. I buried it somewhere up that mountain and deep in the forest, and even with your instinct it will take you days to find it. And you don't have that kind of time."

"How so?"

"Tanki Lowbei keeps all of the news reporters out during the days of Krinama—which today happens to be—but by morning all sorts of outsiders will be here. What do you think will happen when international press gets a hold of a kidnapping story in Tibet's golden town?"

"You're bluffing, if you found it you would have eaten it right away," Marrow said.

"And deny my gracious hosts the right to hold me a proper ceremony?"

Marrow's face returned to a scowl.

"So again, I need your word that none of these people will be harmed."

The redheaded crony chimed in, "C'mon boss, just shoot him, we'll find it ourselves."

"Shut up Smitty, I don't remember asking for the opinion of a dropout who failed to get a G.E.D," Marrow called back.

Smitty looked ashamed. "You said you wouldn't bring that up anymore."

Marrow was studying Jacob's face as if he was trying to get him to crack.

After an excruciatingly long analysis, it seemed that Marrow was finally happy with his decision. "Fine. You have my word that no one else will be hurt."

"Then we have a deal."

Marrow released Sophia's scalp and she shot him the vilest look possible.

"Excellent." Marrow smiled like a child with a bucket of water staring down at an anthill. "You have until sunrise."

"That's crazy!" Clark called out.

"If he already knows where it is, it should be no problem at all," Marrow said condescendingly. "Correct?"

"No problem at all," Jacob retorted, careful not to give anything away.

Jacob knelt down so he was face to face with his guardian, "I'll be back as soon as I can... How bad is it?"

All the color had drained from Diego's face, "How bad is what?"

"Look who's making jokes now," Jacob said with a weak smile.

"No attack," Diego said weakly, the words barely escaping his lips.

"I won't."

"No..." He gently pulled out the white inhaler, which dropped onto the ground. "No attack." He smiled. "Now get going." His eyelids began to droop. "I don't think you can trust him."

"I know... I'll figure something out."

"Tick tock," Marrow proclaimed from above.

Jacob stood and readied himself to run off into the wilderness.

"Wait!" Sophia said.

As if his heart wasn't already pounding fast enough.

"I..." Her eyes were pointed at the ground. "Go to Clark's house and get a flashlight."

"Oh... Ok, I will. Thanks."

"And..." She tightened her jaw and looked onto his face. "Well..." Jetting over to him, she wrapped her arms around his body and embraced him. "Be careful," she whispered. She laid a tender kiss on his cheek, a lot longer and softer than the first time.

He didn't respond; he didn't know how. All that was now careening through his mind was the fact that he couldn't fail, he couldn't let her down.

Sophia removed her arms and he ran.

CHAPTER 38

Luckily he remembered the way back to Clark's. It was quick thinking on Sophia's part; without a flashlight he didn't stand a chance — not that the odds were stacked in his favor anyway. Even with whatever the knack was, he had three hundred and sixty five degrees of option. It was like pin the tail on the donkey, if the donkey was a blue whale.

It had only just gotten dark but the day felt long, which meant he probably didn't have much time on his side until his deadline. All he knew about Marrow was his unconscionable quickness to stab Diego and take Fuki's life. If he didn't succeed, that madman would surely not hesitate to do much worse.

Running right past the small army of Buddhas, he found his bag tossed aside in the front entrance.

"C'mon, c'mon." He flung clothing into disarray. "Jackpot."

Out came a stainless steel LED flashlight with a sticker on it claiming ten times the candlepower of traditional hand-held bulbs. He flicked the power switch on and off a few times to make sure the batteries weren't close to the graveyard.

While there, Jacob figured it wouldn't hurt to bring a few extra supplies. In his pockets — next to his compass and two-way radio that Rosie gave him — went a few Quaker chewy bars and a fresh pair of socks... *hey you never know,* he thought. The night air entering through the open front door was creating a frigid atmosphere, which Jacob tried to combat by pulling his grey hoodie over his head.

The walls were speaking to him. Not in the traditional

sense—he still had no idea what they were actually saying, for he didn't have Clark's prowess—but nonetheless he felt the four enclosing partitions were wishing him luck. Pretending was enough, because in all the mayhem, it helped keep his mind out of the dark.

Jacob stepped over the sill, and the strangest thing happened; the world began to tilt to the right. No houses toppled around him or glass décor fell off the sconces, so he deducted this phenomenon must have been it his head, but he had never experienced anything like it.

"Ok… this is a first," he said hesitantly.

It was almost like when he was on a boat sloped to its port; he felt compelled to slide in one direction.

Throughout this entire endeavor, it had felt as if the world was backing him, and it appeared that it hadn't abandoned him yet. Like Mr. Maddock said, the world is full of the extraordinary and the unexplainable. Maybe this was his true purpose: find the Ancillary and save hundreds of innocent lives. *Ok, maybe saving hundreds isn't on the same level as saving the world*, he thought, *but it sure is something*.

With a quick repetition of his mantra— 'Strength of rhinoceros beetle, heart of a honey badger' Jacob followed his internal push and turned in the direction he was being yanked. As soon as he was standing in the direction that the world was dipping, everything became level again.

Praying that his marbles were still all accounted for, he ran.

He cut through lawns and passed by objects and places he had yet to see. He ran by a homemade two-seater helicopter, a house with a clear half-moon bubble surrounding it, and a garden with white roses the size of bull mastiffs. Along his path was a lawn completely covered in tin foil, Jacob thought about the possible implications of it, and could only come up with the theory that whoever lived there had built a giant grill underground and roasted oversized corn. *Maybe*, he thought, *corn that came from the colossal garden*.

On his far right was the temple they had been inside earlier in the day. Since the river apparently filtered the pollen into the well, Jacob decided to go there, get his bearings, and maybe, possibly, find the direction the water was coming from. Pivoting his front foot, he changed directions, continuing his speed.

It was like trying to run straight up a cliff face. Each step was like dragging ship anchors behind both feet.

He wondered what was going on. It felt like he was a pinball, and the direction he went was out of his control. There must be someone — or something — else flipping the dials.

"Fine," he said to himself. "I guess the temple is unimportant."

Jacob abandoned that pursuit and turned back in the previous direction. "Show me the way."

Again, the world felt right. Actually... better than right. If there was any way of still technically being tethered to gravity but also floating, that was it. The first steps back in this direction made Jacob think of Neil Armstrong walking on the moon — weightless and unfathomably important.

He looked along his decision-less route and noticed it ran straight into the woods. No trail or road, just trees, shrubs and complete engulfing darkness.

"Really?" he laughed to himself. "Not going to be easy, huh? Will I be finding a machete somewhere along the line?"

Just to test the boundaries of this craziness, he made a quick left and tried to sprint. It was like running in quicksand while carrying shopping bags of iron.

"I hope you're right."

He set off towards the dense green.

Jacob was very much aware how insane all of this was, yet he wasn't too surprised. Ever since being told about the Ancillary he knew he would have to accept the strange and embrace the bizarre. A flower that made you reach your potential: that was strange enough already. A plant that bore the same mark as his palm, telling the world that out of some six billion people he and some maniac had the most potential:

that was just plain nutty. After learning about these things he understood the conventional boundaries he knew were a lie and everything that came after would just help to further his new convictions. So, when it became evident that some force was keeping him going one direction—hopefully toward the mystical flower—it wasn't that alarming.

The edge of the town was coming closer and Jacob was ready. His determination was fearsome. The starlight was brilliantly luminescent and the wind was at his back. Normally, that amount of running would have already required a nice long breather, but he was just getting started. If someone told him that invisible hands were underneath his arms, carrying most of his weight, he would have almost believed it.

He expected that his first steps into the Tibetan underbrush would have led him to be bound in vines and hindered by a cacophony of branches; however, he moved swiftly through the cornucopia of nature's booby traps as if they were paper streamers. After only a manner of moments, he was almost a full football field in.

If they were able to bottle this, he thought, *I could make the Olympics.*

"Wait!" he heard a voice in the distance behind him.

Jacob stopped moving and turned his head around, almost to the degree of an owl. It was dark, so Jacob couldn't make out whom the voice belonged to, but it sounded very familiar.

He heard crunching, tripping and cracking until the figure was face to face with Jacob, but with the features hidden in shadow. Remembering the flashlight, he reached into his pocket. It occurred to him that it was quite peculiar not to remove it earlier, as the darkness was near total.

Jacob flicked the switch, and the forest—along with the mystery figure—was revealed.

"What are *you* doing here?"

CHAPTER 39

Sophia trembled on the inside, but refused to let it show.

Even though it had only been a day since she had met him, seeing Diego writhe on the ground was harder then she thought possible.

She kept the pressure even on his wound. Even through it must have been excruciating, it was his best chance of survival.

"Ugghh."

"It's going to be alright. You're a big guy… I'm sure you have plenty of blood to spare."

Back in New York, a stabbing would hardly make the headlines anymore, but seeing one happen to someone she knew would be a memory never forgotten; a memory she wouldn't wish upon anyone… *well, maybe a few people*, she thought, as she glanced back at Marrow and his cronies. They continued their merriment, still refusing to let the hostages go.

CRACK.

Marrow's men all froze. The laughing died.

CRACK. SHOOM.

Something shot into the sky and exploded blue light into the shape of a top hat.

CRACK. SHOOM. POW

More rockets.

Someone was lighting off fireworks.

SHOOM. One unleashed its fury in the shape of a shamrock.

Marrow and his gang looked baffled, and they weren't the only ones. Why someone would be lighting off fireworks now of all times, Sophia didn't understand.

"Check it," Marrow commanded. "Someone might be signaling for help."

The hostages were released and his men vanished into the shadows towards the lightshow. All the women that were momentarily captives ran into the arms of their husbands and children.

"Am… am I… is that real?" Diego asked in a stupor.

"Don't worry you're not seeing things," Sophia said. "I think that one was a pink elephant."

Marrow was left alone with the crowd, momentarily distracted by the fireworks. His back was turned from Sophia, as his gaze was fixed upon the pyrotechnics.

Suddenly, a hand wrapped around her mouth.

Her scream was muffled, like an alarm clock smothered by a thick pillow.

Able to turn her face, she fixed eyes on an old Tibetan who looked strangely like he belonged in front of Clark's house, waiting to welcome guests. An index finger was held in front of pursed broad lips attached to a pleasant and friendly looking face.

She immediately understood he meant no harm. But what was he doing?

The plump fingers were slowly drawn away from her mouth and she didn't make any sound. Her new acquaintance gave a smile of appreciation.

Diego didn't understand the need for silence. "What are you doing? Get your hands off of her," he commanded.

The broad man flinched as Diego spoke. Fortunately another firework blew apart in the sky — a yellow, smiling face — and Marrow's attention was still unfocused.

"My name is Mozu," he whispered. "My friends have created a diversion. I will help. Now hold still and no more talking."

Mozu pulled out a small pouch about the size of a scientific calculator. Its exterior was made of a smooth red material, which he carefully unfolded. Tucked inside were small needles with different colored beads on the blunt end. He produced three green-ended needles, each inserted in the cruxes between Diego's fingers.

Sophia cringed as they were thrust in; however Diego didn't seem to notice, which led her to believe it was a painless procedure. That, or he was doing much worse than she thought. Two blue ones were inserted into both sides of his neck. One particularly long looking red version was set in the side of his abdomen. With utter precision and artistic prowess, Mozu inserted more and more needles making Diego into a human pincushion.

His large body immediately relaxed and all worry drifted off his face like wet paint off a canvas. "Hey! It doesn't hurt any —"

"Shhhh!" Mozu said, putting his finger up to his mouth again. Sophia thought they might have even been larger than Fuki's. At the thought of the gentle giant, her eyes drifted towards the corpse.

Also in the mysterious needle holster was some flesh-colored thread. He strung it through the eye of a medical needle, and, slightly ripping Diego's shirt at the point of impact, began sewing the wound closed.

Ok, she thought, *now that has to hurt.*

To her surprise, the look of bliss remained on Diego's face during the whole ordeal. Mozu was able to stitch him up so fast that Sophia was sure the US hospitals would frame his resume. He cut the thread with a small pair of scissors. Sophia's hand, holding the socks, found its way back on top of the now sutured wound, guided by Mozu's touch.

Mozu pointed at two needles. "Take these out if his mind needs to be sharp. As of now, let him drift."

As he let his hand fall away, Sophia gazed upon Diego's euphoric face. Mozu's needles let her new friend float away to who-knows-where, probably a world of kittens — or maybe obstacle courses were more his speed. In a way she envied him.

Sitting there watching the panic and mayhem that was now Tanki Lowbei—wives crying, frightened children, confused men looking upon a fallen comrade—was sickening.

She thought about how in a sad world, kindness goes miles. Turning her tiny frame, she intended to express her thanks to the gracious man.

"Thanks," she whispered to nothing.

Mozu had disappeared as fast as he had come. She was surprised how stealthy he was for such a large person.

In an attempt to conceal the fix, Sophia closed Diego's fingers together, veiling the acupuncture needles. She figured if Marrow found his prey no longer exactly as he wanted, things could get ugly, hideous in fact. Most of her new friend's body was in shadow, so the beads protruding from his midsection were already well hidden. The only problems were the blue orbs bulging from his neck, creating a Latin Frankenstein's monster. In a bold move, she cupped her hands around them and placed her forehead against his, positioning herself like someone would hold a lover.

Almost as if it was rehearsed, the fireworks stopped animating the sky and Marrow's men came scampering back in the square.

"Couldn't find him boss," said the one with the eye-patch. "Must have lit them and ran."

"Unacceptable," he barked. "Keep looking, idiots. I gave my word I wouldn't hurt these primitives, but I can still do what I like with you morons."

With a collective groan his men receded into the darkness.

Marrow's attention was again brought to Sophia. He swaggered over, looking far too confident, which added to her hatred of the disgusting man.

"How adorable," he said in that same sarcastic tone. "You know, you really are adorable, that blonde hair and that tight body, just..." He inhaled through his nose. "Makes me want to take you away."

"Screw you," she said.

Marrow was unfazed. The hunter's gaze remained firmly on her face.

"Let's just hope your friend gets back in time with my property… or you won't have a choice."

CHAPTER 40

"I snuck away when no one was watching." Clark was severely out of breath. "I figured you would go to the temple first... I was lucky I saw you. When did you get so fast?"

"I don't know the answer to that one. Something very strange is going on."

"That's the case in this town lately."

Jacob saw Clark huffing and puffing and made a quick decision.

"Thanks for offering, but I think I have to do this on my own."

"No." Another strong breath. "I can help... I know the woods... I walk through them all the time."

"Listen Clark, I really appreciate it but you would just slow me down. See there's something weird happening where—"

"Hey!" Jacob was startled by the intensity directed at him. "You might be chosen or whatever, but this is my town. My people, my family are in danger and they didn't do anything to deserve it. And Fuki—don't think I am going to stand by and not do every possible thing I can to help. If I have to die of exhaustion trying to find it with you then so be it... it's worth it. He killed Fuki and for what, some stupid flower... they can have it if it's going to mean my town will be safe. So if the next words out of your mouth aren't 'let's go' then I guess I'll just have to find it before you."

Jacob was flabbergasted. Clark was dead serious.

"Let's go." Jacob extended his hand, which Clark shook vigorously.

"Now you were saying... what is weird?"

"This is going to sound strange but...I think the Ancillary is dragging me to it. I'm being pulled in one direction, and if I stray off the path then I... well, I kind of can't."

This news did nothing to remove the expression from Clark's face. "Lead the way."

"Really? Just like that? No skepticism?"

"What reason would you have to lie? You're talking to a boy who can mysteriously tell you the intricate differences between Sanskrit and Hebrew."

"Good point." Jacob was actually relieved to have some company. *This is going to be scary enough alone*, he thought, *at least I'll have a friend*.

Jacob tossed the tiny powerful flashlight to Clark.

"Don't you need it to lead?" he asked.

"Actually, no... you take it. I can see pretty well."

"There's barely any moonlight penetrating the canopy. How is that possible?"

"This coming from the Tibetan boy who is currently on Princeton's payroll. Stranger things, right?"

"Can't argue there."

Jacob began jogging again. His feet blazed a path through rhododendron, over lichen-infested rocks, and between thick string-like vines. It was too dark to see color, but something about the little light piercing through the treetops let Jacob understand his surroundings — like looking at an ultrasound of the world around him. The underbrush was a vast array of botanical wonders, but there was no time to stop and stare.

A few times, Jacob would halt his progress and wait for Clark to catch up. Even with the portable light device, it was tough for even a native to find his way through the particularly nasty obstacle course that mother earth had devised. Nowhere was there anything even close to a path. Jacob wouldn't have been surprised if it had been millennia since another human set foot where they traveled. The feeling of being reeled in was getting stronger, though unlike what it must be like for a fish,

Jacob felt more and more at peace. It wasn't at all frightening, more like he was going home. He thought about the wonders of what lay ahead of him if he got to use the Ancillary; it was too bad he wouldn't be able to experience any of it. He thought about the idea of potential and the possibilities that hid dormant. If after only drinking the pollen Clark was able to understand all sorts of dialects, his own capabilities must have been unfathomable.

The promise of making a difference was overwhelming. Maybe he was destined to be the greatest actor the world had ever seen... Ladies and gentlemen, accepting his fiftieth Academy Award is a living legend... COB DEER! Sophia would be cheering in the stands in a beautiful black dress — very tasteful — with her hair up in a bun.

Maybe he was going to cure cancer... Ladies and gentlemen, accepting his Nobel Peace Prize... Maybe he was going to be the first astronaut on Mars? Start a fortune 500 company? Become a superhero and stop heinous criminals like that Marrow? That would be good. Helping people always felt right. Maybe kids in foreign countries would be wearing t-shirts with his superhero logo on it. Naturally it would be the image of his birthmark. After a long day of thwarting evil plots he would come home to his beautiful wife, Sophia. Maybe he would just take a small bit and give the rest to — no, he couldn't do that. These people's lives weren't worth the risk. If anything bad were to happen on his account, he wouldn't be able to live with himself.

"Wait up!" Jacob turned and got the unnatural vertigo. Clark was not far behind, but he was tangled in some rather nasty looking creeper plants. The Tibetan native managed to wiggle himself out by contorting his neck and pulling his arms free. With the portable light bouncing up and down, like the headlights of a car going over potholes, Clark caught up.

Still breathing heavier than before — almost at the speed of Lamaze — Clark bent over and put his hands on his knees.

"Do you believe in something bigger than yourself?" Clark

asked.

"Like elephants? I'm pretty sure that they're real."

Clark looked up and smiled. "You know what I mean."

"Am I religious?"

Clark answered, with interjected pauses for air. "Religion is a bunch of borrowed stories. I mean what do *you* think?"

Jacob hesitated and thought about it for a few moments— both so he could phrase it right and to give Clark a much-needed rest. "I think that we are all connected in such a way that there is already something bigger than ourselves. I was always spiritual growing up, but as far as some invisible dictator in the clouds... I don't really think so, but I know that sometimes when I stop and think about the world, I recognize that there's much more to life that we don't understand. It's like if a rabbit tries to comprehend astrophysics, all it's going to end up with is carrots."

"So what do you think all of this means?"

"It's all Greek to me," Jacob smirked. "You speak Greek, right?"

A matching grin. "I'm not sure. I thought the gods picked us, but why would they send these killers?"

"I don't think they did, whoever they may be. That's the thing about free will..."

"You're right, but do you think whatever is happening to you now is because of them?"

"I don't know." A wave of nausea hit Jacob. "But I think if we don't keep moving, the ground at your feet is going to get considerably less beautiful."

"OK, let's keep going, I think I'm ready for round two." Clark made jabbing motions in the air.

"That's the spirit."

Once they starting moving again, the feeling of elation rushed back. Jacob's thoughts were again moving as fast, if not faster than his legs. Was Clark right? Was this the work of some supernatural essence? Or was it like how salmon travel upstream or a flock of birds migrate? Jacob once heard about an experiment where an egg was taken from its flock and hatched in a cage in some laboratory somewhere. The scientists kept tabs on the geese and observed the baby bird as it grew. When the bird was older and winter came — when it was time for the flock to migrate — the isolated bird was restless and kept trying to fly in the same direction as its family. Was it like that? Maybe it was both?

A faint beeping pulled him out of autopilot mode. Jacob stopped right before jumping over the small muddy puddle blocking his way.

More beeping. Was someone in the woods?

Feeling dimwitted, he realized the beeping was coming from the two-way radio Rosie had given him. Fumbling with the device, and almost dropping it in the tiny mud pool, he rotated the top button a few notches.

-TSSSK-"Hello?" he heard the soft voice. "Someone come in."

"ROSIE!" Jacob twisted the volume louder. "You can't imagine how nice it is to hear a friendly voice."

-TSSSK-"COB? Is that you? I thought you would be... hey, well, it's great to hear your voice again, too. What happened?"

"Tanki Lowbei, the whole town, has been kidnapped!"

Clark scrambled up to the puddle and stood next to Jacob to listen in.

"Who's that?" he asked.

"My pilot."

-TSSSK-"You're kidding, right?"

"No," Jacob insisted. "This guy named Marrow and his gang. They came in guns blazing and took hostages... he stabbed Diego."

-TSSSK-"Oh God! I really liked that bloke. Is he alive?"

"I think he is going to heal just fine. He thought he was protecting me. It turns out this Marrow guy is not just another criminal."

-TSSSK-"What do you mean?"

"It turns out that I'm not the only one who's meant for the

flower. This guy has some sort of weird skin disorder, but on his chest it's clear as day… the Ancillary's mark."

-TSSSK- "You must have made a blue. I've never heard of there being two recipients."

"Well it happened. I'm in the woods right now with my new friend Clark and we're searching for it. I have to get it to Marrow before sunrise or he'll start killing the townspeople… he has Sophia."

-TSSSK- "That's like a blind man looking for a bandicoot."

Clark looked confused.

"Don't speak Australian huh?" Jacob jokingly asked.

"Apparently not. I guess I was asleep during that vision."

Jacob again spoke into the radio. "Speaking of, you're an expert on this stuff. Have you ever heard of the Ancillary pulling someone toward it?"

There was a hesitation. -TSSSK-"…No. That's a first."

"I think it's happening, or at least, something is happening. I'm going to find it and bring it to him."

-TSSSK- "… Ok. Keep me posted. Radio me when you find it. I'll meet you in town after that maniac leaves. We'll get Diego to a hospital as fast as we can."

"Sounds good… and thanks again."

Jacob turned the volume all the way to zero and pocketed the radio.

"Let's keep moving," Jacob said.

Jumping the puddle was easy. Landing soft-footed and dry, he looked back and saw that Clark seemed to have become rooted in place.

"What's up? It's only a puddle. Since when is Superman afraid of water?"

Clark only looked back with a blank stare.

Now he was concerned. "Are you hurt?"

"B-B-Behind you dude," Clark said very cautiously.

Jacob revolved slowly and immediately regretted it. Straight ahead—smack dab in his mystical path—was a monstrous bear. Clark had the light fixated upon the beast. No, the world was not going to make this easy for him.

Small white patches were visible on its black coat, and two hungry looking eyes peered back at them. The bulk of it made the largest linebacker look like a ninety-pound ballerina. Walking on all fours, it lowered its head, confused about the miniature sun Clark was holding, and let out a low growl that echoed in their brains.

"Uh," Jacob said. "You didn't happen to pick up bear language by any chance, did you?"

"Let's turn around and find another path," Clark said through clenched teeth.

"I wish I could. Remember how I said I can't turn from this path? We're trapped."

"That's a Tibetan blue bear, they're really rare to see. I don't know much about them but I've heard they are docile."

"Really?"

"…No, that was a lie."

"Maybe—maybe if you turn off the light it will leave us alone."

"No way, bro," Clark said. "And let it stalk us in the dark?"

"Fine, how about we climb a tree until it passes by?"

The blue bear's nose twitched and it slowly moved towards them. The light brought more and more of the bear into view, and it was gigantic. *It must be a great hunter to eat so well,* Jacob thought. He prayed it was just a good forager. The beast let out a grunt and Jacob caught a metallic scent on its breath.

"Ok, nice and slow," Jacob instructed. "We'll both climb up the branches."

As they crept toward the tree, the bear stood on its hind legs and roared. It must have been twelve feet tall. Even in the tree, a small jump from that brute would have them eye-to-eye.

"Apparently it wants us grounded," Clark said.

"Any suggestions?"

"Reason with it?"

Jacob dropped to his knees.

"OH GREAT AND NOBLE BEAR!" Jacob shouted.

"I wasn't serious! What are you doing?" Clark hissed.

"Improvising."

The creature returned to all fours. It's head cocked sideways as if it was confused, or maybe intrigued.

"WE BESEECH THEE TO LET US PASS. YOU ARE A BEAUTIFUL AND POWERFUL BEAR AND WE ARE HUMBLED."

The bear let out another grunt. It ambled towards Jacob once more. Now, it was within pouncing distance.

"I HAVE FOR YOU A GIFT IN EXCHANGE FOR SAFE PASSAGE."

Very slowly, like a robot running out of batteries, he reached into his pocket and pulled out an oatmeal bar. The unwrapping of the silver foil increased the bear's curiosity. It closed in.

Jacob tossed the granola bar twenty feet to the side into the woods.

Thankfully, the bear jumped after it, reminding Jacob very much of how he once saw a ferret run.

"GO!" Screamed Jacob, and they both took off.

CHAPTER 41

"Hey, look!" The excitement in Clark's voice was apparent. "That looks like a stream over there! How serendipitous!"

"Serendipitous?"

"Nice?"

Jacob thrust out his bottom lip. "Actually I like serendipitous better. Let's hope it applies."

"How can we go wrong when I'm following a human GPS?"

They must have run about three miles when they came across the flowing water. The darkness was still complete and less and less sky was able to find its way to the forest floor. The mosquitoes had taken their toll, and because of the thorns, Clark's shirt looked like something you would find covering a werewolf victim. The sound of running water masked the calls of certain nocturnal creatures—*hopefully not werewolves*, Jacob thought.

Jacob remembered the rhyme. "In the place where it starts will be never the same, by worlds' surface will flow untitled to name."

"Sounds like a stream to me." Clark raised two fingers under his chin. "And I'm an expert on cryptic."

"Hey, is it me or is it getting lighter out?"

"It's you, I can't see a thing without the flashlight." He shined it upon Jacob's face.

Jacob instinctively held up his hands for cover. "Ahh," he laughed. "Too bright, too bright. I surrender."

Clark carefully lowered the beam and cocked his head

sideways, much like the bear. "Wait… take your hands away from your face."

"Why? Are you going to blind me again?"

"No… it's just, I think I saw something."

Jacob twisted his body looking for the mysterious something. After confirming they were alone, he said, "Whoa, don't scare me like that. I thought maybe it was a werewolf."

Clark gasped at Jacob's uncovered face.

Jacob's arms instinctively went into a defensive pose. "Where is it? Behind me?"

"Your eyes are glowing."

"Huh?"

"I'm serious. Your eyes are blue… and they're glowing."

"Really?" he said, more curious than surprised. "Blue?"

"Blue—like really blue," Clark said.

"Sweet."

Clark cupped his chin. "I think we're probably on the right track."

"No one told me anything about blue eyes if you're close."

"Maybe no one knew. Think about it, if in the past the person meant for the Ancillary traveled alone, no one would be there to tell them. Or maybe you're the first."

"Valid point. Ok… blue eyes. I can deal with that."

"It's a good look, you should hope they stay that—"

"WAIT!"

Clark jumped. "What?! Did the bear follow us?"

"I HAVE heard something about blue before."

"Where?"

Jacob silently moved his jaw and lips, as if making the motions would help him remember it. He snapped his fingers. "The beginning of the poem! It was something like… look for the place where the blue light will glow! That's it!"

Clark looked confused. "So it's in your head?"

"Sorry?"

"In your head. That's where the blue light is coming from. They did say that flower unleashes your full potential, right?

Giving you your destiny. Maybe there is no flower at all, maybe it's a place… or a time, and the golden flecks in our water really *were* from the gods."

Jacob thought for a moment. "Let's test it."

He tried taking a step backward. It was like trying to walk through titanium.

"I guess I'm not quite done yet, I think it's best to keep moving."

They ran parallel to the stream on the bank. This was a good trade off, as their feet would get a little soaked and stuck in the mud, but the flora was thinner and they could maneuver more easily. Also the stars and moon peeked out of the heavens above, as if watching their progress and giving the gift of their light — Clark was even able to turn off the flashlight. They ran for another mile or so when Jacob's heart sank.

"Oh NO!" Jacob shouted back to his friend.

"What?"

"Don't you see? It's getting lighter! The sun must be rising and we don't have the flower. We failed everyone!" Jacob halted and smacked his hand on the topside of his head. Keeping his face buried, he heard Clark catch up.

"Um… It's still pitch black out. We probably have another few hours until sunrise."

"No! Don't you see… everything is getting brighter!"

"The only thing getting brighter is what's coming out of your face."

"They're getting brighter?"

"Like tiny lighthouses."

Jacob was able to calm down a bit. "I guess that makes sense then… actually no, this is really weird."

"Let's keep moving," Clark said, taking charge. "We do have a while before the sun rises, but we still have to leave time to make it back."

"Right."

As they ran, Jacob noticed the darkness fading. *It's all in your head*, he thought, *you still have time… Don't worry,*

Sophia is still safe. I wonder if Diego is Ok? No time to think about that... just have to keep running. Find the flower—save everyone.

It was a fever. Not only was his body craving the hunt, it now infected his mind. Every step closer was harder and the aching deepened. He imagined it was like the nicotine cravings of a forty-year Marlboro smoker, times a million. There was nothing that could make him go cold turkey at that point. *Can't turn around... have to keep running*, he thought. The yearning only grew worse. He hoped Clark was still behind him, but there was no time to stop and check. No time even to peer over his shoulder. *Faster and faster, have to go faster.* It wasn't even like running anymore—more like a comet being flung around a planet by gravity. *Faster.* He couldn't feel his legs, not that he would want to. He was moving so fast the stream seemed to be flowing backwards. The world was brighter than he had ever seen it. Even at this speed, every vein on every leaf, every pustule of tree rot, every diamond off the wave tops were gleaming out. It was like switching from a black and white T.V. to one in high definition. The sounds were unbelievably clear. Just as Clark put it before, the distractions cleared and he could hear the music of the world. *This is incredible*, he thought, just being close to the plant caused some kind of physical response. He wished more than anything that he could have it for himself.

Then he heard them.

"No way!" It took a considerable amount of effort to stop, but he had to tell Clark—he wanted to share the moment.

It took a few minutes for his friend to reach him, but that was good, it allowed the opportunity to sit back and listen to the symphony of the world. Bach was prodigal, but he could never have captured this.

"Finally!" Clark bellowed from far behind. "Any further (huff) and I would have thought you had (puff) machine parts. I've never (huff) in my entire life seen anyone... move like that."

Jacob burst out in hysterical laughter. He laughed until he didn't think there was a single chuckle left. He laughed until his sides hurt.

"What's so funny?"

"Bullfrogs!"

Wait, Jacob thought, *plenty more laughs to go*, as they escaped him.

"Bullfrogs?"

"BULLFROGS!" Jacob slapped each hand on Clark's shoulders. "I can't believe it. Bullfrogs!"

"So? What's so great about bullfrogs?"

"Mumbo-Jumbo!"

Clark gave up trying. "You are an oddball, Cob."

"They croak louder near the Ancillary. Diego thought it was mumbo-jumbo! It's here! It's got to be here! Bullfrogs everywhere! It's a ribbit rukus! A chorus of croaks! A sonata of —"

"No more time for alliteration! Let's keep going!"

Jacob couldn't argue with that—just standing there was physically painful. He doubted he could have remained in one place for much longer anyway.

Bullfrogs! He couldn't believe it. If only Sophia and Diego were with him. It was so close he could feel it, like surging electricity, reminiscent of the furious lightning outside of Artemis the plane.

He conquered a large hill—full of flattened boulders and tree castaway—and he saw it. Like Moses with the burning bush, the moment was awe-inspiring. It was unexplainably humbling. The culmination of waiting… this was it… this was what he was meant for.

A ball of radiance beckoned him forward, the fruit of fruition. The most perfect cloudless sky on a summer day couldn't compare to the fantastic blue blazing in his eyes. The world had vanished and only blue remained. The severe glow was not unpleasant; in fact, he couldn't take his eyes away. It alleviated all his worries, his hunger, his aches and pains.

It was real.

"It's here!" he yelled to his straggling companion.

"Really? Where?" Came the call from below.

"… Everywhere."

Clark reached the summit and saw it too.

"That small light all the way down there? Is that it?"

The blue rays surged and ebbed and flowed like the mightiest ocean. It overtook Jacob. Waves of color crashed into him. It was a shade unlike anything he could have pulled out of his Crayola boxes as a kid. It engulfed his form and bathed him in a soap of blue beams.

Jacob had trouble forming words, as both corners of his mouth seemed glued towards the sky. "I think we are seeing two different things, my friend."

Clark held out a fist as if he were flying. "What are we waiting for? Let's save the day."

Clark was first down the hill toward the source. Jacob had a hard time making out his friend's form—it looked like the movie version of an alien exiting a spacecraft, with the silhouette squeezed by backlight.

For the first time on this journey, Jacob followed Clark.

"You'll never beat me!" Clark teased. "It's a bird, it's a plane, it's—"

Jacob raced past, not with the intention of surpassing him, but because he couldn't bear being away from the flower.

His flower.

"Oh." Clark's cockiness died instantly.

Jacob stopped short and dropped to his knees.

There it was.

The picture in the book was in a certain respect close, but it was also way off. *To be fair,* Jacob thought, *how could you possible capture beauty like that on a canvas, especially on a cave wall with berry-based ink?*

The flower was no larger than an open palm, but it was like a tiny blue sun pinned to the ground. Through the light Jacob could see the markings on the petals. Sure enough, they matched his palm.

The Ancillary.

It stood short and proud, only feet from the edge of the small stream by a cove. It couldn't have been more than five inches tall, yet Jacob could feel its presence radiating across the entire clearing. It pulsed throughout his limbs. He could taste it, feel it. The hair on his body stood on edge, like grass to the sun.

Next to it, a calm pool gently swayed up and down, the glittering gold flecks floating gently in the water, reflecting the brilliant light. Some sort of geological event left a giant section of a pine damming the gateway downstream.

His attention drawn back to the flower, he again couldn't believe his eyes. It was miraculous. Knowing Clark couldn't see what he was seeing, he pitied his new friend. There was no doubt that a still frame of what he saw could easily surpass the soul-stirring marvel of his favorite poster — the Helix Nebula picture, often dubbed 'The Eye of God'.

He had to have it.

Slowly he reached down toward the miraculous wonder of nature, his finger outstretched like Michelangelo's Adam, adorning the Sistine chapel's ceiling. He needed to caress the vibrant pedals and feel the energy. Only inches now. It called him, beckoned him forward with promises of a whole new life, one full of adventure and clarity.

He finally reached it. Never again would he wait for his real life to find him. It had been found. After five hundred years of growth and maturation, the Ancillary had its recipient. The ultimate gift of nature was in his hands.

Grazing it caused something unexpected. Jacob had never known pain like this. Neurons raged with fury. They fired signals of misery all along his arm as he brushed the plant. A bolt of suffering struck his fingertip, like a steel lightning rod. It was a scalpel digging deep, trying to find something but failing, so it had to go deeper. He howled with pain. His finger jerked back and found its way into his other palm, hiding it, shielding it from that unexpected nightmare.

Now that there was no physical contact, Jacob's body relaxed and the agony subsided.

"What in the…?" Jacob couldn't find the words.

Again, like a yo-yo, Clark was there.

"What was that about? Why did you scream?" Clark asked.

"It… it really hurt."

"What?"

"I tried touching it and I felt lots and lots of pain."

"Um… That's not good."

"You try touching it."

"No way, dude." Clark was adamant about this. "I don't ever want to hear myself making a sound like that one. I think I'll skip the lots and lots of pain. It's probably healthier."

"This doesn't make any sense." Jacob was talking more to himself than to Clark. "I have the mark, why shouldn't I be able to touch it?"

Just like that, Jacob's mind tumbled back into the churning chaos. Trying desperately to rationalize what had happened, he strained his brain to come up with something. His thoughts betrayed him. *This is what I am meant for… right?*

He intended to stand up and walk away from the flower — to get his head on straight — but something kept pulling him in. Turning away was still not an option.

The flower continued to deliver a furious bright light — still enticing — but Jacob no longer had the desire to pick it up. A strange thought found its way into his stream of conscious. He couldn't touch the Ancillary, nor could he leave it there. It was like a gravitational sinkhole. Was he going to be stuck like this forever?

"Maybe we could just scoop it up with something not attached to one of our bodies?" Clark added.

An excellent idea, Jacob thought. He tore off his hooded sweatshirt and covered his hands with the well-worn cotton. He surrounded the small flower apprehensively, making a nest with his outerwear, and very carefully plucked it from its stem.

Even through the cloth, it somehow felt wrong to remove the flower from the ground, like he was taking something from Mother Nature's cupboard, something that he didn't have permission to touch; but there was a town to save. A single petal wouldn't be enough; he would have to bring Marrow the full specimen.

The material allowed him to painlessly lift the Ancillary, and relief flooded through his body. Oddly enough, the light he saw all around him did not die out; if anything it grew stronger.

"Ok," Jacob shied his eyes away from the Ancillary. "We should be able to make it back by sun-up if we hurry, so lets get —"

Jacob stopped short.

"What's wrong?"

"I still can't move."

Clark took a deep breath. Shutting his eyes, his new friend grimaced and held out his hands as if preparing to receive a double amputation. "Try giving me the flower."

Jacob was very careful to make sure the Ancillary was fully nestled inside the sweatshirt and passed it over like a newborn. Clark received the flower and kept it held out, as far away from his body as his arm span would allow.

"Now," he whispered as if keeping quiet would somehow help. "Let's get this over with."

Clark ambled forward with elongated steps, careful where to place his feet, so as not to trip over any of the protruding roots, determined not to introduce his stomach to the ground.

Again, Jacob's mind was in full sprint. How could he not be meant for the plant? Was it all just a coincidence? Everything made too much sense: the birthmark, the bubbles. It was finally all coming together and at last his place in the world was clear. Still confused about what all of it meant, he decided just to focus on getting back to town and ridding them of Marrow and his gang. That was priority number one, making sure the town and his friends were safe — he could worry about destiny later.

Hovering over the spot where he had plucked the mystical blossom, he attempted to lift his foot.

Nothing happened. He was still stuck.

Frustration overtook the music of the world. Nature's orchestra was just a memory. The bullfrogs. *Where did the bullfrogs go?*

Why couldn't he move? What was he supposed to do?

Then it happened.

A revelation.

Why had he not thought of this before?

In an instant, Jacob had solved the conundrum.

Everything was going to be all right, if only he could make it back in time.

CHAPTER 42

Marrow checked the hour on his stolen timepiece. The Corum coin model set in eighteen-karat gold gleamed under the dull light of the streetlamp. Though not his, he had zero grief about taking it from its previous owner — *dead men don't need to know the time*, he thought, *they have all the time in the world*. Two hours had passed. The hostages were still trembling with horror as Marrow had *conveniently* decided to leave Fuki's lifeless body in plain view. Fear was better than respect any day of the week.

It was his winning situation; now he could sit back and enjoy the subtle aroma of fear while that stupid boy did all the work for him. That stupid kid was readily willing to give the holiest of earthly matter for a few teenagers and a town that wasn't his.

What a moron.

The boy had also done him one better. Finding out about the media seemed a critical piece of information he had carelessly overlooked. The guns-blazing approach seemed like a fine idea, but the kid was right, this had 'news frenzy' written all over it. If the press got word, all sorts of complications would arise. Marrow preferred his crimes simple. The fact that today just happened to be a day of Krinama was more gasoline to his fire of conviction. The world wanted him to have the Ancillary.

Marrow's attention turned towards his men. A bunch of primitive fools. After disposing of his so-called help, he would have to be a little more careful who he put in his employ. After using the Ancillary — though he wasn't sure exactly what would happen — he would want to run with a more sophisticated crowd. Lucky for him, these baboons would be easily removed. He had found that in these situations, brains always triumph when locked in conflict with brawn. Marrow had both, tipping his track record vertically. Tying up loose ends was a strong suit of his.

As he watched his cronies gathered in a small group — probably babbling about breast sizes and booze — Marrow sharpened his mind on what was to come.

The power.

Immortality.

———————————

Diego was in heaven... or getting close. The sky didn't seem so dark and the world not so cold. Though he knew a lot of his blood was not where it should be, it didn't really matter. Was he dying? It wasn't so bad. Kind of like being cradled in a silk cocoon, the soft material soothing his skin. There was silky hair too, lying flat against his shoulders. A face materialized in his vision, a perfect face. An angel? Of course — there was no other explanation. Golden locks... and those eyes. He must have been a good person during life to deserve this. The angel's lips were moving but the sound was lost. All Diego could do was smile back. He felt delicate hands on the sides of his neck, a gentle touch that made everything all the more relaxed. Then, as if the thick mist was diminishing, he remembered. The knife, the town, the Ancillary... it all flowed back into his mind faster than a broken floodgate. Physically he remained unchanged, but his mind was no longer in limbo. The angel transformed into a form he recognized. Sophia was staring at him, a look of concern on her face. She held two needles in the clenched palm of one hand.

"Sorry to bring you back down to earth," she said in a whisper. "But something's happening."

CHAPTER 43

It felt early. Like waking in a pitch-black room, but somehow knowing that the day would soon begin its journey. Jacob couldn't remember the last time—if ever—he had dreaded the sunrise. Now, one of his great pleasures in life—along with a laundry list of other things—was being taken from him by that sadistic treasure-hunter.

But the sun *was* going to rise.

It would soon be his turn to do the taking.

Trundling through the brush, the knot that imbedded itself inside of Jacob's stomach lining finally started to untangle. All night spent in fear and hate was not something Jacob was accustomed to. He was unsure of how this morning would turn out; there were so many ways it could go wrong.

"Remember," Jacob said, "we have to play this just right."

"You can count on me, man."

"Don't even let your eyes drift toward it. We can't afford to give him any reason not to trust us." Jacob said this harsher than intended.

"My eyes will be forward bound."

They were en route, hopefully ending up in Tanki Lowbei, at a speed that only adrenaline could provide. Unfortunately, this time Jacob didn't have anything pulling him, and he had to trust that his compass could do the trick.

Though still pitch black, the blue light of the Ancillary shone skyward out of Clark's outstretched arms, which bestowed the light Jacob was navigating by.

A plane of mud, just waiting to steal their shoes, threatened unsafe passage, a dirty road home.

As they trotted through, the creamy dirt squeezed its way under their socks and made a squishing sound very close to that of walking on a wet carpet. Jacob decided to use this opportunity to pull out his radio.

"Come in Rosie! Over."

There was an unsettling moment, and then she picked up.

-TSSK- "Cob! What's your status? Did you find it?"

"We got it. We're on our way back now."

-TSSK- "That's incredible. I can't believe it's real. What's it like?"

"Unbelievable... to me at least."

-TSSK- "What do you mean?"

"It doesn't really matter. I'll explain everything on the ride home. Get to Tanki Lowbei as quick as you can. And try and bring some sort of first aid for Diego."

-TSSK- "Will do, I'll meet you there mate."

Jacob turned the radio off just in time to grab the top of his shoe, preventing it from being lost in the brown abyss. The mud was as thick as chocolate pudding, without the enticing aroma.

There was no sign of sunlight, but they both understood that time was a big concern. *There must be less than an hour before dawn*, Jacob thought. The muddy area was slowly getting shallower as they approached dry and solid ground.

Jacob let the rhyme of the Cronapians roll through his head. It was brilliant. The poetry disguised just enough, but explained it all... to those who were worthy.

Brilliant. It made perfect sense, like hearing an eloquent sentence constructed from a jumble of fragments.

It was the first time all night that Jacob felt some semblance of control. He would make Marrow pay — with something a lot more precious than money. The plan was formulated; they just needed to win the heart of lady luck. The luck of lady luck. If their secret were forfeit, then all would be lost: the town, the Ancillary... Sophia. *I hope she's unharmed*, thought Jacob. If he got through all of this, the first thing he was going to do was tell her how he felt. He would scoop her into his arms and bring her to the giant garden — the most romantic spot Jacob had seen in the whole town — and kiss her under the shade of the gigantic sunflowers. If he could pull off saving Tanki Lowbei and foiling Marrow, he could surely win Sophia's heart.

The moment before he left, Jacob thought there was something hiding behind her eyes. Was it a mutual feeling? Was she as crazy about him as he was about her? Did she want to take him to the Sinung and let Ernie and the other old trees watch as they sank into each other's embrace and —

"We're out!" Clark was exuberant. "I thought we would never get out of that muck. That was awful!"

Jacob gave him a reassuring smile. "It wasn't so bad."

"Maybe for someone who can see in the dark!" Clark laughed. "You're like a hedgehog!"

Jacob stopped short.

"Did...did you say hedgehog?"

"Yeah, hedgehogs are nocturnal. So you're like a hedgehog... you know? Because you can see perfectly fine at night."

"Artemis."

"Who?"

Things just keep getting better, Jacob thought.

"Never mind, long story."

"Hopefully we won't have enough time for you to tell it to me... speaking of which, does any of this look familiar to you?"

Jacob hadn't really stopped to take note of their surroundings; admittedly he was blindly following his compass. "Actually... no."

"Well, we didn't have to cross that dirt lagoon before, so maybe we're just going back a different way. Anyway," Clark pointed upwards towards Everest, "we're on the correct side of Qomolangma, so I think we're going the right way."

"Right, Quo- Quomlava."

"Sorry, I think you would call her Everest."

"Oh," Jacob smiled. "Why didn't you just say so?"

They continued on their journey in that direction for what felt like miles. Though he knew Clark couldn't see it, the blue tint that their environment recieved from the Ancillary made everything look eerily beautiful. The vines were cables straight out of a science fiction movie. The trees look like they belonged on a different planet, while the ground looked like they were walking on some sort of goo. No wonder he didn't recognize anything, he probably wouldn't have even been able to identify his own back yard if the colors were skewed this much. He could only trust that he spent enough time in the Scouts to have learned proper navigation. Now he regretted ever bringing home that bear cub... well, maybe not. They passed through narrow gaps between towering limestone passageways and through wide fields.

They barely talked. There was no need for words; their focus was on one thing—getting back in time. The further they got, the more worrying feelings came to Jacob. Clark could barely make out their surroundings and Jacob was not a native to this land. Silence was necessary for concentrated navigation. If they were going in the wrong direction, then... he didn't even want to think about what would happen.

After progressing through a particularly nasty patch of bramble thorns, they found themselves at what seemed to be an abandoned camp. There were makeshift tents held up by bamboo poles. On the perimeter, old vehicles waited for all of their parts to be cemented with rust. In the corner plot of land were remnants of fire pits with spits roasted black from overuse. It wasn't particularly large and probably housed only about a dozen soldiers when it was in use.

"YIPPEE!!!" Clark shouted. He jumped up so suddenly that he almost let the Ancillary spill out of his arms. With a quick recovery he was able to keep it from falling to the ground.

"What?"

The exclamation sounded pleasant enough, but Jacob didn't want to get his hopes up.

"I know where we are!" Clark held the Ancillary high above his head, like a trophy.

"You do!?"

"Yes, there are plenty of these rebel camps out here, but I would know this camp anywhere."

"How?"

The smile seemed too big for Clark's face. "That!"

Jacob followed his outstretched finger and traced its path to a most unusual object.

Sitting behind one of the tents was a large stone carving in the shape of a dragon holding an egg in one claw, and a skull in the other. The skull looked human-esque, but was elongated and had two curved horns. The proud dragon was sitting on top of a pile of long intertwined snakes.

"This statue is famous among my people," Clark stated. "It signifies how all people are connected and reminds us of our mortality. The dragon is called Mowloc and reminds us of the power we all contain hidden away behind fear and reservations. It reminds us of how important free will is. No one knows who carved it or how it got all the way out here, but this was always a preferred spot for rebel armies. They see it as inspiration and a reminder of why they fight."

"Great sight-seeing aside, I assume you know how to get back?"

Clark's chest puffed out. "Not ONLY do I know how to get back, there's even a nice half-clear road for us to travel on. It will take us straight back to the gates of my town."

"If I weren't afraid of touching that flower again, I would be hugging you right now."

"No time for pleasantries, the path is right past those wooden crates. Let's go home!"

BANG.

Jacob grabbed Clark and pulled him towards the ground. Both their stomachs forcefully hit the grass. The wind was knocked out of Clark with a guttural 'humph' sound. The Ancillary flew from his hand and fell from the sweater-nest, unleashing it's full light, illuminating the forest for Jacob to see.

"Was that what I think it was?" Clark whispered to Jacob.

"It sounded like a gunshot. But I'm not positive."

"What do we—"

BANG.

A patch of grass just inches shy of Jacob's nose exploded in a barrage of green shrapnel. Someone was definitely shooting at them.

"RUN!" screamed Jacob.

They got up and ran to find some cover.

BANG. BANG.

Two gunshots drove them behind the nearest piece of metal they could find. Clark quickly scooped up the Ancillary in the sweatshirt and held it under his armpit like a football. Their closest shelter turned out to be an old camouflage-painted SUV, covered in dead leaves and decayed earth. The front windshield was shattered and the side glass had some sort of brown goop on it, making the window opaque. They had no clue where the shots were coming from, so they quickly opened the front driver-side door and climbed inside. The door was slammed shut just in time, as a forceful impact hit the metal. Fortunately, the bullet did not penetrate the paneling.

Besides the external cosmetic defects, the interior looked to be surprisingly well kept. There was even a slight linger of new car smell.

"What's going on?" Clark was doing his best to stay composed but the fear was quickly manifesting itself as panic.

"Apparently, someone wants us dead."

"Do you think Marrow sent them?"

Jacob pinched between his eyes with his thumb and forefinger.

"Probably... I knew we shouldn't have trusted him." Jacob peeked outside. "It's still dark. I think either he sent a trigger-happy man to track us, or he was never going to honor his pact in the first place."

"What do we do now? Should we wait it—"

Glass shattered and hailed a web of sharp crystals.

Clark shouted and an instinctual fear caused him to briefly hunch over into the fetal position.

Jacob knew he had to keep his cool; there was so much riding on it. *Ok,* he thought, *just relax and think.* Without comprehension—as if his subconscious mind had long before decided the right course of action—his hand reached under the dash and came back dragging a fistful of wires. The multi-colored tangle of Hummer intestine spilled out onto his knees, and he began his search. It was harder than he thought because of the dark and the blue ancillary glow—there was little distinction between the colors. It turned out that being a car mechanic's assistant led to more than grease stains, electrically scorched fingertips, and a bi-weekly paycheck. He hoped that hotwiring a vehicle was universal.

"Let's pray the rebels didn't leave her empty," Jacob said.

"How do you know how to do that?"

Jacob picked up the green wire and shook his head. "I guess it must be the Ancillary working its magic... maybe from when I touched it?"

"Wow, that's incredible!"

Jacob laughed as he tried untangling a particularly nasty twist between the blue and purple wires. "I'm just kidding. It's from an old job I had."

"You were a thief?" Clark looked puzzled.

"No, but a few of the shop customers liked to think the owner was."

He needed to find the two wires that were the same, one from the primary power supply for the ignition, and one that connected to the electrical circuits.

There they were: two red ones—at least that's the color they appeared in the flower's light.

BANG.

They saw the rear side of the car dent forcefully.

"HA!" Clark proclaimed. "What terrible aim!"

Jacob didn't want to tell him that it actually wasn't terrible aim. From a distance, the dark would make it hard to tell exactly where in the car they were, especially since they were crouching under the windows. Marrow's man had finally done the smart thing… he was targeting the fuel tank.

Jacob twisted the two reds together and started stripping about an inch of insulation off each wire. Grabbing the brown one — and following with the same procedure — he got ready to touch the wires.

"Let's hope there's no kill switch, no faulty steering lock… and that I don't get fried."

He brought them together, and after a short sizzle, the engine rumbled, building to an enticing roar. Quickly and carefully, Jacob stuffed the wires back into their rightful place. The vehicle was an automatic and Jacob thrust the shifter into drive.

"Get us out of here!" Clark roared.

They sped off over the rough terrain, the large gas-guzzler taking the obstacles in stride, hopefully leaving the hit man far behind them.

"Hold the Ancillary up!" Jacob shouted. "I can't see where I'm going!"

Clark opened up the sweatshirt and held up their portable beacon.

"Where's the road?" Jacob frantically asked.

Clark squinted. "I… I can't really… OVER THERE!"

Jacob swerved the wheel towards the dirt highway, and with moonlight mixed with the Ancillary lighting their way, they sped off into the night.

CHAPTER 44

"We're leaving," Russell said, his own revolver thrust in Marrow's direction. It was the first time he had ever stood up to his boss, but it felt right. Sometimes even criminals have a line.

"What are you talking about, you buffoon?" Marrow inquired.

"Sometimes you really don't think, do you?"

"Look who's speaking...Shully... pull out your gun and shoot Russell in the face."

Shully pulled out his bronzed pistol and slowly raised it—only it wasn't Russell he pointed it at.

The townspeople all stared in silent disbelief, seeing the first glimmer of hope."What's going on? This is ridiculous, I didn't think you two could get any stupider."

"We're not going to wait around for this kid to bring you a flower. Seriously Tyson... a flower?" Russell scoffed.

"You fools don't understand anything."

"What we do understand is that the kid was right about one thing. When the media gets here in," he looked at his wristwatch, "what can only be very soon, everything here is going to turn loose."

"We are just tourists. If any of these heathens," Marrow raised his voice for all to hear and gestured outwards toward the crowd, "says anything different, they can be sure this large fellow over there won't be the last casualty."

"Yeah, because we all blend in so well," Russell said sardonically. "You're letting this stupid myth cloud your judgment and we're not going to let you bring us down with you. Don't you think that the word is out on that little stunt of yours on the plane?"

"I already showed you the fake passport and gloves, don't you ingrates listen?"

"Maybe *you* had protective measures, but what about the rest of us? The manifest is going to show *our* correct names and when they do a little easy checking into our backgrounds they'll find some prime suspects to question. I can't have the Feds on my back anymore... none of us can."

For a moment, Marrow's words were lost.

"I'll kill you for this treason," Marrow said as he reached for his revolver.

In an instant, all of the men had guns pointed in his direction—even Little Paulo, whose gun did not match his name.

"So it's unanimous!" Marrow bellowed. "All of my men are cowardly scum."

"Maybe so," Shully said. "But we're not your men anymore. Drop the gun."

Marrow spat in his direction.

"DROP... the gun," Shully repeated.

Reluctantly, and with fire in his eyes, Marrow let the gun hit stone.

Truth be told, Russell had been shaking pretty violently on the inside before this coup. The final straw was what Marrow did to Frankie for speaking his mind about an issue that affected them all. There was no telling how a man like Marrow would react to betrayal, but he had crossed the Rubicon and there was no turning back.

"Keep them high, boys!" Russell said as they slowly backed away and got into the rental cars.

With a slam of the door they left Marrow to deal with everything on his own.

"WATCH OUT!" Clark shouted as they hit a moose-sized ditch in the road, making them both get violently restrained by the seat belts. Fortunately they were driving the SUV; anything else would have succumbed to the sizable chunk out of the road.

"You didn't warn me that this road has craters!"

"This road has craters."

"Thanks for the heads up."

"Oh, and heads up."

His eyes scanned the old dash and found the casing had long ago been cracked, leaving the speedometer and clock useless.

"Put the flower up here." Jacob nudged his head towards the windshield. "Right behind the bobble-body hula dancer. I'll be able to see better."

"There's really that much light coming from it, huh?"

"It's incredible, and it's not just bright, it's beautiful, like a pocket sized aurora borealis."

"... Do you think the plan is going to work?"

"If it doesn't, then we're no worse off than we were."

"I don't think that's true, dude. What if he realizes —"

"I know. I was just hoping to convince myself that it was."

The old hummer roared in the night and Jacob was sure all the animals in the vicinity would be utterly confused. It had surely been a while since they had heard such a noise. In the same respect, he wondered what the townspeople would think? What an entrance they would make.

The leather seats were very comfortable and Jacob had to be careful not to get too relaxed; he hadn't slept in a while and he felt the toll of heavy eyelids and tired limbs. Staying sharp was a main factor if he had any hope at all of things going his way.

The flower helped light his way along the lengthy, holed road. His eyes kept glancing over to the petals, which he knew wasn't smart, as it was imperative he keep his focus on the road to avoid a potential totaling. Nonetheless, he kept looking over, still in shock over his realization. It all came together. He felt that old feeling again, the sense the world wanted him to win. There would be no way to recompense Fuki's death and Diego's stabbing—and probably numerous other murders Marrow had committed to get there—but maybe that cavalier monster would finally get what was coming to him.

"How soon do you think the sun is going to rise?" Jacob asked.

Clark stuck his head out of the now-missing window. "Judging by the completeness of the crepuscular sky, I would say we don't have much time."

"Crepuscular?" Jacob asked.

"It means darkness."

"Wow, this thing is powerful," Jacob said, nodding his head towards the flower.

"To quote the old cliché, the night is always darkest before the dawn."

Jacob thought about that line for a minute. In regards to the situation, he hoped for all their sakes that the darkest part wasn't over and the dawn decided to sleep in.

"How far are we?" Jacob asked.

"Not far at all now." Clark's hands clenched his knees and he began to rock back and forth.

Jacob stared outside and saw the bordering trees whisk by in a blue blur. He tried to stay clear of the roots penetrating their path. The scenery was so strange that things didn't seem real anymore—actually nothing felt real anymore. Just days before, Jacob was still at home going day-to-day just waiting for something, anything to define his life, and show him what he was meant to be. Time is so fleeting, he used to think, yet he continued to wait for his *actual* life to begin.

Many books that he treasured reading—including his favorite series with his favorite Elven hero—all seamed so fantastic and unbelievable; but here he was, smack dab in the

middle of his own wild adventure.
The suspense was killing him.

CHAPTER 45

For the first time in his life, Marrow was dumbfounded. It was always him doing the betraying—he never would have dreamed the thick-skulled monkeys of his would have the gall to abandon him. Caesar, at least, had warning from his wife before his unified stabbing.

He quickly picked up his revolver and held it out towards the circle of townsfolk.

"This doesn't change anything for you! If Cob isn't back in time, I WILL be taking hostages, so you better all pray to whatever *GOD* you like… but just know, I will get what's rightfully mine, and you all are going to help me. If he doesn't beat the sun—and lets all hope he does—you will alert all those swarming media locusts that a jealous rival came in and killed that man, and fled right away."

He slowly ambled over to Cob's pretty blonde friend. Grabbing her by the arm, he dragged her away from her rather large companion. He lied to Cob before; most likely the Spaniard would be dead within the hour. He punctured deep, which didn't give the young man much hope, especially without medical attention.

"You will give me a house for the day and tell the outsiders that another 'Krinama' will be held tomorrow."

The girl was struggling; however, Marrow was markedly stronger and her wiggling was easily quelled.

"This girl will be keeping me company and if any of you mention the fact that I am hiding… well, I have extensive practice and am quite good at creating situations where death would be an act of charity."

The crowd said nothing.

"Do you understand me?" Marrow asked.

The old monk once again stepped forward, and like a dominant dog encountering a bigger alpha male, put his head down and muttered, "Yes, we comply."

In the distance, Marrow thought he heard the low buzz of an engine. *No*, he thought, *the reporters couldn't be there yet, it was still early.* Even so, they wouldn't be allowed into the town. It was still dark. It seemed the boy had failed and he wasn't surprised. Even though Cob had the mark, Marrow knew that he alone was truly chosen. Cob's mark was small and insignificant. Like a mosquito on an elephant, it wouldn't make any difference. His mark, on the other hand, traversed his body proudly, a painting covering the full frame, the mark of a true artist who knew exactly what image he wanted to create. A masterwork.

The drone continued to grow louder until they all heard the distinct crash of metal on metal, which Marrow assumed to be something large totaling the town gate.

Why would someone crash through the gate, unless....

"Who did it?" Marrow screamed as his nostrils flared and his mouth quivered. "Who called for help?"

The monk picked up on his desperation.

"No one," the old man said, "we would not."

The roar was getting louder: *Only certain vehicles make that kind of noise*, he thought, *military.*

"You have all made the wrong decision!" Marrow howled and grabbed Sophia tighter. "I'll kill her! I'll kill you all!"

Then he saw the SUV and his suspicions were confirmed.

"You are all dead!" Marrow cried, "I'll burn this town!"

The armed forces machine drove recklessly, tires screeching, heading straight for their gathering. It looked old, very old. *Turns out*, Marrow thought, *the Tibetan government don't have much money, or they don't care for this town as much as I previously anticipated.*

The headlights found Marrow with his captive and changed course towards them. It was only a few hundred yards away, yet it showed no signs of stopping. It zoomed off the road and into the large square. Were they willing to kill her just to get to him as well?

He thrust his gun into the side of the girl's head, violently, and from behind grabbed her chin and held it tightly forward so her eyes were locked with the barreling vehicle.

"Do you want her dead?" His voice was going hoarse because of his screaming, but it didn't stop him.

Suddenly, now only a hundred or so feet in front of them, the car hit the brakes and came to a screeching halt. It slid for a while and, though it was dark, Marrow knew it left a nasty tred-mark on the asphalt.

The SUV came to a stop, and two figures came jumping out almost immediately. Marrow could only make out their silhouettes, but assumed these were the first wave of army officials and were going to try and negotiate. There would be no negotiating, only pain.

They came running towards him, at a speed too quick for negotiators. The two mystery figures were running as if an avalanche were dashing to swallow them whole. The shorter one was holding something in his arms; Marrow wasn't too keen on not being able to see what it was.

"Don't come any closer or I will shoot!" Marrow bellowed into the murky darkness.

They stopped short.. Marrow couldn't make out the figures; they were still hidden in the shadows.

"Wait," one of them yelled, "don't shoot! It's Jacob!"

No, Marrow thought, *it can't be. He couldn't have made it back just in time. It's too perfect.*

"Step closer and let me see your faces… slowly," Marrow yelled back.

They crept forwards, taking long strides until the light of the streetlamp finally revealed them.

It was Cob, and by his side was the short kid with the

Superman shirt who must have slipped away earlier while he wasn't looking.

The first sign of day appeared to the left; the sun peeked out as if to see what all the fuss was about.

"We have the flower!" Jacob yelled. "Just let her go and I'll give it to you."

Marrow couldn't believe it. Was the boy toying with him to buy some time or did he actually have it? Was his obsession, the object which he spent countless years tracking and imagining, about to be revealed? It had to be real, all those ancient cultures couldn't have independently known about it. The stories were all too similar. The God plant, Messianic Burgeon... Satan's Shoot. But did he actually find it?

Marrow's life's work and dedication was about to pay off. He would know power. A new level of control, a stranglehold over mankind was just the beginning. He would entrap, ensnare, and enslave the world. He would reach his ultimate potential.

Tremble world, for thy maker weeps.

"Show me!" Marrow said.

The Tibetan slowly took the cloth package out from under his arm, and started removing the folds. Marrow's heart was beating so fast he wouldn't have been surprised if the thumps were audible. *This is it*, he thought.

Suddenly, the world brightened. A powerful source of light ignited everything around him... but it wasn't originating from the sun. In fact, it was drowning out the natural white light. It was true: the Ancillary glowed blue.

Glowed was an understatement. At once, Marrow realized the truly awesome power that was soon to be his. The light was spectacular. It coated everything and everyone in a deep hue richer then any water he had ever seen. The blonde hair in front of his face no longer looked golden, but reflected back the pigmentation of the Ancillary.

As he took in his surroundings and stared at the faces of the townspeople, he realized something strange. None of them seemed to be shocked by this eruption of light. They all stared curiously at what the boy held in his arms, yet they did not revere the overwhelming spectacle.

As if Cob could read his mind, the boy said, "We're the only ones who can see it. I see it too, it's... incredible."

"And you brought me the whole thing?"

"I didn't alter it at all. It's real and it's all yours, just let Sophia go."

"Bring it here."

Cob nodded towards his shorter friend and he slowly began creeping forward. *That's it,* Marrow thought, *only a few feet more and I'll finally have it.*

The Ancillary.

After what felt like a lifetime of searching, the greatest treasure the world has ever given man was to be his. The name 'Marrow' would strike fear into the heart of humanity for all eternity. His name and deeds would echo into the darkness of forever. Religion would be erased from the world and everyone would pray to a single mortal deity.

The light was almost unbearable. As the young heathen brought the Ancillary closer, an unbelievable lust came over him. It swept his across his body as quickly and fiercely as a sandstorm. He knew what he had to do. He became famished; a hunger so complete that its remedy could only be one possible thing.

He pushed the girl with all his strength and she collapsed onto the ground. His hands needed to be free.

The Ancillary was at arms' length and he grabbed for it. When he finally touched it, his world immediately changed.

Never in his life — not from any encounter with a woman or drug — had he felt that amount of ecstasy. From his fingertips outwards, wave after wave of euphoria sent his body into a complete state of pleasure and tranquility. It was at that moment, that he truly understood why the Ancillary had been worshipped and remembered through the esoteric whisperings of history. *A feeling like this defies words,* Marrow thought, *it defies logic.* It was all too good to be true. Karma be damned, he was about to receive the greatest prize the earth had to offer. The pleasure started to become overwhelmed by the need for the Ancillary. It was primal, a beastly feeling which he had to quell immediately. Only one thing mattered now.

The hunger was excruciating.

He lifted the Ancillary, the flower of legend, up towards his mouth in preparation for his earthly metamorphosis.

The world went dark.

CHAPTER 46

Jacob couldn't believe what he saw.

Who knew the old man could move so fast? Or so stealthily, for that matter.

Right before the flower reached Marrow's lips, his head jerked to the right.

The Bone-man collapsed.

Clark let out a lengthened, "Duuuude!"

"MR. MADDOCK!" Jacob yelled with delight.

What in the world is he doing here? Jacob thought.

The word warden hid behind a rather large statue of an elephant, biding his time until the perfect moment. While Marrow was distracted by his perceived good fortune, the old librarian crept up behind and let out a swing that Babe Ruth would have envied.

Jacob and Clark rushed over.

Mr. Maddock helped his granddaughter to her feet and embraced her with all his strength.

"It's OK now, sweetheart, it's all over. You're safe."

While still in the midst of a giant hug, Mr. Maddock released one hand and beckoned Jacob inward.

"Cob my boy, what a great pleasure it is to find you unharmed. Unbelievably filthy, but uninjured."

"Wh-What? How—"

To ease Jacob's struggle to find the right words, Mr. Maddock began to explain everything.

"I stumbled across a critical piece of information that I had yet to discover while going through my books. In all my years of research and understanding of Ancillary lore I can't believe I had yet to realize it. There were clues, however I was in a certain mindset and I guess this stubborn old brain only saw what it wanted to. I tried to phone Rosie numerous times but I couldn't get through—I hope she's all right. I knew that this knowledge was too important for you not to have, so I raced around the world, and from the looks of it, I got here just in time. What an adventure! I saw this cretin holding my Sophia captive and the rest is history. That man I clobbered *was* the bad guy, correct?"

"That's an understatement," Jacob said.

Mr. Maddock released Sophia and Jacob, but kept a hand on each of their shoulders.

"Hey man, I'm Clark. It's nice to meet you!"

Jacob's enthusiastic young friend squeezed in and extended his hand towards the librarian.

"And what a pleasure it is, young man. Tell me, how did you learn to speak English so well?"

"Hmmm," Clark said, his face bright and smiling, "from what I've learned…I guess it was from the pollen."

Mr. Maddock's eyes filled with wonder. Mostly to himself, and to affirm what he already knew, he said, "It was your potential."

"Yup!"

"Where did you all get the pollen from? Was it airborne?"

Clark seemed delighted to be answering all these questions. "From our well. The Gods sent it to us to drink."

"This town is incredible," Mr. Maddock said loudly towards the Tanki Lowbei natives, who were now starting to rouse. Everything was happening so fast, and they were reluctant to let down their guard. That, and the gruesome corpse of their leader was still in plain sight.

"By the way," Mr. Maddock said. "Where is Diego?"

"I'm over here, sir!"

Diego was sitting upright against a stone wall, watching everything progress. His hands were clutched around his stomach, but besides his slightly green tint, he looked cheerful.

"Come over here and give this old man a hug, then!" Mr. Maddock said.

Diego moaned, "I would love to sir, but if I move I might pop my stitches."

"He let you get stitches?" Jacob asked, surprised.

"No… long story."

Now that he knew his protector was going to be all right, it was the moment Jacob had been waiting for.

Sophia.

As he swiveled to look over at her, and saw that she was already staring straight at him, waiting to catch his eye.

In a move that, until today, Jacob knew he wouldn't have had the guts to do, he walked straight up to her, and without saying a word, kissed her with all the passion he could muster.

The world melted away as he pressed against her soft lips, and the best part was, she was kissing him back. Her hand wrapped around the back of his head, grabbed his hair, and pulled him in harder. All Jacob's frustration and anxiety of the day evaporated into the morning mist of the Tibetan highland. She held him firm against his face until they both ran out of air and had to part.

Jacob let out a, "wow."

She smiled and whispered in his ear, "I think we have our next adventure to look forward to."

Whatever Jacob was trying to babble was cut off by another kiss.

"How charming!" Mr. Maddock said.

"So what was this critical piece of information?" Sophia asked her grandfather after she let Jacob go. "I think we ought to know since it's about time the Ancillary went to its rightful owner. He did save the day and all."

"Ah!" Mr. Maddock replied, "You see…"

The old librarian carefully bent down to examine the flower, which to Jacob was still giving off the bright blue glow.

As Mr. Maddock stood back up with the flower, so did

Marrow.

Tightly locked in Marrows fingers was the large revolver. His hand was shaking and the barrel was aimed right at Mr. Maddock. Jacob had never seen a face so contorted with rage. His eyes were bulging, teeth clenched so hard that he could almost hear them cracking, eyebrows pinched so tight that they formed a single entity. The blood racing down the side of Marrow's face only added to his demonic appearance.

"Yes!" Marrow said, as spit dropped down his face landed on the namesake line. "It is time for it to be returned to the rightful owner."

The bone man tightened his forearm and lined his gun up with Mr. Maddock's forehead. Jacob's stomach sank.

The shot echoed off the statues and buildings, resonating for much too long in their ears.

When Jacob was finally able to open his eyes and accept the horror, he saw something he couldn't believe.

Mr. Maddock was still upright, but Marrow was crumpled on the ground, his entire lower jaw missing and a red puddle oozing out of the lower half of his face. What was happening? The shot was so loud that in these close quarters, the origin of the blast was undeterminable, but it surely didn't come from Marrow's gun.

It seemed to Jacob a fitting end to Marrow; he finally got what was coming to him…but from whom?

CHAPTER 47

Rosie Gruffentree let the rifle's end smoke for a while until she was ready to reveal herself. The firearm was quite powerful and the butt had bruised her shoulder, however the smarting pain was the smallest of prices to pay. It was the first time she had taken a life, but it needed to be done. She stood up and brushed off the knee she used to position herself on the ground next to her building of choice. Stepping out of the shadows and letting the rifle hang from the shoulder strap, she began her first steps toward a new life. The sun had begun its full ascension; she was ready to start her own.

Slowly, she walked toward her old friend and young acquaintances. *I cut it too close*, she thought. *Who knew the boy would be so cunning, or so lucky*? She hoped that bogus story about how 'the world wouldn't let the chosen one go so easily' would ease his mind and throw him off his game.

Much too close.

"ROSIE!" Jacob yelled. "It was you! You saved us!"

The entire crowd of townsfolk erupted in cheering and applause. Their faces reminder her of joyous children at a carnival. People were hugging and kissing and laughing as if their greatest nightmare was finally over. Only a few people crowded around some dead body on the ground refrained from celebrating.

"My dear!" Teddy shouted. "What a splendid sight!"

She didn't reply; there was no need. No false pleasantries would be exchanged. She was finally free to reveal her true motive. She came for one thing and one thing alone: the

Ancillary.

Now only a few strides from her prey, she re-raised the rifle.

"Hand it over, Teddy," she commanded.

"What are you talking about? Stop joking and give your old pal a hug," he said.

"No one's joking, you old fool. Hand it over or I finish the job that freak over there couldn't finish."

"This is not funny," Teddy said as his smile faded.

She let a round off into the air. Everyone jumped.

"Why are you doing this?" Jacob asked.

"You really haven't figured it out? Wow, you're thicker than I thought."

"What are you talking about? And what happened to your accent?" Sophia barked at her.

Rosie grinned. "Do you really think I don't know how to correctly pack a parachute?"

Blank stares.

Though she really only wanted the flower, Rosie decided to explain herself. It would be fun to see their spirits crushed.

"I've been using Teddy for years, trying to get closer to the Ancillary. The only way I was able to put up with his unbearably peppy attitude was because he is the only one who seemed more knowledgeable than myself on the subject. He had the resources and lord knows he had the time. But when he mentioned you," she motioned her gun towards Jacob and noticed he didn't flinch, "I knew I hitched my horse to the right wagon. It was fate. I also knew I had to get you out of the picture."

"How can you say something like that?" Sophia cried.

"Ok, ok, so I don't have 'The Mark' but it really doesn't matter; anyone could benefit from its power, and that person is going to be me. I'm not about to let some pubescent snot take what I have spent most of my adult life craving, regardless of some stupid birthmark. It is my obsession, it is my reward. When Ted called me up, talking a thousand miles an hour, telling me all about his new theory on where it was, I concocted my plan. Years I spent learning how to fly that shotty plane out in the bush, and it was going to pay off... If I could play my cards right."

"But you helped us," Diego moaned.

"No, I helped myself. Once Jacob found out about his rightful treasure I knew there was going to be no stopping Teddy from doing everything he could to get his golden boy and the Ancillary together. I had to get rid of the risk he posed, but I had to make it seem like an accident. First I brought you to the island noted for their Ancillary cults. Some people there think the one should be united with it, others think he or she should be destroyed. I had plenty of conversations with the locals about it in that little restaurant I sent you to. I figured that when they saw the mark, they would hold him there — either to help him or hurt him, didn't matter to me, as long as he was out of the way. I was about to leave when you somehow got back to the plane. Given, it was a stupid impulse to let you back in, but I was panicking. I thought about it afterward and I should have just left you there, they couldn't have gotten into the plane. Since that moment of mercy left me in the same position, I knew more serious measures needed to be taken. I decided to give you a faulty pack. If I just plain-out shot you, I would be facing all sorts of problems, but if it looked like you just... happened to be out of luck in the air... I could continue my searching with no questions asked."

"Why didn't you give us all faulty parachutes?" Sophia asked, disbelief in her voice.

"*That* wouldn't have been suspicious."

Sophia gave her a look of unreserved contempt.

"You three didn't even need to chute down. I landed my plane in a large, grassy field only a few miles away. I'm actually surprised that you didn't see me land. I turned off my phone and radio and laid low. Then I could take my time. I figured that after a while or so I would try to get in touch with those other two, but I waited to make it seem like I wasn't too anxious about hearing how Jacob had died in the fall. But what do I find out? That somehow Jacob is still alive and that some other fanatic is looking for the Ancillary. I would never have thought to go the whole kidnap a town route, but hey, to each their own. I knew I had to swing into action."

Jacob seemed to finally believe her. "That's why you seemed surprised when I answered the radio!"

"You're catching on... By the way, that's not *just* a radio. There's a small tracking device concealed inside. Very simple but very effective. I figured since you all still trusted me, which I'm surprised you did," Rosie said, while Sophia gave a humph, "I would use you to my advantage. I had heard a rumor that the chosen one would be drawn toward the Ancillary, but I never believed it... until you told me what you were feeling. Once you radioed me that you had found it, I went into the woods towards your signal. Since my first plan didn't work, I had to do something even more... draconian. I couldn't kill you in town, but in the woods, no one would be around to find you for who knows how long. By the way... who did you think was shooting at the abandoned rebel camp?"

"That was *you*?" The little Asian boy asked.

"Yes, and you lucked out for a second time... hotwiring a hummer... once again I underestimated you."

"Is it really worth all of this Rosie?" Teddy asked. "Is it worth your soul?"

"You of all people should know how much it is... now hand it over."

Mr. Maddock looked over towards Jacob.

"It's ok, Mr. Maddock, I was ready to give it up once before, I'll do it again."

That's the spirit kid, she thought, *hand it over and I won't kill you all.*

The old man hobbled slowly towards her, cane in one hand, mystical flower in the other. Each knock of wood on stone was almost an aphrodisiac for her. She needed the

Ancillary; she needed the power.

Beneath the layers of greed and selfishness, she truly wished it hadn't come down to gunpoint, but that's just the way it was, and there was nothing she could do about it. That, and the fact she hadn't listened to that portion of her personality in a long time. It was more vestigial than anything.

Mr. Maddock was now close enough for her to smell his breath. She saw pity in his eyes; she needed none. Long ago her path was chosen and, in her opinion, the end highly justified the means.

Holding her rifle with one hand, she stretched out the other and received the flower. It was finally hers... she would experience what billions, living and dead, could never dream of. Her name would be immortal.

It was smaller than she thought, and it gave off a soft blue glow.

"Now get back over there, and all of you get on your knees. I want the whole town to witness my transformation."

Teddy hobbled back and the onlookers all obeyed.

She let go of the rifle and let it hang across her chest. With both hands she examined the flower. It was beautiful. The marks lay proudly on each blue petal. It deserved to be lovingly adored; however, there was no time to waste. She knew all the media clowns would be closing in and she had to be back to her plane as soon as possible.

With both hands she raised the flower to her lips and in one bite devoured the petals, stamen, everything. She chewed slowly and swallowed.

It was done.

The feeling of accomplishment was greater than anything she could have hoped to feel. The revolution would soon being.

Her hands dropped to her stomach. *Was it supposed to hurt?*

Then the fire erupted.

It started in her feet. It was like standing on hot coals. What was going on? It crept up her legs. It felt like a power sander was rubbing off her skin. It reached her midriff. She vomited. Her body wanted it out, needed it out, but it was too late, the poison was spreading. Her chest was next; it felt like unmerciful hands were wrenching her insides, trying to steal her organs. Her arms were no longer in her control and her shoulders no longer felt attached. The real pain began when it reached her face. She felt hundreds of hornets in her cheeks. Her tongue began to swell and her air was cut off. She would have given anything for it to stop.

Everything turned red. Blood started pouring from her tear ducts and ears. *Make it stop!* she thought, *I'll do anything, just make it stop!*. She was violently shaking and, without realizing, hit the ground. Her limbs were rigorously twitching and misery filled every cell in her frame. *MAKE IT STOP!*

And as if her prayers were answered, the torture ceased.

Along with the world.

CHAPTER 48

Jacob felt no pity. It was her own damn fault.

Watching Rosie end her life was hard, but it was the path she chose. She lay motionless on the ground. Her death must have been excruciating.

He prayed that it was finally over. All he wanted was a warm bed. Sleep was a gift he would be happy to receive; that, and a warm shower.

He glanced over at Sophia. She looked confused. Her eyes turned towards him, full of concern.

It took his best effort to smile. So much death, even to enemies, takes its toll.

He scanned the faces of Tanki Lowbei and he could tell that they also had no idea how to feel. It seemed the only unsurprised faces in the crowd were himself, Clark, and Mr. Maddock.

Even though there were a few kinks, his plan had worked.

"I don't understand," Sophia said. "What happened?"

Jacob finally felt the weight lift from his shoulders.

"The Ancillary has two parts."

"You knew!" Mr. Maddock said elatedly.

"In one of the books you gave me, there was a poem called the rhyme of the Cronapians."

"Ahh, one of my favorites and—" He cut off his own words, "... Of course!"

"Will someone fill me in over here?" Sophia asked. "I am so lost."

"Of course," Jacob said, "the poem was right about a lot of

things. Glowing blue at night, the golden pollen, the water... but there was one line that didn't register with me until I was at the flower itself. It was true, what Rosie said. The Ancillary pulled me in towards it. It actually pulled me in so forcefully that I physically couldn't walk away from it. When I touched the flower it really hurt, which was the first sign. I tried to come back but I still couldn't move, the second sign. That's when I thought about the poem and the fact that Marrow and I both have the mark. The answer was clear."

"What line?" Diego asked.

His eyes glanced towards Mr. Maddock who was beaming with pride.

Jacob quoted, "Ground is the lock for man's quest for the key, the *root* of it all will be man's destiny."

It seemed to click for Sophia. "No way!"

"Yes, way. Marrow was meant for the flower, and it turns out I was meant for..." He withdrew the root from his pocket. "This."

It looked sort of like a blue potato. Smack dab in the center of the tuber was Jacob's mark: the Ancillary's Mark. The root wasn't very large, nor was it particularly aesthetic, but when it touched Jacob's skin, the feeling was perfection.

"Wow," Sophia said. "That's incredible."

"And," Mr. Maddock said, "it's what I came here to tell him. It took my entire life for the truth to come to me, and for Jacob... a matter of days. You are truly a remarkable boy and the world chose one hundred percent correct, but it seems like you have more cleverness than I assumed, and my services were unnecessary."

"Are you kidding?" Jacob said with a smile. "You saved the day!"

Mr. Maddock's beaming smile somehow grew.

"So what I assumed," Jacob said, "was that if *my* portion guaranteed my destiny, then *his* portion would take destiny away."

"That was awesome when you said that to me in the

woods, dude! It was like Sherlock Holmes. You rule!" Clark said.

"AND," Jacob's voice rose so that the whole town could hear, "I don't think I would have had the courage to face the woods alone, and I definitely wouldn't have been able to find my way back in time without Clark. My faithful companion here deserves all the thanks I can muster."

Clark raised his fists into the air in triumph. The crowd roared with applause.

"And my new friend, Diego," Jacob said. "Now I can say you would truly have taken a bullet for me... heck, you took a knife. You are the best muscle and brain a guy could ask for."

More applause from the crowd.

Sophia almost tackled him to the ground as she kissed him. Each time their lips touched was more amazing than the last.

"So," she said, "you saved the day and got the girl. Only one thing left to do."

"Oh yeah," he said. "I almost forgot."

He reached inside his other pocket and pulled out a sock.

Turning the sock over, he poured its contents into his hand. Out came wet, golden pollen.

Jacob turned towards the townspeople of Tanki Lowbei. "I wasn't sure if we would be able to find the spot again, so I gathered all the pollen I could get out of the water and brought it back for you all. I just wish Fuki could have gotten some."

The old monk stepped forward and bowed to Jacob.

"Thank you, young man," he said. "The Gods knew what they were doing when they put mark on your hand. Fuki would be so very proud."

"So why didn't you let Marrow eat the flower?" Diego asked Mr. Maddock, "Wouldn't that have solved the problem?"

"I guess it was selfish, but if Jacob eats his portion and that maniac ate his, there would be no proof that it ever existed. I wanted the flower to go to a museum and then everyone could have known just one of the extraordinary secrets the world has yet to reveal. That and... if there is proof... then my son..."

Sophia ran over and embraced her grandfather.

"Now that you're done thinking about everyone else," Clark said with glee, "it is time for you to accept your gift."

It was time.

Jacob walked over to Clark and placed the small root into his new friend's hand.

"What... what are you doing?"

"I want you to have it."

"But... but you are meant for it," Clark said.

"If I am meant to do great things, then I will. My whole life I have been waiting for something...but it wasn't the Ancillary."

"I can't possibly let you give me your flower!" Clark said, trying to hand it back.

"Exactly," Jacob smiled, "*my* flower, *my* rules. Besides, someone is going to need to lead your people. I've already seen a portion of what you have inside of you; I can't imagine the good you are going to do. You truly are a superman."

Clark's face hardened, followed by a nod.

"Oh," Jacob said, "by the way, Diego... there were bullfrogs near where it was growing. Hundreds of them."

Diego burst out laughing and then immediately stopped and grabbed his stomach.

"So it's not all a bunch of mumbo-jumbo then, huh?" he asked.

"Nope...it's all real."

EPILOGUE

Washington, D.C., The White House, 20 Years Later

"My fellow Americans. What a country we have become. I cannot express enough how proud I am to be holding the position I have. In only a year, we have seen crime rates at an all-time low, and beneficial technological breakthroughs at an all time high. War has ceased around the globe and we are living in a true utopia of freedom and love. My fellow Americans, I know it was not an easy transition, but you trusted me and my policies, and in the end, what a difference we have made. The arts are booming and the people are happy. With the cooperation of President Chi Chung Hupuenang of the new democratic China, international relations between the west and the east are stronger than history has ever seen. Inside our own borders, unemployment is a word we no longer have to associate with a healthy portion of our patrons. We did it, America, we are finally here."

"Hey, Sophia," Jacob called to his wife. "Come listen to this… does it flow?"

Into the bedroom came—in Jacob's opinion—the most stunning first lady the White House had ever seen. Her hair was longer, but it remained the same shade of beautiful blonde as they day they met. *Wow*, he thought, *it feels like a lifetime ago*. Her face had matured, and the only thing that came with age was a deeper beauty.

Jacob looked at his wife, and even after years of marriage and through two births—a boy and a girl—Sophia never failed to bring a boyish, puppy-dog-love grin to his face.

"You worry too much. You're going to be fine."

"I know, but these things always make me nervous. What if I choke?"

"You are the youngest president in the history of the US. I think if you mess up a few words in a speech the public will cut you some slack. Plus I think with what you have accomplished…well… I think a few words that don't flow won't hurt your reputation too much."

Putting on her favorite peace sign earrings and purple jade necklace, she gave him a cunning smile and said, "But that part about trusting you and your policies does sound a little pompous."

Jacob erupted in laughter, ran over to his wife, and embraced her—with a little playful tickling just to get her back.

"Pompous, huh?" Jacob said. "I'll show you pompous."

"DAD!" Clark Deer laughed. "What are you doing? You're wrinkling your suit."

Jacob released his prisoner and straightened his tie.

"Worth it," Jacob said.

His son was fifteen, tall and handsome. His son's blue eyes strengthened Jacob's feeling that one day, his boy would be a head-turner.

"Are you all set for the banquet?"

"Yeah Pop, it's going to be fantastic," his son said.

"And your sister?"

"Playing with her dolls, but she's ready."

His daughter was six and fortunately had gotten her mother's good looks.

In ran Fuki—his trusty German shepherd—who proceeded to jump up on Jacob as if determined to shed fur all over his new suit.

"Down buddy!" Jacob said with a laugh, "We won't be gone all night. You don't have to worry."

"C'mere boy!" Jacob's son took the dog downstairs.

"So how do I look?" Sophia asked him doing her best twirl.

"Prettier every day."

Diego Ramirez stuck his head into the room. "Mr. President

sir, we should get going. We don't want to be late."

Jacob turned to the head of his secret service. "Will I ever get you to call me Cob? We have been through a lot, you know."

Diego laughed. "Probably not, sir. That would make me feel less professional in front of the others."

Jacob smiled and shook his head. As he and his wife began leaving the house, he glanced over at his boy and recalled one of the fondest memories he had.

A few years ago, Jacob had told his son the story of his quest for the flower and all that went along with it. Young Clark's eyes widened with fascination.

"That's incredible, Dad!"

"It is. I was very lucky."

"Well, what does the word Ancillary mean?"

"It means secondary, unimportant. It's actually an ironic name for what it does."

"Not really…"

"What do you mean?" he asked his son.

"From what you told me, it means that you already had all this potential inside of you. You could have accomplished all this with or without the Ancillary."

Jacob was flustered. In all his years since his great adventure, he had never heard it put into words that way.

"Thanks, son," Jacob said as he kissed the top of Clark's forehead. "I guess that's true."

Breinigsville, PA USA
21 December 2010
251958BV00004B/1/P